Screaming For Peace

Horror Writes For The People Of The Ukraine

Dear Reader.

First and foremost, I would like to thank you for buying a copy of Screaming For Peace. This is a non-profit anthology, as all the money we raise through sales will be donated to aid the victims of this senseless, illegal war.
What shocks me most about what's taking place in eastern Europe is that we, as a species, never seem content with what we have. Take Vladimir Putin as an example. He's a billionaire in his 70s and ruler of the largest country on Earth. I want to think that were I a rich man in his twilight years; I'd be at peace with the world, sitting on a yacht and sipping cocktails. But greed is a destructive drug, and consequently, innocent men, women and children are being blown to pieces; and why? For a few thousand more square miles of land.
Sadly, while there are men like Putin, the world will never know peace or security. And now we find ourselves thrust into another Cold War.
We, the horror writing community, spend our time thinking up gruesome and horrific ways of torturing and killing our characters, yet the horrors of the real world are always far worse than anything we could conjure.

We at ReelHorrorShow wanted to do something to help, so we reached out to some amazing and talented writers who were more than willing to give up their time and contribute to this anthology that you now hold in your hand. I don't know how much it will raise. I hope it does well, but anything is better than nothing at all.

So, once again, I thank you for making this purchase, and I hope you enjoy the deliciously ghoulish and gory tales within.

A huge thank you goes out to all the authors who contributed to this project. You're all awesome, beautiful people and wonderful writers.

Let's keep our fingers crossed that this senseless bloodshed ends soon.

Oh, and in case Vladimir Putin happens to get his grubby, blood-stained hands on a copy of this: Fuck You! The blood on your hands will never wash away. History will remember you in much the same way as it remembers the likes of Hitler, Pol Pot, Blair and Bush. Just remember, every murderous dictator eventually ends up very dead.

Lee Richmond

Screaming For Peace (Title Only) copyright © ReelHorrorShow Publications, 2023.

The copyrights to the stories inside belong to the authors. ReelHorrorhow claims no right to the credited authors works. All rights reserved. No part of this work should be reproduced, distributed or transmitted in any other form, including photocopying, recording or any other method without prior written permission of the authors, except for the use of brief quotations in reviews and other non-commercial uses permitted by copyright law.

All characters, events and places in this publication are fictitious unless otherwise stated by the author. Any resemblance to persons living or dead is purely coincidental.

Mirror Image © J.D Allen 2023
Don't open the Door, Harold © Kelvin V.A Allison 2021
I Will Save You © Stephen Cooper 2023
Let it Be the Devil © B.E. Goose 2023
Between the Spaces © Mark MJ Green 2023
Inside © Ayralea Lander 2023
Haunted © E.B. Lunsford 2023
Ukrainian Chimes © Ronald McGillvray 2023
Sweet Tea © Leigh Pettit 2023
Plastic – A Love Story © Lee Richmond 2023
Open House © Rebecca Rowland 2018
Uncaged © Jesse Thibodeau 2023
The Missing Return © Adam Watts 2023
I Hide in the Shadows © Kristen Vincent 2023

Cover art by Elly Wilson

Screaming For Peace

I'm visible but can't be seen,
Screaming but can't be heard,
All alone and surrounded by people,
I am dead but still here breathing.

You can't hear the voices yelling inside,
Constant reminders of my dark past,
Like salt rubbed into wounds not fully healed,
Never letting me forget the horrors I survived.

I feel like I'm broken, pieces of me missing,
Condemned in my own eyes, even hating myself,
Nothing I do or say is ever good enough,
I blame myself for what was never my fault.

The truth is I've suffered through hell,
Scars hidden deep inside, only I can see.
I've been left to die, alone and afraid,
Now I'm drowning inside, stuck in my past.

Haunted by trauma, it follows me everywhere,
Refusing to let go, I can never escape it,
Eating at me daily, my own mind my enemy.

I'm losing myself, don't know who I am anymore.

I need to move on, finally conquer my demons,
Vanquish my doubts and fears, remember my strength,
I saved myself once, why can't I do it again?
The past is gone, why I am unable to move on?

It's time to find myself again, remember who I am,
I'm stronger than I know, nothing is stopping me,
Broken for so long, I don't remember how to be whole,
Why can't I just be me again? Why can't I be happy?

I feel broken even now, the pieces are still there,
But they don't fit together anymore.
I'm not the same person, unrecognizable,
Why did I put up with the abuse for so long?

The past always seems to repeat itself,
An endless loop, ending in the same situations,
The best of intentions becoming our worst mistakes.
Why do I always get the short end of the stick?

This hell I'm living has to end soon,
Something has to give, my mind or will.
I don't know if I can take anymore,
I'm screaming for peace, but no one else hears.

E.B. Lunsford

"Those who cannot remember the past are condemned to repeat it."
-George Santayana-

For The Brave People of Ukraine

-The Authors-

Stories

Mirror Image	J.D. Allen
Don't Open the Door, Harold	Kelvin V.A Allison
I Will Save You	Stephen Cooper
Let it Be the Devil	B.E. Goose
Between the Spaces	Mark MJ Green
Inside	Ayralea Lander
Haunted	E.B. Lunsford
Ukrainian Chimes	Ronald McGillvray
Sweet Tea	Leigh Pettit
Plastic: A Love Story	Lee Richmond
Open House	Rebecca Rowland
Uncaged	Jesse Thibodeau
I Hide in the Shadows	Kristen Vincent
The Missing Return	Adam Watts

Edited by Lee Richmond & Mark MJ Green

Mirror Image

-J.D. Allen-

Mirror Image

You'll think I'm crazy, but I'm not. This really happened.

Looking back on it, I can't remember… I'm just a little confused about what I was even doing at the Sunrise Mall that morning. I was probably out Christmas shopping. I remember the stores. They were decorated with the festive signs of the season: pine trees adorned in silver and gold tinsel, blinking lights of red and green, and an abundance of candy cane stripes.

I parked my old blue Mazda in the underground parking garage – level D, for some reason I still remember that – and I rode the elevator up to the main floor of the mall. I had been walking around for quite a while, window shopping, when I spotted the coffee shop and decided to stop for a 'Starbucks Fix'. As usual there was a line at the counter, and I took my place at the end of it. Tapping my left foot impatiently, I tried to ignore the annoying Christmas music blasting from the mall's speakers.

At first, I didn't see him, standing in the very same line as I. I was too busy assessing the availability of vacant seating around the tables scattered throughout the bustling coffee shop hoping to find a place to sit once I had my coffee in hand. When at last I did see him, I froze in shock.

He wore the same sneakers on his feet as I wore on mine; his socks matched those on my feet. His faded blue jeans were the same style as mine. His white, buttoned-down, cotton shirt was rolled up at the sleeves just as mine revealing the same dragon swirl of a tattoo on his forearm that was identical to the ink on my forearm. His hair, his posture, even the way he impatiently tapped his left foot while waiting in line, identical in looks and manners as to the ways of myself. But that wasn't the worst of it.

His face was my face.

His eyes were my eyes.

He was an exact duplicate of me.

He hadn't seen me. I was shocked that no one else seemed to notice that two of the same man, identical in every way, were standing in line just a few feet apart from each other, as if nothing were strange about it whatsoever! I guess everyone else was too busy with their faces buried in their laptops, or in their

Smartphones, to notice anything outside of their own screens.

    I had occasion to think of that old movie, 'Invasion of the Body Snatchers' as I watched my double and I remembered how people were being replaced by duplicate imposters from outer space in that old black and white thriller. I shuddered at the memory.

    When his turn came to place his order, my double stepped up to the counter and I heard him ask for the same type of coffee – chi latte, two sugars, extra cream - that I always ordered and I nearly gasped when he also bought a piece of sesame bread, my favorite pastry confection in the case.

    When he left the counter with his order, I stepped out of line and followed him out of the shop with my 'Starbucks Fix' now forgotten. I stayed back a safe distance as I followed my duplicate as he went from shop to shop, drinking from the steaming paper coffee cup, moving and gesturing with a familiarity I felt within myself instinctually, as they too were my very own movements and gestures.

    He purchased my wife's favorite Michael Kors perfume at the Macy's counter, and he bought the 'Little Wheels Indy 500' racetrack and 'turbo' car set my son had been begging us for Christmas at The Toy Barn. From the Hickory Hut he purchased a single Teriyaki Beef Stick, and I watched him eat the whole thing as he continued roaming the mall, disposing of the evidence of the wrapper in a nearby trash-receptacle as I was supposed to be on a diet and was hiding these types of little food-cheats from my wife.

    I had been following him around the mall for about an hour, and just as I was beginning to get hungry, he went to the food court and he ordered my favorite meal – two regular cheeseburgers, small fries, and a diet coke – from McDonalds.

    I ate the same meal as he as I sat a few tables away watching my double behaving as I behave while eating alone at the food court. Neither of us making eye contact with the strangers around us as I was prone to keep to myself in public. Neither of us differing in demeanor from the other.

    I worked up my nerve and when I felt safe doing so, I took out my Smartphone and acted like I was reading something on its screen while I zoomed in with the phone's camera, and I covertly snapped a close-up shot of the man who was my twin. Just in case I needed proof of his existence.

    When my double finished eating, he discarded his tray at the trash station, and he walked through the mall to the elevators. I followed him down to the parking garage – level D – where he climbed into an old blue Mazda parked adjacent to my old blue Mazda. The dent on his back left bumper matched the one on mine which was created over two years ago when my wife backed into a poll at this very mall.

 I left the Sunrise Mall following my double at a pace of a few cars behind, just far back enough to be lost in the sea of other cars should he look back in his rearview mirror. He had other stops to make that day as I had many errands to run, and I cautiously followed my imposter from place to place around my hometown.

 At my bank, I stood at the courtesy counter away from the tellers, and I listened as the man who was pretending to be me recited my account number and withdrew a small amount of cash from my savings.

 At the post office, I watched through the large windows at the front of the building as my duplicate accessed my private P O Box and extracted what, I can only surmise, must have been the latest batch of my incoming mail.

 As I followed him to my house, my heartbeat quickened.

 When he turned onto the driveway of my home, swerving around my son's bicycle lying near the sidewalk, I decided to park down the street, as a precaution. I watched as the automatic door of my garage rose up and the man who was my double drove his little blue Mazda into my garage.

 I climbed out of my little blue Mazda and approached the house.

As was my habit, he left the garage door up, and I caught a glimpse of him as he stepped out of the car and through the narrow white door between the garage and the interior of the house. He disappeared inside my home.

I approached cautiously and as I stepped onto my property, I could see my double through the wide picture window at the front of the house approach my wife in our cozy living room and my heart stopped as my wife rose from our sofa and gave the phony me a kiss on lips that resembled mine.

For a moment, I had cause to wonder if my wife were a duplicate too.

I watched them from the bushes outside my home as they briefly spoke in our parlor, and then hand in hand they moved into another room out of my sight. In a panic, I flew to the front door, grabbed the door knob, and twisted and turned it to no avail. It was locked.

Walking stealthily beside the porch railing, I stepped into the shadows of the open garage and as I approached the narrow white door that separated the garage from the kitchen to gain entry into my home, the door suddenly opened and the stranger that was me appeared in the opening.

I ducked into a darkened spot between my work bench and the water heater before my duplicate could notice me and I heard him say; "I'll be out in my workshop, call me in when dinner is ready" as he closed the narrow white door and stepped into the garage.

    He approached, stood at my workbench, just three or four feet next to where I stood, but he did not notice me. He turned on the small transistor radio that sat on my father's workbench for over thirty years when I was growing up before sitting on my work bench for the past fifteen years – don't ask me how I've kept it in working order – and rockabilly filled the air from the small circle of holes that served as its speakers broadcasting from one of my favorite radio stations.

    I stepped out from behind the shadows of the water heater holding a claw hammer I had picked up from my workbench and I struck the stranger who impersonated me with the flat end of the tool.

    My blood spouted from the crack in his forehead, and he fell to his knees. He looked up at me with a confused expression in eyes that looked like mine.

    I turned the hammer, gripped in my right hand, to the side with the claw, and I struck the imposter again and again until his face no longer resembled mine. He lay motionless on the concrete floor of the garage in a puddle of my blood and brain tissue.

    As I looked down on the dead and phony version of myself, I once again had occasion to wonder if my wife – and perhaps even my own son – were now also strange imposters and I turned from the bloody, lifeless mess on the concrete floor and I gripped the doorknob on the narrow white door between the garage and the kitchen, but the door was locked.

The radio had stopped playing rockabilly and was now broadcasting a news report about the local police's search for a criminally psychotic patient who escaped from a local asylum and was believed to be responsible for a series of brutal, random slayings. I ignored the drone of the radio as I had my own problems to solve.

What if there were more duplicates of me out there?

I tiptoed around the crumpled, battered thing that had disguised itself in a copy of my skin, now lying dead in a pool of my blood, surrounded by chunks of my brain, and I left the shadowy confines of my garage in a daze.

As I stepped into the blinding glare of sunlight, I half expected to also be hit with the sobering effects of reality, but I was still transfixed by my shock. My mind still reeled struggling to comprehend the unbelievable events of the day.

Walking backward down the driveway, staring into the dark cave of the shadowy garage and nearly tripping over the discarded bicycle; I stopped and stood dumbfounded on the sidewalk.

From the corner of my eye, motion caught my attention. I turned my head just in time to see a young boy, perhaps ten years old, come peddling around the far corner of the block on an old blue bicycle headed right at me on the sidewalk.

His sudden appearance startled me and when he got closer, I called to him;

Hey, Kid!

He stopped and looked up at me startled.

I snapped his photo with my Smartphone.

He rode away quickly.

I looked at his face – my face - on the screen of my Smartphone; a young boy sitting on my bike. His shoes were like mine; his socks were like mine. His Spiderman shorts and X-Men T-shirt matched my own. But that wasn't the worst of it.

His face was my face.

His eyes were my eyes.

He was an exact duplicate of me.

I swiped the screen with my finger and the photo of the boy on the bike was replaced with a photo of a man sitting at the Sunrise Mall food court. His face was my face, his eyes were my eyes.

When I swiped the screen again, the photo of the man in the food court was replaced with a photo of an elderly woman in a bank. Her face was my face, her eyes were my eyes.

When I swiped the screen again, the photo of the elderly woman in the bank was replaced with a photo of a little girl on a school yard playground. Her face was my face, her eyes were my eyes.

When I swiped the screen again, the photo of the little girl on the playground was replaced…

Photo after photo, all were mirror images.

You'll think I'm crazy but I'm not. This really happened.

I returned the phone to the pocket of my X-Men T-shirt.

Looking back on it, I can't remember… I'm just a little confused about what I was even doing on that street in front of that house that afternoon. I guess I was probably out looking for my lost bike.

I took my bike from the driveway where I found it, hopped on, and I peddled in the same direction as the kid who was my exact double. I spotted the imposter just up ahead a little ways – maybe about a block and a half away – riding my bike on the sidewalk ahead.

When he turned the corner at Second Street, I instinctively knew he was headed to my neighborhood, to my house, where I also instinctively knew my parents would be waiting for me to soon return home to them.

Could my parents be fooled by this creature pretending to be me?

I peddled faster and eventually I caught up to the kid disguised in my skin, riding my bike, grateful to have kept, still clutched in my right hand, the bloody claw-hammer.

About The Author

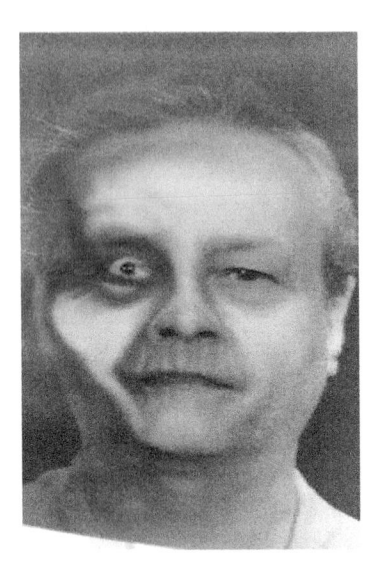

J.D. Allen

Born after midnight on the evening of Halloween, 1963, Joseph Dean Allen stalked the foggy enclaves of the San Francisco Bay Area, by moonlight, for much of his youth. Currently he haunts the rainy Pacific Northwest with his husband, Kyle, and the two gremlins, disguised as house cats, with whom they live.

Don't Open The Door, Harold

-Kelvin V.A Allison-

Don't Open The Door, Harold

"Don't open the door, Harold!"

The words were spoken with such conviction and terror that Edgar threw the novel he was reading into the air, his lean form twisting in terror as he lurched up and away from the sofa where he had been comfortably sat.

Heart hammering within his chest, he turned his head slowly, searching for the speaker that he knew without any doubt could not be there.

It was eleven PM, and he was alone in the large home he had recently purchased with the royalties from his latest novel, a former eighteenth-century farmhouse nestled amongst wetlands on the Yorkshire coast, far from his birthplace in Hastings, to the south.

Edgar had chosen the home for its remoteness.

Never a fan of people, the remote home seemed perfect for him, isolated from everyone but the occasional twitcher venturing into the wetlands to spy a

Lesser Speckled Muff or some such bird, and the polite if somewhat strange villagers of nearby Little Ogdon.

He had moved in during the first week of spring and had gone out of his way to make himself known in the village as a polite newcomer to their area. It was almost Halloween, and despite his very best efforts, he still felt like everyone stopped talking when he would enter the small shop or the villages only public house.

He didn't for one moment think that their standoffish behaviour had anything to do with homophobia, despite his best friend's claim when he had mentioned it to him but viewed it rather as a general distrust of all outsiders.

In fact, he hadn't seen anybody in the last week except the postman, Roger, and old Ms Johnson in the post office, the pair being the closest he had to local friends.

So, who had spoken?

The obvious, logical answer was nobody.

Yet Edgar had heard the voice clearly, that of a young woman, as if she were standing right behind the sofa.

Had he fallen asleep and dreamed the voice?

That had to be it.

Smiling, he shook his head and turned to look for the book he had thrown across the room, spotting it underneath the coffee table against the French windows.

Sighing wearily, chuckling at himself for being so jumpy, Edgar moved to the book and bent, picking it up and smiling down at the cover, reading the title aloud as he did so. "Drab House…an extreme ghost horror novel!"

Still chuckling, he moved back to the sofa and sat down, curling his tartan pyjama-clad legs up beneath him, picturing the book's author. "Henri, you crazy man, this book is absolute fire."

The smile slipped from his face as a sudden knocking sounded at his front door, his head turning to stare at it on the other side of the lounge, past the blazing fire.

Swallowing the sudden tightness in his throat, he rose to his feet, his gaze drifting to study the designer clock above the hearth, a unique, one-piece creation by Tennessee artist Kayda, his nerves jangling in alarm.

It was ten to eleven at night.

He had been so engrossed in reading his friend's latest novel he hadn't noticed how quickly the time had gone.

Who would be at his home in the middle of the night?

Why would someone be at his home this late?

'They've come to murder you,' his overactive author's imagination whispered in the dark recess of his mind.

He gasped in shock, a hand leaping to his heart as the knocking came again, insistent this time, the heavy oak door seeming to shake within its frame, and for the second time that evening, he launched the novel through the air, cursing as it landed in the middle of the hearth. The flames hissed and crackled about it, the pop of the wood making him jump again as the pages began to curl up, the novel blackening right before his eyes.

Filled with a sudden anger, Edgar surged towards the door, crossing his lounge in long strides, his fear gone.

Shaking his head, he reached out with a hand, fingers curling about the old iron handle, then screamed as the voice sounded directly behind him, ice-cold breath upon the nape of his neck. *"Don't open the door, Harold!"*

Still screaming in terror, he flung open the front door and rushed out into the dark night, shuddering as he felt the ice-cold touch of a fine rain-like mist touch his face.

Heart hammering in his chest, Edgar continued to back away down his garden, eager to get as far away from the bright rectangle that led inside his home as he could, only stopping when he stepped from the ornate paving stone path and felt wet mud squelch between his toes.

He flinched at the cold touch, hastily stepping back onto the paving stones, then seemed to realise that he was stood in the almost encompassing darkness that the remote location of his home afforded. Heart in his mouth, he turned, staring out across the bottom of his long garden, past the low hedges to stare out across the wetlands that he knew were there watching him back.

The memory of the knocking at the door returned to him in a rush, and he cursed beneath his breath, his blue eyes staring into the darkness, searching for the visitor.

Why had they not been standing outside the door when he had wrenched it open and fled into the night?

Had they left? Surely not.

The last series of knocking had prompted him into accidentally throwing his book into the fire, and he had ran from the house shortly afterwards.

Wouldn't he have seen the visitor walking away towards the narrow road which led to the nearby village?

Wouldn't they have heard him and come back?

Unless they hadn't left and were watching him?

But why would they do that?

He was certain that whoever it was meant him no harm.

Why would they knock if they had intended to hurt him?

Surely it would be far better to break in and kill him.
Kill him.
Oh, God.
No longer so confident, Edgar began to walk back towards the open door of his home, deciding to take his chances with the phantom voice rather than a potential killer.
Taking a steadying breath, he began to walk towards the rectangle of light, focusing on the interior of his lounge, then froze as a soft shuffling sound came from the darkness several feet to the left of his open front door.
Releasing a shaky breath, Edgar took another step forward, his eyes locked to the darkness where he had heard the noise and tried to sound manly, hating how scared he sounded. "Is anybody there?"
A stick snapped, and Edgar screamed and ran for the door, his arms pumping by his sides, filled with a certainty that strong limbs were going to grasp at him at any moment and drag him back to the wet grass, then stab at him repeatedly with knives, axes and machetes.
His leading foot stubbed hard against the doorstep of his home, and he stumbled face first, sliding across the wooden floor of his lounge, then somehow made his feet.

Shaking his head in denial, he threw himself back at the open door, hands slamming it shut and locking the bolts.

Head dizzy with stress, he leaned against the heavy door, desperately trying to listen for any sounds on the other side, then stepped quickly away as he pictured a mysterious figure hammering upon it once again.

He screamed as his mobile phone, forgotten until that moment, suddenly began to ring, the intro to Yorktown from the musical Hamilton filling the room, and cursing, he staggered over and snatched it up. "Hello…hello?"

"It's me," the cheerful voice replied, and Edgar pictured his friend and fellow author, Martin Lakemore. "What's up? You sound like you are crying. I take it the reviews of your latest novel have started landing?"

"Martin, you have to help me!" Edgar lowered his voice, his eyes drifting to the front door. "There's some weird shit going on here. I think someone's trying to get in!"

Instantly the smile was gone from Martin's voice. "In? In your home? Jesus Christ, are you alright? Who are they?"

"I don't know," Edgar shook his head, aware that his friend couldn't see him do so. "I didn't see them."

"What?"

"I heard them knocking on my door!"

"And…?"

"And that's it!" Edgar shook his head, his gaze glancing at the clock above the hearth. "It's just gone eleven! Wait, how don't you know this? Where are you?"

"Portland, Oregon," the reply came. "I am here for the convention…I asked you to come, remember?"

"Author Fest!" Edgar nodded in understanding. "Right!"

"What did the police say? Are they on their way?"

"The police?"

"You've called them, haven't you?"

"No…I…well…"

"Are you insane!" Martin raised his voice, and Edgar could picture him standing up in shock. "If someone is trying to get in your home, call the police now! Hang up and call them!"

"Wait, no," Edgar was suddenly on edge. "Don't go!"

"What? Call the police, Edgar…do it now!"

The line went dead.

"No!" the word came out in a whine, and head shaking in denial, Edgar began to phone his friend back then ended the call, knowing that Martin had been right.

He had to call the police.

Moving his thumb over the phone keyboard, he paused, brow furrowing as he suddenly considered what to do. He had never had to phone an emergency number in his life before and was unsure what number to phone.

Was it 999 or 911?

No, 911 was American. Wasn't it?

Nodding confidently, he was about to press the first number nine when he paused again, certain that there was another number people were encouraged to call.

Was it 111?

But 999 was for emergencies, wasn't it?

This was an emergency.

He needed help.

Without waiting for indecision to strike once more, he pressed the three nines and raised the phone to his ear.

"Hello, which service do you require?"

"Police, please…police."

"I am connecting you now."

There was a series of beeps, and the phone rang again and was immediately answered by a woman. "Police emergency line, what is your emergency."

"There's someone trying to break into my home."

"And who am I speaking to?"

"Edgar," he nodded, then winced. "Sorry, Edgar Jacobs."

"What number are you calling from, Mr Jacobs?"

"What?" he blinked, then recited his number, amazed that he could remember it for once, then reeled off his home address too. "Please, send someone!"

"Can you see the intruder, Mr Jacobs?"

"No, no, I can't."

"Do you know how many there are?"

"I…no, I…I haven't actually seen them, but…" the creak of a floorboard from upstairs snatched at his attention, stealing the air from his lungs as he glanced up, the phone moving away from his ear. "Oh, God no…"

"Mr Jacobs?" the voice on the line sounded suddenly concerned. "Are you there?"

"I think there's someone upstairs…"

"Are you alone in the house?"

'Obviously fucking not!' he thought.

"I should be," he said, his eyes tracing across the landing as another creak sounded, as if someone were walking.

"Mr Jacobs, I have contacted your local station, and an officer will be with you within the hour…"

"The hour?" he nearly screamed down the phone line.

"Your home is quite remote, and all the local officers are currently attending calls," the woman explained with the patience of one who had shared countless calls before. "Mr Jacobs, I am going to need you to find somewhere safe and hide until the officers reach you."

"Hide?"

"Yes," Edgar could picture the faceless woman nodding calmly, perhaps sipping a cup of coffee while he stood there, ready to defecate on his highly polished wooden floorboards. "Is there somewhere you could hide?"

He almost dropped the phone as the scream came from upstairs, shrill and drawn out, the sound of a woman in complete agony. "Oh, my fucking God, did you hear that?"

"Mr Jacobs? What is wrong? Has the intruder got in?"

"No, no…there is a woman screaming upstairs!"

The woman sounded confused. "You can hear her?"

"Can't you?" he asked, tensing as the screaming sounded once more. "She is doing it right now!"

There was a long, drawn-out silence, and then the voice returned. "Mr Jacobs, have you been drinking or taking any form of recreational drugs this evening?"

"What? No, of course not! Why are you asking me that?"

"Please stay calm, Mr Jacobs."

"You can't hear her screaming?"

"Mr Jacobs…"

"Can you hear a woman screaming?" he all but shouted.

"No, no, Mr Jacobs, I ca…"

Edgar ended the call, head shaking as he closed his eyes.

So that was it then.

He had gone insane, just like his mother.

A nut job at the age of forty-two.

She had been two years younger than he was now, before they had carted her away to a secure psychiatric unit, screaming that she could see people that weren't there.

That was the last time he had seen her, the unfortunate woman taking her own life the next year.

With shock, Edgar realised that the screams that he had been imagining upstairs had ceased, probably because he had realised that they weren't real in the first place.

Just like the knocking on the door.

Just like the woman's voice whispering in his ear.

Don't open the door, Harold.

Yet where had he got the name, Harold?

He hadn't known anyone with that name in his life, nor could he even think of a celebrity with the same name.

Shaking his head, he cast a rueful look at the remains of the book that he had been reading, little more

than a blackened mess of ashes in the fireplace now, and then began to slowly walk up the stairs to his bedroom.
What he needed now was a good night's sleep.

Edgar lurched awake, his heart hammering in his chest as he fought with the creature atop him, trying to divest himself from its smothering grasp. With a grunt of triumph, he kicked the sweaty duvet away from his body, realising just what it was as he did so and propped himself up on his elbows, his eyes scanning about the room, trying to work out what had just woken him.
Had it been a nightmare?
He couldn't remember having one, but sometimes dreams were like that, fading as a person awoke, sometimes returning to them over the course of the next day, sometimes vanishing forever with no trace.
Had that been what had happened?
Sighing wearily, he laid back down on his bed and grabbed his phone from the bedside table, a flick of his thumb revealing it was just past three in the morning.
The hour of the witch.
He shuddered as the thought came to him, his lifelong fear of witches resurfacing in a rush, and cursing, he sat up and flicked on the small bedside lamp for some light.
The bedroom lit up, but he felt no better.

Beyond the window of his bedroom, the mild rain of the previous night had turned into a storm; heavy rain lashed at the lead-lined panes while the wind howled around the house as it came off the North Sea and raced unhindered across the open expanse of the wetlands.

"Fuck this," he groaned and laid back down once more.

The sudden banging upon the front door of his home had him sliding from his bed, eyes wide as he stared at his bedroom door as the handle suddenly turned, and it swung toward him, revealing the dark hallway beyond.

Once more, the hammering upon the door sounded loud and insistent before fading away to be replaced with the creak of floorboards as someone moved in the hallway.

Edgar gasped in terror as footsteps suddenly sounded as if someone were moving down the stairs in a hurry, and as if in a dream, he moved to the door and peered out.

"Don't open the door, Harold!" the slender woman at the top of the stairs called down to someone, her body barely clad in a silk, pink negligee that seemed to move like smoke about her form, barely covering her breasts.

"Harold!" the woman began once more, hurrying out of sight, and stunned, Edgar moved to the oak bannister and peered over to the dining room below, watching as the stranger reached the bottom step and then hurried out of sight, her voice insistent as the knocking began once more. "Don't open the door, Harold!"

Heart in his mouth, Edgar edged along the landing towards the head of the stairs, hands gripping to the bannister in a vice-grip as he peered at the room below.

He heard the click of locks being unfastened, the voice of the woman repeating her pleas, followed by the creak of the front door as it opened, a man's voice starting to speak. "What the devil do you think...

The voice turned to a choking gurgle, and the sound of something heavy hit the floor. As the woman gave a scream of terror and denial, the front door slammed shut, and her screams turned to a raw howl of pain.

Eyes wide, Edgar stared down at the corner of the dining room where it led through into the large lounge, barely daring to breathe, and unable to believe what he was doing he started to descend the stairs on shaky legs.

He slipped and fell as the woman suddenly lurched into sight on her hands and knees, one large breast hanging from her negligee, a large cut in the flesh of her left arm.

Back pressed hard against the wall of the stairs, the author watched in horror as the woman began to climb the stairs on her hands and knees, her long black hair hanging about her features like a curtain of crude oil. As she drew level with where he sat in terror, she turned her head back, her good arm rising to brush the hair from her face, and Edgar felt his stomach lurch at the terror in her wide eyes, snotty mucus dangling from her nose, while tears stained her now pale features.

The clump of footsteps made Edgar turn, his hair rising on end as he saw the tall figure in the black robe and white collared vestments of a priest move to the bottom of the wide staircase, a plastic vacuum-formed mask painted to look like a lady complete with bright red lipstick and black eyelashes covering their features. The towering height and shoulder-width of the figure had screamed of brutal masculinity, and the voice of the intruder was confirmation as it began to sing softly, the long knife it held in its left-hand scratching along the bannister as it began to climb the stairs behind the sobbing woman. *"Ring-a-ring-o'-roses… pocket full of posies…a-tishoo, a -tishoo…we all fall down…"*

Without another word, it leapt upon the woman, dragging her by her heel back level with where Edgar lay, strong hands rolling her over to lay upon her back.

The blade swept up and down, slicing through three fingers of the hand that the screaming woman had raised defensively, the digits dropping down the stairs.

The blade came down, stabbing deep into her exposed breast, sheering the nipple off so that it hung on a strip of muscle, then the knife rose and fell repeatedly, rupturing her left eye with the point, sending blood and fluid cascading down her cheek, punching through her tongue as it poked from her mouth as she screamed, severing the end to fall and stick to her bloody breast.

On and on it went, the figure moving to kneel astride the dying woman, taking their time now as they worked at her, removing each of her eyes in turn.

She had found the ability to scream once more as the blade had cut into her mouth, slicing her full lips from her face, then began to saw at the front of her throat, cutting through the thick muscle so violently that it severed her spine, her head bouncing down the stairs.

And all the while, Edgar screamed in terror, and the killer sang, oblivious to his presence. *"Ring-a-ring-o'-roses…"*

"And so, he left, just like that?" Roger, the postman, eyed Old Ms Johnson in confusion several months later as they stood in the post office, he nursed the cup of coffee that she had made him, and her nodding at him wisely.

"Oh yes, I heard it all from one of the removal men that helped him ship his stuff out."

"Did they say why?" the postman raised an eyebrow.

"Ghosts," she gave a soft chuckle, her head shaking.

"Ghosts?" Roger gave a snort of amusement. "The ghosts of who? No one has ever died in that house, have they?"

"No," she confirmed. "Not a single person."

"How strange," he took a sip of coffee. "Shame, he was a nice man. Still, I expect it was all that horror he wrote that made him think that way…it must get a bit much."

"I honestly wouldn't know," she gave him a smile. "All I do know is that the new owners are arriving today."

"New owners?" Roger was shocked. "That was quick!"

She nodded, opening her mouth to speak, then nodded towards the window of the post office. "This must be them now…don't stand gawking, away with you."

Chuckling, Roger passed her the half-empty cup and bid her farewell, then left the post office, smiling as he saw the couple that were approaching. "Good morning."

The man, several decades older than the dark-haired beauty at his side, frowned at his words, seemed to think better of it and nodded. "Morning."

"New in the village?" Roger was unable to stop himself from asking the couple, enjoying the fact Old Ms Johnson would be watching and cursing him for a fool.

"Yes," the woman answered before the man, and Roger felt his heart and his loins lurch at her beauty. "We have just purchased Drift House down to the south of the village. It looks out over the wetlands."

"It's a lovely place," Roger nodded at her. "Truly lovely."

"We hope to make some amazing memories there," the woman smiled, her eyes as bright as her large smile.

There was a moment's silence, and then the man nodded and began to walk on towards the post office, and smiling awkwardly, the woman began to move after him, her voice reaching back to Roger as he began to move away. "It was lovely meeting you."

"Likewise," he nodded, a hand rising in farewell, then he turned as a shadow fell across him, his grin returning as he found old Ms Johnson's son, Sebastian standing there, the large youth's features blank as he studied the couple.

"The new owners of Drift House," Roger jerked a thumb towards the departing pair, chuckling as he heard

the woman tell her husband Harold to hold the door for her, then he began to walk away, humming to himself as he went, while behind him, Sebastian began to sing one of his nursery rhymes, his deep voice almost mournful.
"*Ring-a-ring-o'-roses…*"

About The Author

Kelvin V.A Allison

Hailing from Portsmouth on the south coast, horror author Kelvin V.A Allison has made the north-east his home for the past fourteen years and has written a staggering thirty seven horror novels in that time, including the ten book World of Sorrow series which is in talks of being made into a graphic novel, and five short horror novellas, as well as co-writing the RPG system Edge of Darkness. His sci-fi horror novel, Juggernaut, a cross between 28 Days later and Star Trek is currently being converted to a script by a Danish screenwriter in the hopes of it being picked up by a television network. Currently living in the paradise that is County Durham, he has swapped the hustle and bustle of the large southern cities for a peaceful village existence in the home he shares with his fiancée and their four children, where he spends his days writing, eating fruit filled sugared pastries, lamenting the loss of his waistline and wearing an assortment of masks.

I Will Save You

-Stephen Cooper-

I Will Save You

A shovel crunched into the roots protruding from the ground deep in the woods as a man lay still in the dirt a few metres away. His face was stained with blood while his battered and bruised body remained motionless. His clothes were capped in mud, as were his hands. His swollen eyes were tightly closed above his busted nose, and for all intent and purpose, he looked dead with his barely visible breaths and laboured heartbeat. The skinny guy above him digging his shallow grave certainly thought he was. But he wasn't dead, not yet anyway. He still had some life left in him as he partially opened his puffy eye to take a peek at the man hovering nearby with the shovel in hand.

Dan (the man holding the shovel) checked his bruised jaw, which now had a constant click to it, before driving the spade into the ground once more, not noticing the would-be-corpse's half-opened eye.

Digging a hole, even one this shallow, was tough work in the summer heat and had sapped all his attention and energy. The tall thin trees around him offer some protection from the late afternoon sun, but not enough. His fishing hat helped too, but neither of those things aided the burning in his arms as he plummeted the shovel down once more. His knuckles ached as well while he held the wooden handle, all of them dented and bloodied from the tough son of a bitch on the floors fucking iron jaw. He did not go down easy.

He took a breather from the digging as he lent on the impaled spade and eyeballed the asshole on the deck beside him. A hatred swirled making him want to kill the fucker all over again, not realising they'd failed the first time round. The Man kept perfectly still, his eyes once again shut, praying the shovel didn't come down on his prone body and finish the job.

Dan gave the carcass a swift kick in the gut, but the man held in his groan. Gritting his teeth, he took the cheap kick. What other choice did he have? The skinny guy, satisfied with the extra punt, continued his digging. A second guy approached from behind the man, but he couldn't risk swivelling his head to take a look, and still wasn't sure if he could move it anyway. For the moment it was best to remain perfectly still and play dead, while hoping he didn't actually succumb in the meantime.

"You think it's deep enough?" Dan asked the new arrival taking deep breaths from the exertion.

The dying man on the floor couldn't see Eric but could hear his voice as he spoke to the gravedigger.

"For this piece of shit." He too gave the downed, nearly dead man, a kick that he had to refrain from reacting to. "Yeah."

"Check with Tony that there's nothing else to go in the hole," Dan concluded.

Eric left as quickly as he arrived, heading back through the trees as Dan sized up the man and looked back at the hole. '*Fuck*,' the hole definitely needed to be slightly bigger he realised as he continued to dig in the sweltering sun. The dude hadn't looked the biggest of guys at first, but laying in the dirt he was definitely bigger than Dan remembered, and certainly bigger than the hole he'd dug. Taller, rather than bulkier, although everyone looked taller and bulkier than Dan. He wiped the sweat from his eyes after plunging the shovel down a few more times and tossing the dirt beside the shallow hole before he looked down at the man's body once more… but it wasn't there. What the fuck? Where'd he…?

Dan didn't get a chance to complete his line of thinking as the Man cracked him with a rock, right on the button. Both hit the ground. The Man's legs buckled underneath him as he remained at death's door, while

Dan crashed to the dirt after being knocked out cold. The Man took stock of the situation. The surprise blow hadn't given Dan a chance to yell for help, and the sound of their hard landing had been muffled by the leaves and shrubbery on the earth. Plus, the woods were alive with birds chirping and a stream flowing nearby to help mask any noise. For the moment, he figured he was safe.

The Man briefly let go of the rock as his hand gravitated towards the back of his throbbing head. He had been unaware of the pain a split second earlier, but the strenuous action of getting up and clobbering that motherfucker had relit his senses. Now he felt the pain and fuck did it hurt. His fingers dabbed at the back of his skull, and when he pulled them away, he noticed the shine of the bright red blood covering them. There was something else there too, some clumpy substance that he hoped was mud and not brain, but he couldn't't be sure as the searing pain definitely pointed towards the latter.

His eyes began to fade as his balance went despite being sat on the ground. He was on the verge of passing out but knew if he did, it was very unlikely he'd ever wake again. Either the pain and his injuries would take him, or that piece of shit digging his grave would regain consciousness and bury him. The Man took in a couple of gulps of air before going the other way and taking a few deep breaths as he tried to restore some sense of calm. He checked his surroundings from his seated position and spotted the footprints Eric left which led away from his grave. The heavy rain of the last few weeks had provided the cast despite the scorching sun quickly drying the area. As the footprints led north, the Man decided he was going south.

He tried to stand, ready to make his getaway, but while he held the back of his damaged head, images began to flicker before his eyes and invaded his mind making him stop in his tracks.

He saw a young woman screaming with tears streaming down her face as he stood in front of her, fending off three guys. The skinny fucker on the floor was one of the three, and he looked pissed off and ready for a fight. The other two he couldn't place, but assumed one of them had to have been the gravedigger's buddy who had called him a piece of shit. That left one unaccounted for. Was he still with the young upset woman? Was she still in trouble? What were they doing to her?

So many questions entered his mind before realising he had a lot more. He couldn't remember what the fuck had happened or even who he was. He tried to recall his name, but it was out of reach. He pawed at the back of his head, only now registering the full extent of the damage. Those assholes had done a real number on him. No wonder they thought he was dead. He barely believed he was alive himself with how foggy his mind was. And what of the girl? The one he'd been protecting from these cunts.

He looked at the inviting woods leading the opposite way from the tracks but knew he couldn't leave the girl. He had to save her. If she was still alive, she needed his help, he was certain of it. He retook the rock from the floor he'd used to knock his would-be undertaker out and slapped Dan awake with his other hand as he mounted him.

"Where is she?" the Man asked with extra vigor in his voice. He still felt weak and ready to die at any given moment, but a surge of adrenaline had taken over since the recalled memories, and his body was willing to put in the extra work to keep him alive a little longer.

"Where is she!" he asked again, slapping Dan hard across the face and getting his attention this time.

Dan groggily tried to shout for help but couldn't form the words. If his jaw had felt somewhat dislocated before the rock connected, now it felt like the damn thing was dangling from his face. Blood spilt from his lips as he tried once again to cry for help but only managed a pathetic gargle.

"What the fuck have you done with her?" the Man asked once more. His patience already waning. He knew time was running out for both him and the girl. He needed answers, but the piece of shit beneath him had no intention of offering any as all he could mumble was something resembling 'help me' that was barely loud enough for the Man to hear, let alone any would-be saviours.

The Man held the rock above his head which took a lot more energy than it should have. His arms felt weak, and the grip was loose, but the pose itself at least looked threatening and let the guy beneath him know he meant business.

"I'm not telling you," Dan somehow forced from his mouth in barely a whisper. *Wrong answer.*

The rock dented Dan's forehead as the Man brought it down in a violent rage. The hideous depression sent Dan's eyes rolling back in his head. The second blow broke more of the skin, and the third cracked Dan's skull sending the jagged edge of the rock through the bone. He repeated the action several more times, with his attacks landing randomly. Each strike no longer just crashed into Dan's demolished forehead. He took his fucking left eye out amongst the repeated blows and made a complete mess of his nose. The already hanging jaw fell off Dan's face. His cheekbones crumbled. They'd need to identify him via fingerprints by the time the Man came to his senses and stop mashing the paste underneath him. *No further questions.*

He left what used to be Dan on the floor and followed the footprints towards the thicker trees in the woods. They'd left the beaten path in order to bury him someplace he wouldn't be found, which meant the prints quickly disappeared within the undergrowth. There was no clear path to follow, so the Man moved forward on pure instinct, hoping luck was on his side. His condition suggested he hadn't had much of that so far, *so maybe he was due*. Holding the back of his head as he navigated the trees, he let the bloody rock fall from his other hand. He was unaware he had even kept hold of it and just as absentminded about dropping it. He was on autopilot to an unknown destination, but at least his mission was clear. *Save the girl.*

Fallen tree branches and loose roots tripped him several times as he struggled to keep his footing. His head rocked back, taking in the barely visible blue sky above him as the canopy obscured his view and night began to make some ground. The sky and trees merged in his hazy view as his brain pulsated and felt ready to explode inside his broken skull. But he continued forward. Determined, and with a single purpose in mind. *He had to save her.* Nothing would stop him. Not the roots trying to snag his feet or the branches trying to send him crashing back to the ground. Not the setting sun trying to lose him within the dense forest or the assholes who fucked him up and tried to bury him alive. He would go on!

Another slip ruined the illusion of being able to succeed and sent him tumbling to the forest floor.

Images once again invaded his mind as he lay on the ground with his eyes closed. He remembered punching that dickhead Dan in his weak-looking face fucking up his jaw before he was kicked from behind by the second guy, Eric. He regained his footing quickly after the kick and continued to shield the girl, ready to carry on the fight. But something happened, and he'd lost. The memory skipped forward to Dan and Eric dragging him through the woods. They both looked a mess, but he was worse. He remembered his skull already being fucked at that point as they pulled him by his feet across the muddy ground and through the shrubbery to the place they intended to bury him as his mind faded.

He opened his eyes and saw drag marks that told him he was on the right track. The displaced dirt came from a small incline in front of him. He struggled with the slight climb as he pulled himself across the muddy floor, still unable to stand. His vision blurred as the pain in the back of his skull intensified. The blood was no longer a bright red, but that did little to alleviate his fears, especially with everything spinning and fading and his body temperature nosediving. At the top of the incline, a thin gravel path weaved between the trees and up ahead the Man spotted Eric for a fleeting moment before he disappeared from the horizon.

Knowing now that he was definitely on the right course, the Man willed his malfunctioning body to stand. He was no longer running on fumes but on empty. His legs felt like lead, his steps painstakingly slow, his balance compromised with every movement. His mind was still foggy, and his vision was absolutely fucked. He regretted not taking the shovel and using it as a crutch, but that had only occurred to him now. Too late to go back. He'd passed the point of no return.

He continued onwards, even picked up the pace a little as he reached the spot where he'd seen Eric. His breathing got raspier. His eyes flickered as his head switched between falling back and dropping forward. His gaze caught the mud on his boots. The dirt running up his trousers. His filthy mud-caked and blood-soaked hands.

The Man tenderly touched the back of his damaged head, pulling away dried blood and clumps of hair. More dirt too, and something that may well have been skull fragment, but he didn't want to inspect too closely.

Tears formed in his eyes as he knew death was coming for him, but he swatted them away. No time for them now.

"I'll save you," he mumbled as he staggered passed the point he saw Eric and hoped his potential killer had stuck to the path. If he had deviated further the Man didn't fancy his chances of spotting the signs. He kept on though, despite all the obstacles. His faculties were murky but still somehow focused on the one task at hand.

"I will save you."

As he took a bend in the pavement, the Man stumbled. His feet giving out from under him for no other reason than pure exhaustion. Hitting the floor his eyes noticed a long strand of blond hair stuck to some plants sticking haphazardly from the ground, having recently been trod on. He reached forward and took the stray hair. Gently examining it in his fingers, another memory came rushing back to him.

He was fending off the three attackers as he slugged Dan to the ground once again with a vicious haymaker. The skinny fuck was resilient but wasn't in a hurry to get back up this time. The Man swung wide and busted Eric's nose wide open, bringing tears to the guy's eyes and staggering him backwards before he awkwardly fell, landing high on his shoulder and dislocating it. He elbowed the third man (who he didn't know was named Tony) and sent him spiralling towards the woman. As Tony reached the woman the Man darted forward to stop him doing anything to the petrified girl. Swinging his fist down once more, he swiped a lock of the woman's hair with his fingertips before he clenched his hand into a fist and knocked Tony to the floor.

"You stay away from her," he roared at the three as they regrouped, all looking worse for wear.

Again, his vision jumped forward to being dragged. This time it was at the very spot he now laid. He'd kept ahold of the woman's hair purely by accident until the plant ripped it away from him while his hands dangled by his side. They continued to drag him before turning off at the slope.

He wrapped the strand of hair tightly around his index finger as he achieved the monumental task of climbing to his feet. His legs altered between lead and jelly, but he continued on. He could see the outline of Eric ahead of him, unaware that he was being followed by the Man. The sun had lowered further, bringing an extra darkness to the woods, but if Eric looked behind him, he'd still be spotted. The Man didn't care. There wasn't time to play it safe. His life force was seeping from his body, and his will could only drag him so far.

In the end, biology would rule over mind, and his depleted tank would accept defeat. But not quite yet.

"I will save you."

He took a few more laboured steps before briefly falling to one knee then standing again.

"I will save you."

Another couple of steps and the other leg buckled.

"I will save you!"

His voice was louder that time. More determined. More belief. He didn't know how the fuck he'd save her, but he would. The trees began to thin out as a clearing slowly began to appear in front of him. Despite the sun falling, the light got better as he neared the end of the woods.

"I will save you," he repeated once more as he stumbled and fell. He dragged himself towards the edge of the forest as he heard voices.

His fingers dug into the ground as he clawed at the dirt. His body felt like dead weight, but the sound of the voices drove him on. He had to see them for himself. He had to see who the voices belonged to and where the girl was. Then he had to save her! He knew he didn't have anything left, but one more feat of superhuman determination surely wasn't impossible. One last action to ensure her safety, and then he could let go. But not yet.

As he made it to the edge of the tree line everything stopped. The anger and frustration. The acknowledgement of death and the fatigue of his body. The blood, sweat and tears. All ceased to be for a brief moment as he caught a glimpse through the long summer grass and saw her face.

Sitting down on a fallen log ten meters back from the edge of the forest was the Woman. Her face was bruised, and her lip busted. The little makeup she had on had run, and tears still trickled from her worried eyes. Her summer dress was grass-stained, and her knees cut and dirty. The dress was ripped in several places, and her hair ruffled. Her hands were trembling as she held something in them, but the Man couldn't quite see what it was or why it was so important for him to know. He dragged himself a few feet further until he could get a better look. In her hands she held a broken blood-tipped shoe, one of her own.

Eric approached the woman and sat beside her while Tony rested his back against the big log on the other side of her, cradling a broken arm. Eric delicately put his arm around her as she leaned her head into his shoulder with the rate of her tears growing. He comforted her as she sobbed, all while the Man looked on with his eyes fixated on the bloody shoe and his hands reaching for the back of his damaged head once more. The touch brought back the last of his memories of the events leading up to him waking up next to the shallow grave.

 He remembered watching the woman from afar, following her on her stroll through the beautiful woods. He remembered licking his lips as he focused on her long sexy legs and beautiful blonde hair. His lengthy dick stiffened as he drew closer to her, keeping quiet and out of sight the whole time. Once he was close enough to smell her perfume, he took a look around the clearing and realised they were all alone.
 He pounced, covering her mouth with his hand before she could scream. He tossed her onto the long grass with a hungry, cruel smile planted across his lips. She bit his finger as he covered her mouth again, and he smacked her for the indiscretion busting her lip and reddening her cheek. Truth be told, he enjoyed the little bit of fight she offered. It got him even harder. Tears streamed from her eyes as he ripped at her dress and tore away her underwear. His monster cock was buried deep in her dry pussy before she even realised what the hell was happening, eliciting an ear-piercing wail that the Man found amusing until he heard people shouting in their direction. The place wasn't as deserted as he'd thought.
 He continued pumping his stiff dick inside her as the woman tried to fight him off, all while screaming at

the top of her lungs. No need to keep her quiet now. She was no match for him, but the three guys rapidly approaching might be, so he had to climb off the whore and face them. At a glance, they didn't look much. Three men dressed to fish but had let go of their rods and tackle boxes as they'd sprinted towards the endangered woman. Three wannabe heroes, the man thought as he stood without fear or regret to face them after stuffing his horsecock back in his trousers. He relished the challenge and cracked his knuckles like it was go time.

He punched Dan to the ground first and then knocked Eric aside after he'd been kicked by the flexible fucker. Tony was a different matter. He could handle himself and soon proved it, making the Man realise he was in a fight. To begin with, he thought he'd take care of the three saviours and get back to raping the pretty blonde with no problems, but Tony was a problem. Tony had let rip with a few punches that knocked the Man back, but he made sure he kept between them and the girl making it clear that she was his. 'Go find your own pussy,' he joked as he spitefully kicked her back to the floor when she tried to make a break for it.

That had incensed the three guys as they regrouped and attacked again as a team this time. Eric landed another flying kick like he was some kind of kung-fu guy rather than a middle-aged man in a fishing vest. Dan *stood back up for the third time, ready to go again despite his dislocated jaw. Tony was moving looser, like he was warmed up now and really ready to turn it on. The Man, however, was unfazed. He snapped Tony's arm at the elbow as he came close to breaking through and protecting the vulnerable woman. It was a delightful sound for the Man, sickening and pleasing at the same time, with the added bonus of Tony's painful roar. If he wasn't already hard from the bout of raping, he would have been after that.*

He punched Dan in the gut, taking the wind right out of him and dropping him to his knees before blocking Eric's latest stupid fucking kick and was about to break the asshole's leg when something connected with the back of his skull.

The Man's memories of the event changed their perspective. He was still seeing what happened in his mind, but it was no longer from his own eyes. The memories were directing themselves, and his mind filled in the blanks as he watched the end of the fight unfold in third person.

The Woman had climbed to her feet and taken off her boot. It had a slight heel to it, nothing huge, but enough to cause some damage, and that's exactly what she'd done. She'd slammed it into the back of the Man's head, and the corner of the heel busted him open. He didn't realise she'd then hit him twice more before he fell forward. The back of his head bleeding all over the place as she found the sweet spot.

She mounted his back and brought the shoe down, over and over again, like he had done with the rock on Dan. Every blow tore another chunk away from the back of his head as she went fucking ballistic on him. The three men sat watching from the position they'd been knocked to as her war cry and explosive rage continued. Eventually, the blows weakened as she lost the remaining strength in her arm, and floods of tears took over at the realisation that she'd just killed a man. Albeit a scumbag fucking rapist that had attacked her.

The Woman composed herself a little more, moving away from Eric's shoulder as Tony offered her his jacket from his seated position.

"You did the right thing," he offered as he passed the jacket to her after seeing her shivering.

"No one's ever going to find that cunt. No one's gonna miss him," Eric added. She didn't look convinced about that, but the main thing was he'd never put his filthy hands on her ever again. She'd seen to that.

The Man took one final look at her with tears in his eyes. His anger and determination deserted his face in favour of remorse. *Had he really done that? Was that who he really was?* He was glad he'd forgotten everything about himself. Maybe it was better that way. During his final look, he knew she was safe, that his mission was complete. It hadn't been him who saved her, quite the fucking opposite, in fact, but now she was safe, and that was all that mattered.

He climbed gingerly to his feet and took several steps towards the impossibly black woods behind him. *When had it got so dark?* he thought as he collapsed for the final time.

The End

About The Author

Stephen Cooper

Stephen Cooper is an extreme horror writer from Portsmouth, England.
Having spent the last 20 years writing film scripts and directing MV's he made the move to books in 2022 and has no intention of looking back. His debut novel Abby Vs The Splatploitation Brothers Hillbilly Farm is heavily inspired by the video nasties, B-movies, and slashers flicks he loves, as well as the splatterpunk and extreme horror he's began to read.

His debut novel Abby Vs The Splatploitation Brothers Hillbilly Farm is heavily inspired by the video nasties, B-movies, and slashers flicks he loves, as well as the splatterpunk and extreme horror he's began to read.
He has since released three more books. A torture-porn called Near Death, a brutal wrestling novella, Blood-Soaked Wrestling and his nastiest work to date, The Rot. A second book in the Abby Vs Series is on its way in 2023. When not writing horror, he can be found talking about it on his YouTube channel 'Splatploitation,' in which he covers a wide range of extreme horror splatterpunk.
For more on everything splatploitation check out
https://splatploitation.com

Let It Be The Devil

-B.E. Goose-

Let It Be The Devil

It wasn't the collapse of wood and mortar, which had been consumed by the engorged flames, that awoke Clara. Nor was it the insatiable, unearthly bellowing off in the distance as the perpetrator who had left her home in rubble flew off into the silhouetted, snow-covered pines. It was the wetness she felt dripping on her face that awoke the young mother within the wreckage. All of her senses jumped, brought back to reality again; however, blinded by the lack of light as she was buried alive. Clara thought about what had happened before she eventually blacked out.

    She and Clyde had heard the beast let out its otherworldly shriek. Before they could fathom what they had just heard, the aroma of smoke had coated their nostrils with soot. She ran to the newborn, baby in hand, then nothing.

Until now, the weight lying on her chest was warm, bundled in love and blankets held against her heart. Clara had her youngest of three, Annie, not even four weeks out of the womb, the one who needed her protection the most. As Clara dug herself and her newborn out of the debris, she prayed that her other two, William and James, might have been quick on their feet to hide or run. Something their infant sister couldn't have done.

Illumination of fire and what the clouds in the night sky would allow revealed the crumbling of her home, the desolation of their animal pens, everything burning and dead. Moaning into a scream, Clara dropped to her knees, holding her beloved Annie. She could see the burnt, steaming outlines of her two small boys facing down in the snow. They had run but weren't quick enough to escape the Devil from above. Somewhere in the back of her mind, a chime rang out. A moment of her motherly instincts telling her to look down at her baby, who hadn't moved or made a sound. She pulled Annie away from her chest to find her face blue, her mouth oozing blood. What Clara had thought to be vomit or spit-up wetting her own face was gore from the trauma of having a house fall on her now-dead baby. She blacked out again, if only for a moment of anguish, her entire life burning and dead.

What had she done to deserve such an evil coming out of nowhere and destroying her life and family? It could've taken her and Clyde, but why the children? What had the four, and six-year-old William or James done? Or better yet, Annie? Why did such evil come to wreak havoc on them? Then, off in the distance, she heard the terror from above wail again. It sputtered in its flight amidst the trees, twisting and turning like a maple seed pod in the wind, whirling down deep into the pines.

Unhinged and enraged, Clara picked herself back up. Her eyes and cheeks stung as the cold breeze of New Jersey turned her tears to ice, soiled from dirt and char, bonnet escaping in the whirling winds. She set her baby down on top of her abode's wreckage, re-wrapping poor Annie back up with the blankets, as she thought that if the child's soul still lurked, it should stay cozy and warm. Amid the scattered remains of her life, she found Clyde's rifle, a reminder of his time serving the Army of the Potomac, the bayonet still attached to the muzzle. Wrought and rotten with emotions, Clara, ill-equipped for the pines, followed the bright jam-red pools sinking into the snow, her tattered dress and ash hair waving with the trees in the current, feet and fingers already growing numb.

She wasn't willing to retreat or turn back to the town miles and miles away. If she would die from the elements, she would take down the devil with her.

Blind rage turned into soft weeping as the widowed mother of none progressed further into the dead-silent pines. Clara fought back the need to scream, wail, and announce herself to all who might be awake and thriving off the bones of the unfortunate here in these woods. In a split moment of thought, she lingered on the idea of how shooting without declaring oneself presence was a vulgar or even barbaric action. But the thought ceased as quickly as it came. It was vulgar and barbaric to attack from the skies in the middle of the night and kill her fleeing children. It didn't even make a meal of them...

The thought that this creature, this evil, vile abomination, hadn't even hunted them for food but for fun. Sport. Just because. Had her family died for nothing? Had her boys suffered a gruesome fate out of sheer misfortune? Clara straightened up her shivering posture and trucked onward.

Not an echo of an owl or any movement other than her own. It felt like the heavy snow, barely supported by the branches it set upon, was holding onto dear life so as not to draw attention to itself. The only sound was the wind from the west, and even it seemed to try and muffle its bellows. Crunching snow under her thinly covered shoes was the loudest sound within the woods. This lonely silence would've had her thinking she was walking into a trap, wolves out in the distance, but even they made movement. They existed and exerted life, letting others know they were being prayed upon, even if they couldn't see them. However, Clara didn't feel any of that. She was the only living thing for miles, alone in a place that normally still wiggles with minimal life, even when desolated by the cold of winter.

As she continued to follow the trickles of blood, she tried to think about the last time she had felt so isolated. Maybe when she went out into an autumn brush, too young to realize the dangers of being lost, only wanting to follow…

She was found late in the evening by a search party of her family's parish. They had caught a shadow standing in an opening in the forest, standing in the middle of an area dry and brittle. The tears streaming and the sorrowful whine like a ghouls as her mother ran up, arms open and engulfed her, like a web to a fly. She hadn't understood why there were tears streaming from her mother's face. Father had gone off into the unknown, and she never greeted him the same way. Naivety, a sweet poison.

The same wail and distortion of her features, like her mother's that night, had twisted Clara's. Sobbing expelled itself from the freezing woman. She would never have the relief that her mother was granted; she could only hope for revenge. That is, if she ever found the devil again.

Shivering and wiping the tears and snot from her face with the palm of her hand, the red drips were becoming smaller and thinner. She muttered her desperations and hurried around the bend of trees. A gust of wind forced itself across Clara's frame as the red trail ended in a large crimson goop, pooling at the bottom of a tree. In a slow ascent, she brought her head up. She hoped, she prayed to see the creature stalking the top of the small, crooked tree.

Entangled in the rigid limbs was half of her husband's corpse. His torso stuck within the finer veins of the tree. His left leg still wearing his shoe, dangling as the creature tore through muscle and de-jointed bones, the right leg completely missing. Frozen by more than just the temperature, Clara buckled. It was then she realized how numb her most distal digits were becoming. She whimpered as she approached the tree, finding the missing right leg dangling just above the mangled corpse, the boot still strapped. With her feet turning to stone, she braced herself for what she would have to do.

With one boot equipped, she poked at the body hovering so close but miles away from her with the bayonet. The one-time Clyde's refusal to remove his work boots in their home brought her grace. Prodding brought more than just the boot; the cracking and breaking of branches dropped the entire torso. Lungs frozen and mouth dry, she could only let out a muffled yelp rather than the full-blown cry that Clara would've let out in any other state of being. Ropes of intestines were still stuck within the tree, streaming down, still attached to their base, blowing in the unforgiving wind. She took the left boot and ran to the other side of the tree, sobbing.

The trunk of the tree let Clara rest her weight against it while she slipped the boot on, all the while a wreck, a quivering sham of a human being. Darkness loomed above. Between it and the frigid weather, calling to her, asking politely for her to close her eyes, to be out of steam. It almost won. The sweet embrace of a sleepy, cold death was alluring, to wake up in heaven with her family like nothing had ever happened. But something had happened, and she wasn't about to let it happen again to someone else, to another set of children.

Mom would be home shortly, after she held the heart of the beast that killed her life and love.

Clara pushed herself forward off the trunk.

In luck, she found that on the other side of the trees, in the imprints in the snow, were markings of a struggle, like the beast had fallen. Black goop, thick and oily, searing through the pure white ground. It reminded her of what her boys would do during the first fall of winter. Snow angels. Only this might've been an angel at some point, but was far too twisted to be one now. Cloven hooves marked the new trail to follow. The creature must've stood on two legs when not flying, but it seemed it didn't prefer land as its main form of travel, tripping and falling every hundred yards or so, the oily substance following.

    Clara didn't want to stop to inspect the black goop. She knew she might lose the monster's trail if she took too much time, but it struck her as strange, like something long forgotten.

    The snow left a riddle pressed within it as she followed. The path of hooves straying from side to side, like the creature was drunk, or better yet, injured. She couldn't count on it, but she hoped, with how the monster moved, that dear Clyde had stabbed the damned thing and done something to bring the devil down to the ground. She hoped that if he were watching, he would know his death had not been in vain.

    Frozen tears and mucus were aiding the wind in damaging her fragile skin as Clara pursued. If her reason for being out here was any different, she might have found the surrounding nature beautiful. Tall trees dead, snow-covered, untouched by even the animals, only her and the trail of hooves to follow, so peaceful, so alone. Too alone. She stopped for a moment, trying to block out the howling breeze. Nothing, no animals, no movement, not even unclaimed howls in the distance. Just her and the beast. She would've been afraid if she knew she was returning home, but having nothing to return to removed any trepidation. An odd quietness plagued the world. It was never this still. She swallowed deep, her chest like a corn kernel ready to burst. She screamed.

    Nothing, not a bird, or a rustle to hear. She wasn't in the pines of her home in Leeds anymore. She was elsewhere, in the home of the unknown. She felt so small, so insignificant. Doubt was beginning to soil her. Clara fell to her knees, the rifle's butt keeping the gun upright, her hands bracing it. More tears. How would just a woman be able to take down such an evil? The realization that her anger could only keep her warm for so long, that the truth was she would freeze to death before finding the monster. That would most likely be her fate. Warm tears, followed by cold hands, wiping her sadness away. She pulled herself up with the rifle and continued. Nothing would stop her.

    As she continued her pursuit into the desolate wasteland, she began to trip over frozen objects, the condensation too deep for her to explore and discover what she kept stubbing her toes on. But the vast amount of these 'stones' gathering on the bare ground had her curious. Around a bend in a natural shaping of the woods, these stones, covered in snow to mask their details, were forming mounds, like the tales of pillaged castles she had been told about in nighttime stories. First, the mounds grew to walls, then to a collection of small pillars. The cold was getting to Clara, and she took a moment to rest.

The oily substance she had been following along with the imprints in the snow, its placement in her memories, and why she couldn't let the thought go...

Maybe it was the hypothermia setting in, as when she was sane and warm, she could never remember the time she spent as a child in the pines alone. She remembered wandering off and the way her mother's face contorted when she was returned to her, but the time between those two events was a blur, until now.

It was much like now, a silence uncanny and time unmoving, her child-like wonder with the pines amazing her with every step. The way the trees with their coats of leaves rustled in the autumn season, the colors of nature so subtle yet bold and bright, alluring. No wonder she had run off. But now, in retrospect, the lack of sound, of insects and the noise that accompanied them, the smells of the pines lacking, a clear path that the woods wanted her to follow. This was a trap her childlike mind couldn't comprehend. So, she wandered aimlessly without much thought of time passing, as the sun refused to move and she only knew to go home when it was dark out. Clara wandered seemingly alone for countless hours, each one so similar to the last. That is until...

Skulls. They were skulls she was tripping over. Human remains stacked neatly on top of each other, glued tight by the frozen meat still clinging to their host. She wanted to pray to God but feared this was a place which was blind to his light. The track of goop led her down the path of the morbid pillars. She again questioned her reason for continuing. She was already dead, so why make her death more gruesome than necessary? The taste of revenge caked her sinuses and reminded her why she must continue.

She tried not to focus on the skulls, to keep her eyes on the path, but her gaze would wander over to the side, and she would find herself stuck staring at one that still had an eye attached, mouth agape. Where did all these poor souls come from? Clara asked herself. Were they like her? Following the path to the beast that would soon be putting her skull onto a pillar? Or were they attacked and dragged off into this awful place like her family? She knew she would never have the answers to the questions she asked, and with great control, she pulled herself away.

As she followed the morbid path, the shadows in the distance grew thicker in her peripheral vision. Was her body slowing down? Succumbing to her eventual end? Not yet. She wouldn't let it. Shivers jangled her nerves, and each step was becoming deep and booming. The darkness of the void moved to more than just the outskirts of her vision, now swirling like a whirlpool within the center. Regret sputtered from the void as she approached. She could hear them, the voices of the otherworldly forest. Whispers of violence, of her own mistakes, like they held her darkness and were projecting it out of her. There were no more imprints to follow nor oily goop to lead the way, only Clara now, on the path of an effigy of skulls.

The mounds, two small thin pillars, then two columns thick and decaying, the trees turning to flesh; the bark pulsating like veins under stress. They said things to her that turned her stare blank, and her soul blanched, her blood sour and skin sore. A quiver, the calm before the storm, failed to hold back what her body could no longer brace.

"I was just a child!" Clara exclaimed to the ether. The shadowy sponges trying to soak up her vision went along with the flesh trees, but the skulls remained. With a jittering heart, she spun around to check her surroundings; gun pointed and ready to fire. Failing to see a host to the voices brought her lungs to gasping. It had to be the cold getting the better of her, and there was nothing but her here.

With no leads to the creature, she continued on the path of human remains, hearing a crack and caving in what was once a face, under her step, the sound frothing her stomach every time she heard it. She had to think of something else.

Sitting in the front row of church after being found wandering the woods, her parents knew something she didn't understand. Waiting like a good little girl, studying her hands to keep her mind off what they and the priest were discussing. This was the first time she had experienced the same silence she was beset with until now, the absence of a clock ticking or the snapping of flames, just nothing but the wind.

"I don't care what you say, she's our daughter," her mother's urgent whispers echoing from beyond a wall.

"There's nothing we can do, Emma," the hushed words of her father, the little girl feeling smaller and smaller with every step of her approaching parents, the wick of one of the candles sinking and extinguishing, another desperate plea from her mother.

The drip of thick fluid into the padding of snow made Clara snap her head to attention, rifle raised and ready. The pang came from one of the mounds of skulls behind her. Clara debated whether or not it was worth inspecting. She figured not. Just because she hadn't heard a sound here yet didn't mean they didn't exist.

She was back at the church waiting for her parents, the sobbing of her mother twisting the girl's posture and hands, waiting for them to return to her, an impending doom presiding over her. Another candle giving out.

Another drip, closer than the one before taking her attention away from her memories, Clara again turned to check. Nothing but the mounds of death, the wind upskirting the snow and blowing it in her face.

Another candle, another drip. When her mother and father walked back into the main hall, Clara saw the blackness of her mother's eyes rolling up before her hand could reach her mouth. Her father pulled his wife back to brace her. How her father's gaze had turned, as if he was looking into evil itself, incarnate of the void itself. True fear, the likes of which she would never see again on a human being.

"I didn't know what I was doing," Clara said to herself, as if she could jump into the memory and change it. "It came out of nowhere. I just remember it being so big, and it looked like it had stars all over it. I didn't think anything with stars on it could be bad."

Her mother's weeping was with her now, following behind Clara as she pursued further down the snowy path. She knew not to look back, to not let whatever was picking her mind apart to have the better of her.

Sobbing turned into the incoherent words of a ghost, asking why Clara had done this to them, to everyone. Why she brought this evil upon her family and community? Over and over again, her mother's voice became more desperate with each plea. Until the sorrows of the dead woman were too much for her daughter to take. Clara turned around.

"Because I wanted more!"

All of the skulls behind her were bleeding, the drips of gore coming from their hollowed-out sockets, pooling and mixing into the snow. A twinge of relief hit that her dead mother was not going to be popping up behind her to bemoan her disappointment with her only daughter, but the relief was short-lived. When she turned back around, she saw it.

Off in the distance, its silhouette hovered. Even for the few inches between it and the ground, Clara knew the monster had towered over her husband. Its head mounted on a long neck like that of a horse with horns, eyes unseeable but staring her down like she was but an inconvenience. Its forked tail lashing back and forth like an angry cat's. The sight stopped Clara in her tracks. Somewhere within her, she had told herself this wasn't going to happen, but here she was. She hadn't frozen to death and was now given a chance to take revenge. She readied the rifle and charged, wanting to make sure the bullet found its target.

An inhuman roar escaped the beast as the bullet met its victim. It shuttered and spread its wings wide before disappearing from Clara's sight. She quickly brought the rifle down to reload the way Clyde had shown her, struggling to do it with her frozen fingers. The frozen ice-cold ramrod stuck to her palms as she rammed the bullet and powder down, ripping the skin off as she hit the bottom of the barrel. She pulled the hammer back, lifted the rifle to her shoulder, and managed to get another round out, only this time failing to land the shot and being knocked to the ground, slapping her body down into the skulls, the bones crunched against her back.

She was back in her parent's home; womb engorged, ready to burst. She was hidden away in the basement for the last nine months, barely spoken to by her family, cared for but no longer cared about. That day had been a blister-inducing June evening, the oppressive heat only broken by a heavy rain coming in from the Atlantic Ocean. She didn't know that the creature without a form, filled with stars and the abyss, would put this evil into her. She had only stuck her hand out into the nothingness. Hadn't they said angels come in many forms? Hadn't they praised the event of the Immaculate Conception? Why was this a bad thing?

It was the humming buzz of night insects that Clara remembered focusing on when her water broke. It was supposed to be a trickle of clear fluid, like she had lost control of her bladder, but instead, a slick of black oil came gushing out. Every contraction she was alone for, every wave of pain and panic made her regret going out into the woods alone, following the distortion among the leaves, reaching her hand into the unknown. Huddled in a corner, the thing, using her body to grow, to feed off, was almost out. Then, with one last gut-wrenching push, a monstrous evil came into the world.

Within mere moments Clara heard the locks of the door unclamped and wood slamming against wood. In a sweat of delirium, she thought she saw her father, shotgun in hand, pointing at the monstrous evil that lived in his daughter. She heard the click of the gun, waiting for her ears to ring from a gun being shot in such close quarters.

Clara woke up, staring at the clouds of the forever-night. She was back, not yet taken away by the pines. The rifle laid a few feet back. She rolled herself over and told herself she wasn't done yet. That the monster was staring because it didn't think anything of her. It pitied her like a cat watching a mouse run in between its paws. Stark throbbing radiated through her shoulder as she crawled towards the rifle, soon retrieving the gun and propping herself up. A warm stream of heat centered at the back of her head gave her cause for alarm. When Clara pulled back her black fingers, they were stained with her blood. She wondered how long she had been out for, how much this injury took away from her remaining time on this earth.

    Nevertheless, she pursued, knowing now that the beast was close and injured. She had that in her favor, giving her the extra strength to follow after it faster. If Clara had been paying attention, she would've noticed the expanse of the amount of skulls now making archways and figures, the trees breathing and pulsating, turning to flesh and bones. She was no longer in Leeds, New Jersey. She was where the preacher might call Hell, but to her, she was exactly where she needed to be.

    The path of bones ended at a concave clearing. The sky above was clear with stars like white confetti, sprinkled and wondrous in their positions. However, any other part not under this ethereal realm was bedeviled by cloudy gloom. Immersing most of the area was a lake like glass, and even where Clara stood, she could see out into its depth like the water had never been swum in or tainted. In the middle, the beast lay curled up as her youngest would do after a frightful nightmare. Clara readied the end of the rifle, the rusted bayonet ready for one last kill, and descended towards her target.

Each step panged her heart like a deep drumming from below. As she approached the shore, she knew she wouldn't have the range from where she stood to get a clear shot of the beast. She checked the strength of the frozen surface. It held her weight, and slowly Clara tried her best not to slip and slide into a weak point of the ice. She tried to keep her rage in check. She had come so close; she had the upper hand, and if this luck kept, she could shove the sharp blade so far down into that sick creature's brain.

She heard it weeping from afar.

"I'll give you something to cry about," her uncontrolled muttering escaped like smoke from the fire within. "You killed my parents, my brothers… I thought I was rid of you until now. Why'd you come back? Why my boys? Why my husband?"

The feeling of being watched ramped Clara up even more. She was doing everything she could not to scream, to charge like a mad woman, until she saw it blink. At first, she thought there were eyes in the lake, buried deep and frozen under the water. Specks of eyes staring her down and blinking until she realized that she was looking at the sky's reflection. Above, thousands of pupils stared like they all wanted a piece of her. Well, if that's what they wanted, that's what they were going to get. She ran forward, bracing the rifle with all her weight so that whatever the bayonet made contact with, it would jab with the most force she could give.

"WHY DO YOU NOT LOVE ME, MOMMA?"

The evil spoke to her in her mind, causing Clara to lose her footing, balance and momentum, crashing down with a thud, the bayonet's point wedged deep into the thick ice.
"Why did you kill my family!" Clara began to sob. "I thought I got away from you! I thought I could get away from all this. Why is this happening to me?"
She was breaking down. No more hope left in a woman who had nothing more to give. The beast rose up and slowly turned its horrific form towards its attacker. She was beaten, and with that, she began to pray.

"THEY TRIED TO KILL ME WHEN I WAS BORN. THAT'S WHY I KILLED THEM"

The beast floated forward. Clara kicked and screamed, trying her best to retreat, all attempts in vain. It paused in its pursuit of her.
"I didn't know… I didn't know." She wept in fragments. "I didn't know I'd become pregnant if I put

my hand in that thing. My family locked me up, and treated me like I was carrying the devil himself."

The creature slowly floated forward and then down towards the woman it called its mother.

"Please, just kill me. Make it quick!" She sobbed. "Let me be with my family."

"YOU LOVED THEM MORE THAN ME. WHY DID YOU LOVE THEM MORE THAN ME?"

Her crying came to a halt.

"Because I didn't think you needed love," she answered. "You're a monster. What monster needs love? Is that why you came after my kids and husband?" She paused. "You were jealous?"

"YOU CALL ME A MONSTER, BUT I DON'T KNOW WHAT THAT IS."

It continued forward, Clara's tears dripping again as a primal fear took over, making her kick and squirm in a failed attempt to escape.

"I WANT YOU TO LOVE ME, BUT I DON'T KNOW WHAT THAT IS."

The beast, foul-smelling like rotten wood and spoiled death, its fangs and mouth in a state of decay as it snarled.

"YOU DID THIS TO ME. YOU PUT THESE THINGS INSIDE OF ME,"

She was cornered, done. The death she had been dreading in her face, with teeth like a viper, attached to a regret.

"I AM EVERYTHING YOU PUT IN ME. I AM YOU AND YOU ARE ME, AND NOW WE'RE GOING TO BE ONE TOGETHER. YOU ARE PART OF US."

Everything was black when Clara regained consciousness. She couldn't feel her bleeding hands or the lacerations on the back of her head anymore. However, she could feel her eyes rolling side to side under heavy lids. Her thoughts returned quickly, and much like every other time she had woken up, she opened her eyes.

Above so high, in the ether which felt like between heaven and earth, she stared down at the monster eating away at her body. A panic spread in what she could still feel of herself. Worry in her pupils, frantic vision darting back and forth at the scene, unable to scream until an eye caught her peripheries. She was staring down from above, along with the rest of them.

About The Author

B.E. Goose

GROW STRONG & GROW STRANGE

https://linktr.ee/B.E.Goose

Between The Spaces

-Mark MJ Green-

Between The Spaces

The thudding of feet coming through the ceiling caused Aleksandra to look upward in annoyance. The heavy steps had seemingly pounded their way from one side of the room to the other, carrying enough force to set her delicate lampshade swaying.

What is it they do up there? She pondered.

There was always something from the flat above. Music too loud, doors slamming, and now, heavy footsteps sending muffled booms reverberating into her apartment. It was as if Jack's giant nemesis from the fairy tale was angrily tromping atop his beanstalk castle. Aleksandra always thought of Jack as being the villain in that tale. The giant was occupied with his own business when Jack turned up and started stealing his belongings. And then, he murdered the poor giant by cutting down the beanstalk and sending him plunging to his death. It was a nasty tale with an ending she didn't like. Why have a story that ends in death when life is a blessing that deserves value above all else?

Thinking of stories caused her to look at her meagre bookshelf. It wasn't spartan due to lack of funds, more that she didn't enjoy reading as much as she used to. Words were strange things that could hold contrasting meanings for different people. They made intent and, by extension, conversation, tricky beasts to master.

Having emigrated to the UK from Poland, English was not Aleksandra's first language, and she had initially found the double meanings of many English words confusing. After only a few lessons, she quickly took to the new dialect, surprising herself as her broken English vocabulary had expanded dramatically. Yes, homophones would occasionally trip her up, or the confusion of strange local idiolect that could also vary from one person to another, but on the whole, she thought she managed well.

The footsteps resumed bumping and dancing, a tarantella of sound culminating in a crash that shook her room enough to send a couple of the books she had been perusing sliding over. A shout rang out from one of the other flats, and the annoyed expletive, "For fuck's sake," carried through the thin walls. The voice was clear, but distance gave it a slightly muffled quality, as though the speaker lay buried under layers of cloth.

Aleksandra stood still, almost holding her breath as she tried to keep the air circulating in and out of her lungs to a minimum. She listened, her ears focusing on the room above, trying to filter out the subdued sound of her neighbour's television set, the Countdown theme drifting through the thin brickwork. Music drifted from another room, further down the corridor. Outside, a motorcycle engine roared as it sped past the building. Closing her eyes, Aleksandra sought to blot them out. She pushed them into the background until the only prevalent sound was the persistent yet almost always unnoticeable buzz of electricity in the air.

Strange. The hum of electrical energy seemed louder now she was becoming aware of it. Was it always like this, only she hadn't noticed it before? Concentrating on the sound, Aleksandra began to hear something else within the drone. Buried behind the noise, tucked far into its depths, a murmur of - voices? No. That couldn't be right. It must be the sounds of another television or music system. And yet, the pitch and tone were different from the familiarity of sounds that usually drifted throughout the apartment complex. There it was again. Voices. Aleksandra tried to focus all her attention on them, but it was so hard to make out. Like trying to identify a specific whisper in a room filled with murmurs.

If she strained, she could almost make it out. A ghostly susurration that beckoned. Hidden promises that tantalised the senses and hinted at something forbidden yet pleasurable. A secret only for Aleksandra and no one else. There was a certain lyricism to the words, giving the impression of a prayer or hymn.

Aleksandra stumbled, her eyes springing open as she realised she had taken an involuntary step toward the wall upon which her bookshelf was affixed.

What happened? Had she fallen asleep standing up, the voices nothing more than a jumbled illusion spun by her dreaming mind? She couldn't hear them anymore. Not over the sounds that swirled around from the other tenants and her own heavy breaths.

Reaching toward her shelf, Aleksandra picked up one of the hard-cover autobiographies, surprised at the coolness of the wraparound against her fingertips. She placed it back where it belonged, among the other similar titles. Doing the same with its fallen companion. Autobiographical tales were her preferred reading material. She found it fascinating and exciting to read about the struggles of people who were now rich and famous but came from humble beginnings. They offered hope that perhaps anyone, even her, could one day hear the call of greatness. Hear the call? That thought led her back to the whispering she had heard. Could that have been her call toward something greater? A whisper of a hitherto unknown future that was waiting, almost within her grasp, to whisk her away from a noisy flat and her minimum wage cleaning job to something wondrous? If only. But such flights of fancy weren't worth dwelling on. They were dreams, and all dreams have to fade in the glare of morning lest they disturb the bleakness of reality and paint it in pictures of unattainable beauty.

Aleksandra's melancholic thoughts were pulled away by another noise upstairs. Not footsteps this time, more of a dragging or scraping sound. Again, Aleksandra found herself wondering what the people above her were doing. As she raised her head to look up at the ceiling once more, something on the wall caught her eye. Was that mould? A single black speck, looking like a perfectly shaped circle, stood out against the light-coloured magnolia paint that unimaginatively coated her four walls.

She stepped forward to inspect it in more detail. It didn't look like mould, more as if the paint had cracked and something beneath it was showing through. Did that noisy fool upstairs cause damage to the wall with the crashing about earlier that had caused her books to topple?

Now she was closer, Aleksandra could see a sheen to the black circle that gave it a greasy, oily-looking texture. What was it?

Deciding to try and clean whatever was marring her wall, Aleksandra stepped into the kitchen and removed a cloth from her cleaning supplies. She considered using a chemical solution to wipe the stain but hesitated, having learned from previous experience that the paint on her walls was so thin and watery that even a weak mixture could strip it from the wall. Rather than risk it happening again, she instead dampened the cloth with warm water from the tap.

Armed against the forces of dirt and grime, she returned to the living room and approached the mark on the wall. She stared at it, unmoving, hesitant to touch the dark circle within the paintwork, but unable to tell why she felt so nervous.

Aleksandra took a deep breath, held it, and then let it slowly roll out of her lungs. She repeated the process twice more, then raised the dampened cloth and wiped at the speck.

Nothing happened. At first. But then, Aleksandra recoiled when she realised the moisture seemed to have been drained from the cloth. She knew the material hadn't simply dried out. The black stain had absorbed the fluid it held. She felt a compulsion to touch it, to press her finger against its surface, but fear of what would happen kept her from giving in to the urge. What if it drank the moisture from her? No. That wouldn't -

couldn't - happen. Her imagination must be playing tricks on her. She hadn't wet the cloth enough, and it had dried out, that was all.

Shaking her head, Aleksandra returned to the kitchen and gathered together a variety of supplies. Cleaning sprays, gloves, bleach, soap, and a bucket partially filled with warm water. Who cares if she ended up stripping some of the paintwork? She wanted that stain removed.

She pulled on a pair of bright yellow gloves and dunked the cloth into the soapy water, squeezing out the excess liquid but leaving it wet enough that it couldn't possibly dry out before she had finished her task; because that must be what happened. It had dried. The stain *did not* drink it. Before she could change her mind, she slapped the wet cloth against the dark smear and rubbed the rag vigorously back and forth.

Nothing. The stain hadn't been erased, nor had it even faded under her assault. She examined the cloth, relieved to find it was still wet. The moisture had not been drained by whatever was marring her otherwise pristine walls. Sighing, Aleksandra debated what she should try next. Perhaps if she examined it, whatever *it* was, more closely, she would have a better idea of how best to remove its presence.

Leaving the chemicals where they lay, Aleksandra reached out and placed a gloved fingertip upon the blackness. She pressed her digit against it, feeling cold emanating through the wall. Enough that she could sense it through the textured latex of the gloves. Not only that, but it seemed smooth, similar to marble. As she ran her gloved finger across the mysterious spot, she brushed loose a scab of plaster. "Shit," she swore as the painted flake tumbled free and fell to the floor.

Looking back at the wall, she saw the missing sliver had exposed more of the blackness lurking within. How much is there? She wondered.

She removed her hand, and for a moment, it felt as though there was a tacky, adhesive quality to the spot. As if it was reluctant for her to take her finger away. Aleksandra stared at her fingertip, half expecting to discover a piece of the substance clinging in place, finding herself somewhat relieved when all that met her gaze was the textured yellow of her glove. Removing the gloves, Aleksandra used a chipped fingernail to scratch at the plaster. It fell from the wall with little effort, almost as if it were too eager to escape the clutches of the blackness beneath.

From somewhere far away, the choral resonance could be heard once more.

Time slipped away from Aleksandra as she scratched and picked. A confetti of plaster and paint chips now littered the floor as she uncovered more and more of the strange darkness inside her walls. Soon, her hands became tired and sore, uncomfortable from the fragments stuck under her nails. Aleksandra headed back into the kitchen, returning with a metal-bladed spatula.

It took over an hour, but Aleksandra managed to clear all of the material that covered the spot. Although, calling it a spot was no longer accurate. A circle of absolute blackness, one meter in diameter, had been revealed. No, not a circle. A sphere.
A jet-black orb extended into the wall. But how could that be? Examining her discovery, Aleksandra realised the dimensions of the thing were wrong. It couldn't be taking up as much space as it appeared to, or it would be protruding into the neighbouring apartment. She stepped back, shaking her head, clearing it of the haze that seemed to enshroud her mind. The realisation of the damage she had caused within her flat struck her. She mumbled, fully observing how much of the wall she had carved away. Paint and chunks of thin plaster littered the floor, as did her shelves and books, which she had removed during the process. Studying more intently, she realised that although brickwork surrounded the object, it was as if the walls had been built around the thing. No, that wasn't right. It was more as if the blackness had grown within the wall, absorbing

the brickwork as it swelled, unseen between the spaces. But the size of it? Did it extend into her neighbour's home, too? Surely not. It couldn't, else she would be able to look through and see her elderly neighbour as she sipped tea and watched the telly.

    She wanted to go and look, but her feet were reluctant to move. The whispering chant held her in place, an otherworldly siren song that compelled her to stay in its presence.

    She had to move away from it. What had happened? Why had she destroyed her wall?

    Muscles straining, sweat beading her forehead, staining her armpits, and slicking the centre of her back, Aleksandra took a single, reluctant step away from the living shadow. And another. And another.

    The shadow rippled. A liquid vacillation as if a gong had been struck, disturbed the surface and what once was a three-dimensional sphere now appeared to be concave.

    The song increased in volume, and Aleksandra's steady retreat halted.

    From within the inky mass, arms unfurled, as jet black and ominous as the void itself. Each limb ended in a formless blob from which fingers sprouted like a sped-up film of seedlings bursting from the ground. They latched onto the wall. Feathery strands of mycelium spread where they touched, and from each 'wrist,' another arm grew. These new limbs unfolded as had the ones before them. The process repeated, each arm growing a hand and fingers, followed by another limb unfolding from that one. And another.

The chant swelled and billowed, a swelling of vocal hypnosis that filled the room before switching to a slow diminuendo as the voices became a whisper. The now hushed and muted song had a narcotic effect upon Aleksandra, and she barely registered the multitude of arms taking her in their embrace. Cradled by the limbs and the soporific choir, Aleksandra gave herself over to them as they pulled her into the blackness.

Mary turned the volume down on her television. Was that a noise from next door? It was hard to tell with the sounds that filtered through from the other residents. Oh well. It was probably nothing. The young lady next door was usually so quiet. Pleasant too. Shy but polite. Reaching for her remote, Mary turned the volume back up. She loved watching Countdown, smiling in agreement as on-screen, Susie Dent informed the contestants of the eight-letter word they could have made with their letters.

Picking up her cup and saucer, Mary sipped at her tea, lips smacking in satisfaction.

The television shut off as a loud thump issued from next door. The noise caused Mary to jump in fright, her cup and saucer clattering in her hands. From across the hallway, she could hear someone swearing in complained response to the sound. Either that, or their power had gone out as well, and they were complaining about the inefficiency of the energy company. Wait, that couldn't have been it; she could still hear the muffled sounds of televisions and music competing with one another. That was the only problem with the apartments; the walls were so thin. Placing her cup and saucer on her small side table, Mary tried the television remote. Nothing. Sighing, she stood up and went to examine the socket. Perhaps the plug had come loose from the thump? Moving closer, she spotted a stain on the wall. That wasn't there before. Where did it come from? She had only cleaned the room yesterday. Peering at it, she examined what appeared to be a black speck of mould.

From across the hallway, she heard the same neighbour swearing again, their voice rising in pitch before abruptly cutting off. Damn thin walls. Whether it was noise, or the scent of food being cooked, sooner or later, everything filtered through.

END

About The Author

Mark MJ Green

Bald and bearded reviewer, and writer. Mark likes the spooky side of life and things that go bump in the night. Although that's usually him wandering into something as he didn't bother to turn a light on.
Mark was found as a child, wandering through the Fens of Cambridgeshire in the UK. He was a strange, feral beast that subsided on a diet of reeds and whatever small creatures crossed his path.

Attempts were made to civilise him, but he tends to amble around resembling an annoyed orc.

He writes horror fiction in a variety of styles within the genre.

To create your own version of Mark, take one, Mr Potatohead and attach his angry eyes - preferably placing one of them at a slightly different angle to the other. Affix a beard and leave the head barren of growth. Congratulations. You now have your very own Mark Green. Caution. Product may swear at random moments and for no apparent reason.

Despite his gruesome tales and grumpy exterior, Mark is a friendly chap who enjoys spending time with his family. He currently resides in Lincolnshire. You can find his reviews at reelhorrorshow.co.uk

You can also find him on amazon:

https://www.amazon.co.uk/Mark-Green/e/B086MK7WYS/

And Goodreads:

https://www.goodreads.com/author/show/20176631

Inside

-Ayralea Lander-

Inside

Chapter 1

The beach was mostly deserted at this time of the day and season, and Wendy knew an area that was even more secluded. It was her favorite place, and she had never been disturbed there. As she walked along the warm, soft sand, she could feel it pushing up between her bare toes. Her sandals had been removed the instant she had reached the sandy beach, after she crossed the scrubby grass between the parking lot and the beach. Gulls wheeled overhead and cried against a backdrop of drifting clouds, the sky a gorgeous blue like the faded denim of her shorts. The waves breaking upon the shore, washing up seaweed, and the sound of the water drawing back over the empty shells of the sea creatures that had formerly occupied them was like music to her ears.

  The sun beat down; even though it was no longer summer it was still warm enough, and felt great on her skin. She pulled her tank top off as she strolled toward her destination, stuffing it in the oversize beach bag she always brought with her. Under her shirt was her bikini top, which she planned to lose as well when she got to her spot.

She only passed two other people, both together, sunbathing on a large beach towel, a cooler close by to them stashed under a large, brightly colored umbrella. They didn't stir, and she was happy that the beach was practically hers.

She soon arrived at her secluded spot. It was accessible past an area where the trees grew closer to the beach, that was rocky and harder to pass through. Most folks turned back at this point and set up spots where the beach was more tantalizing. But one day, Wendy pushed past it and found a sandy spot perfect for privacy.

This is where she found herself now. She pulled a towel from her bag and rolled it out on the warm sand, followed by a dog-eared paperback she retrieved next to read as she bathed in the rays of the sun.

Settling down, she stripped off her bikini top before wiggling out of her shorts and bikini bottom, then rolling onto her stomach and retrieving the paperback from the corner of the towel. She took her wide-brimmed hat off and opened her book. Reading contentedly, she soon found herself lulled off to sleep with the sounds of the gulls and the surf relaxing her.

She woke up with a start, checked the time and saw she had been asleep for almost an hour. She was getting warm, so she decided to take a dip in the ocean.

She walked down to the water's edge and felt the surf suck her toes and then her feet down into the sand as the water surged around her as she stood watching the waves rolling in. Wading out to meet the surf, she stayed close to shore but deep enough that she could tread water and not get carried out too far. With no one around, she had to be extra cautious as any mistake could cost her her life. This was the danger, but also the allure, of the ocean to her.

As she got deep enough to buoy herself up in the tepid water and tread, something tickled her foot. *Seaweed,* she thought to herself as she kicked her foot. The tickle moved upwards; it felt like tiny fish were bumping against her calf and up her thighs. She wasn't too alarmed, but she wasn't fond of the sensation, either, and tried to look down, but the sun glinting off the surface and her arms keeping her afloat but stirring the water denied her curiosity any closure. The tickling moved upward, and she felt something wriggling past her buttocks and between her thighs, which caused her to panic and start thrashing. She accidentally inhaled some of the brine and started to choke as she tried to orient herself and stay afloat. She felt something tickle her labia and push past, penetrating her as it invaded her vagina, and the sensation made her grab at her pudendum as she sank under for a second. Not feeling anything with her probing fingers, she surfaced, sputtering, and swam as fast as she could to the shore.

She half swam and half pushed off with her legs when she was closer to shore, dragging herself onto the beach and standing up, her legs quaking. She examined her vagina closely, running her fingers along the labia and pushing one digit inside, but nothing was amiss. She wondered if it was just an anomaly, a phantom sensation; what else could it be?

She had had enough, though, so she went back up to the beach towel and dried herself off after shaking the sand from it, donned her swimsuit, pulled her tank top on and shimmied into her shorts. Stuffing everything else in the bag, she traced her path back to the parking lot where she had left her car and swung by the store for some groceries for that night before heading home.

Chapter 2

Wendy busied herself with preparing dinner in the kitchen of her small bungalow, as her boyfriend Gabe was coming over after work to join her.

She had showered earlier and put on fresh, casual clothes. Another tank top and a pair of workout shorts.

She did the prep ahead, knowing he enjoyed cooking with her, but she didn't want to spend too much time not relaxing with him.

She peeled the shrimp and set them in a bowl to marinate in the fridge. The steaks were marinated as well and set aside. She made the salad ahead of time, chopping all the veggies but waited to add the dressing later so the lettuce wouldn't get soggy. She set up the rice cooker as well, ready to be switched on at the appropriate time.

Finished her prep, she retired to the living room to wait for Gabe, turning the TV on and flicking to a random sitcom in the background. She really wanted to continue reading her novel but enjoyed some background noise for company. She settled into the comfy, plush couch to read while the TV droned in the background.

    She felt distracted, though; her sex was a bit sore still. Frowning, she decided that maybe a visit to the doctor would be in order soon if it continued.

    Who knows what was in the ocean after all? She swam a lot and had never had an issue before, but her experience earlier was unsettling her.

    Just as she decided she should call the doctor, her doorbell rang; it was Gabe, and she went to let him in.

    For now, she forgot again about her experience in her excitement to see him.

    They enjoyed dinner, laughing and relating to each other their day and week in general. Wendy didn't get to see Gabe a whole lot, he was busy with his job, so they made the most of their time together when they could.

    They had been seeing each other for a year, and Wendy's friends teased her about when it would get "serious," but they were happy to date for now. Both enjoyed where they lived and didn't want to move in with the other, at least not yet.

    They retired to the living room after cleaning up dinner, loading the dishes into the dishwasher and stashing the food in containers. They brought their wine glasses and the bottle in with them, and Wendy felt a warm buzz from the alcohol that was pleasant and seemed to heighten her libido.

    As she ran her fingers up Gabe's arm to his hand, she gently took the wine glass from him and set it on the table. With a lascivious smile, she leaned in and kissed him, something she usually left to him to initiate. Tonight, however, she was on fire and felt an almost aggressive urge to couple with him. She didn't know what had gotten into her as she nipped at Gabe's full lower lip and unbuttoned his shirt.

    He was surprised too, but not in a bad way. He moaned in between kisses that he liked her being assertive and taking charge, which was good because she was having trouble holding herself back.

    With his shirt unbuttoned, she pushed him back, so he was laying with his head on the cushions, and straddling him, she ground her sex onto the rapidly swelling bulge in his pants.

    "Oh God, baby, this is hot," he said as he gazed at her. She pulled her shirt over her head, dropping it to the floor. She removed her bra, which followed the shirt to the ground, her full breasts swinging free. She cupped them in her hands, running her fingers around the large areolas before twisting her nipples, licking her lips and moaning, head thrown back.

Gabe moaned beneath her, spellbound. His arms reached up and replaced her hands with his, stroking her hard nipples as she curled forward and ran her hands over his pecs before sliding her nails down his abdomen, not enough to hurt but enough that he felt them.

"Oh yeah, Wendy, you're like a cat in heat. I don't know what's gotten into you tonight, but I love it."

Standing up for a moment, she removed her shorts She was not wearing any panties beneath, and slipped herself back over him, undoing his belt and unzipping him, wasting no time slipping her hand inside to pull his rock-hard penis out that was already oozing pre-cum. She stroked him, using the pre-cum to lube her hand while she stroked. Gabe could barely manage to stay focused on playing with her breasts as his eyes rolled in his head, and he murmured appreciatively to her.

She scooted back, his hands reluctantly parting from caressing her breasts, as she leaned down and took him in her hungry, wet mouth. He moaned and twined his hands through her dark, curly hair as she eagerly fellated him, her lips and tongue making him hiss in pleasure.

"Baby, let's go to the bedroom. I wanna..." he started to say, but she interrupted him by taking his cock in one hand and slipping herself over him and down so quickly that it was like she was impaling herself on his throbbing rod. His words faltered, and his eyes bulged as she rode him, snarling in a guttural tone.

"Jesus Christ, Wendy, you've never been like this before. I'm not complaining but..." he started to say again, but she silenced him with a finger to his lips, that she ran the nail down his throat and then propped herself on his chest with her hands as she continued to jackhammer herself on him as if she was using his flesh as a means to an end, and Gabe himself was just a meat puppet. Gabe felt this, and it half turned him on, and half made him feel weird. After all, this wasn't usually like her to be this way. She normally loved to be made love to, with a good, long session of cunnilingus before his penis was even near her vagina.

She moaned and started to buck and shudder, a clear signal that she was getting close to orgasm.

Something suddenly felt like it *pinched* his dick, and he wondered if it was her IUD for a moment before pain seared through his groin. It felt like something was biting him, for fucks sake!

"Wendy, stop!" He yelled, but it was too late. She was climaxing, and he was pinned beneath her writhing form like a butterfly in an entomologist's collection. As he felt her vaginal muscles clench, he was helpless as his cum was practically milked out of him, and another bolt of pain ran the entire length of his organ and blossomed across his belly.

"FUUUUUUUCKKKKKKK!" he screamed and pushed himself backwards and almost over the end of the couch in a panic to withdraw himself from Wendy, and she was shoved back and off him, a fountain of cum, and to his horror, blood sprayed in an arc from his deflating prick as it popped free of her.

Wendy's face twisted in anger at first, and she intoned, "What the fuck, Gabe! What do you think you're doing? I almost fell off the couch..." before she noticed the blood.

Gabe curled up and cradled his genitals in his hands, afraid to look but he had to.

The amount of blood wasn't as bad as he previously thought. It was now just seeping and mixing with his cum. He asked Wendy for something, so he could clean himself off and appraise the damage. She grabbed a kitchen towel and came back, handed it to him, and he wiped himself clean with great care.

There were four neat puncture wounds that blood welled up from as he wiped it away, two on each side of his shaft just under the sensitive glans. *What the fuck did that?* He thought, his forehead creased and a frown upon his face. Wendy looked concerned, and she thought with increasing alarm about what had happened in the ocean. Not wanting to alarm him, she kept the incident to herself for now.

"What the hell Wendy, did your pussy *bite* me?" he said incredulously as he examined the small wounds. Wendy laughed nervously but was loathe to admit what seemed impossible.

"Maybe it was the string from my IUD..." she started to say, yet it sounded unlikely even to her. But maybe the device itself had slipped out and cut him? She mentioned this to him, and he begrudgingly accepted it. He couldn't think of anything else himself.

"I'll make an appointment to see the doctor tomorrow and have it checked out. I'm sorry, Gabe. Will you be OK?"

He replied that yes, he was mostly OK, just shaken up by the pain and the blood.

They got dressed, and Gabe helped Wendy clean up the blood that had spattered across the couch. The stains lifted out nicely, and they settled back down with a blanket on the couch to keep them dry, finishing the wine and cuddling as they watched some TV.

Gabe knew Wendy felt terrible about him getting injured, and he assured her that all was well. His penis really did hurt though, and he figured he may have to get checked out. Maybe antibiotic ointment to prevent an infection was in order.

Wendy was deep in thought; she didn't know what had come over her sexually. She was never aggressive, but she had been overcome with a *need* to have Gabe inside her. Recalling her straddling him before he was even out of his clothes, she winced to herself, feeling almost like she had raped him. She was glad he was into it that time, but still, why had she been controlled by her urges in such a way? She had no answers.

As the night wore on, Gabe needed to leave and get home, shower, and head to bed so he was fresh for his early shift at the hospital. He figured he may even be able to get checked out while he was there but didn't think he wanted a colleague seeing his punctured penis. He chuckled to himself, in spite of the strange injury, as he got into his car and returned to his house.

Wendy retired early with her book to read, but the wine and her strange sexual desires had worn her out, and she quickly fell asleep.

Inside her vaginal canal, something stirred. It had fed on blood earlier but was hungry for more. It had found a suitable host to call home, so it busied itself making that home like it needed it to be.

Usually, the *Cymothoa exigua,* more commonly known as a sea louse, would sever the blood vessels in a fish's tongue, its usual host, causing the organ to rot and fall off. The parasitic isopod would then attach itself to where the tongue used to be in order to feed.

It found a suitable place that it would attach itself to now, so it busied itself by severing the blood vessels of her cervix. Wendy moaned and rolled over in her sleep but did not wake. The slight pinching sensation wasn't enough to rouse her.

The isopod need only wait now.

Chapter 3

Wendy woke and stretched, two days later after her date with Gabe, yawning as she observed the morning sun streaming through her curtains. Getting up, she opened them and gazed out at her manicured backyard. She frowned as she scratched idly at her vagina. It itched, and she could feel a dull ache from inside it.

Heading to the bathroom, she relieved herself into the toilet and decided to check her IUD to be sure. She pushed a finger into her vaginal canal and grimacing, she pushed deeper and felt her cervix, but something wasn't right inside. It felt spongier than the usual firmer texture, and as she tried to find the IUD string, her questing finger found a hard lump.

Frowning, she moved her finger deeper when she felt a stabbing pain like her fingertip was being lanced. She gasped and yanked her finger out.

As the digit popped free with a wet, sucking sound, she heard something *plop* into the water of the toilet bowl.

She was first concerned with her finger, and as she pulled her hand out from between her legs, she saw that her middle finger was oozing blood; it was running and dripping on the seat of the toilet and the floor. She grabbed some toilet paper to staunch the flow and rose to see what her second concern was; what she had heard splash into the toilet bowl.

She grabbed the toilet brush to move the toilet paper aside in the watered-down urine of the bowl and spotted something in the bottom of the toilet. Grimacing with slight revulsion and glad she hadn't pooped too, she reached her hand into the bowl and felt something soft and slimy and retrieved it. Standing over the bowl, her forearm and hand dripping pee-water, she examined it. It was a lump...of something? It looked fleshy, dark pink mottled with maroon. Could it be a clot? She no longer got heavy periods because of the IUD, but what else could it be?

Not knowing what else to do, she placed it on the lid of the toilet tank, washed up, and went to grab a resealable sandwich bag. She dropped the lump into it and placed it in the fridge before fetching her phone to call the doctor to make an appointment. It would be a week before she could get in, and the receptionist advised her if things got worse, she should go to the emergency room.

Satisfied, she got into the shower and prepared for the day.

She worked the next two days, but luckily the next day, she had time off, and Gabe was free as well.

They had made plans to get together at his place this time for dinner and see a matinee during the afternoon.

Wendy was uncomfortable at work at first. She could swear she had an itchy, burning sensation that moved inside her vagina throughout the day, but upon arriving home, the discomfort had appeared to pass. She slept well that night, and the next day was uneventful.

She had almost forgotten about the incident with the toilet, other than seeing the lump in the Ziplock baggie in her fridge and giving herself a mental reminder to bring it to her upcoming doctor's appointment.

Chapter 4

Her day off arrived, and Wendy ran some errands and cleaned the house while waiting for Gabe to pick her up so they could go to the movies.

They had both decided on a horror movie, and Gabe had his arm around her as they watched. She jumped several times, popcorn spilling down the front of her low-cut shirt and into her bra on one occasion. She laughed, slightly embarrassed, as she retrieved the kernels and fed them to Gabe.

They both enjoyed the movie and chatted about it as they headed back to Gabe's place, stopping at a Chinese restaurant to pick up an order they had phoned ahead for.

Arriving at his spacious house, they grabbed plates for the food but opted for the chopsticks that accompanied the food; instead of using forks.

Eating in the living room, they enjoyed a bottle of wine and put a low-budget B-horror movie on in the background that they chuckled at while dining.

Wendy was feeling a similar sensation to the last time she had seen Gabe, only this time, she was even more sexually aroused. She could barely focus on the movie and ate faster than usual because all she could think about was touching Gabe and feeling him inside her. She controlled herself this time, not wanting to be pushy and aggressive like before, but it was getting more difficult as they brushed up against each other as they boxed up the leftovers, rinsed the plates and put them in the dishwasher.

No sooner than Gabe turned to her and started to say something about heading back to the living room and the movie before Wendy pulled him to her and purred into his ear, "I have a better idea. Why don't you take me to your bedroom?"

Gabe's eyes widened. Once again, Wendy was randy as hell, and he remembered the last time when she had aggressively ridden him. He started getting hard thinking about it. Something about how she had practically used him like a living flesh-doll was something he had been thinking about since their last date. He felt more turned on than weird about it now.

They kissed passionately until she, not him, took his hand and led him to the master bedroom down the hall from the living room.

They stripped each other down between kisses and caresses, Wendy almost panting in his mouth as she kissed him with a hunger like in their early days when they were discovering each other and what turned them on.

Both fully nude, Wendy pushed Gabe back so he was sitting on the bed, and she instructed him to lay back and enjoy himself as she took him into her mouth. Already hard, he needed no coaxing and moaned as she fellated him in all the ways he loved.

She practically was eating him, devouring his dick with her tongue and lips, taking him deep enough that she gagged on him yet didn't slow her ministrations of his member. It only seemed to increase her pace.

Gabe knew he was going to blow his load right down her throat if she kept it up, so he suggested they 69 so he could concentrate on her and hopefully have her slow down. She slithered up the bed as he positioned himself, so his head was on the pillow, and he eagerly sought to make her cum.

It didn't take long before Wendy felt a climax approaching, and it was all she could do to try and keep sucking Gabe as she moaned and sobbed around his girth as an orgasm rolled through her body.

Not wasting any time, she felt like she was in heat and needed to feel him inside her. This time, she rolled onto her hands and knees and beckoned him to mount her, which he did, as she let out an animalistic growl at his penetration.

She had forgotten all about her injury.

Gabe had forgotten all about the last time his penis was inside her.

He thrust into her, taken over by her writhing beneath him and thrusting back to meet him, the sound of their wet flesh connecting, bringing him close. He felt Wendy getting close for the second time that night. She usually didn't cum so fast, especially a second time, but he wasn't going to complain. He could hardly hold off himself.

She pushed herself back to meet him as she climaxed, as Gabe did simultaneously as well, and unfortunately, inside her, something that was now attached to where her cervix used to be latched onto him when he ceased thrusting, buried deep so that he could empty his balls inside her clenching pussy.

The pain was like nothing he had ever felt before. It paled even to the last time, which he was reminded of succinctly.

Her vaginal muscles clamped onto him, and he was unable to withdraw himself from whatever was causing the pain.

He folded up on top of Wendy, pushing her forward and flat onto the bed. He felt something wet and gushing as his bladder emptied inside her in his loss of control at the pain and terror that had seized him and threatened to make him black out.

Wendy, pinned under him, cried out his name and gasped, "Gabe, what's wrong? What's happening?"

Her voice was full of confusion and fear, and then, suddenly, Gabe was free.

He rose up on arms shaking, kneeling on the bed, cold sweat pouring off his body, to see blood spurting from his groin and gushing from Wendy's vagina.

This time, his penis was a ruined mess. Fatty tissue bulged from rips and tears along the gore-streaked shaft. He wasn't even sure that most of it was even intact. As he held his mangled cock in his hand, he felt a hot rush to his head as blackness overwhelmed him, and he passed out cold, blood and urine soaking the sheets and duvet.

Wendy turned as she felt Gabe's weight lift from her, her hands flying to her face in shock at the sight of all the blood and the mess that was Gabe's mangled penis. She wasted no time trying to rouse him, and unable to, rushed to her phone to call an ambulance, sobbing into the phone.

She grabbed towels after unlocking the door and hastily wiped herself off before donning her clothes as fast as she could before attending to Gabe, unsure what to do other than to apply pressure to his bleeding groin.

It felt like forever, but the ambulance arrived quickly, and she yelled for them to come in and that they were in the bedroom.

They attended to Gabe before taking him out on a stretcher, and Wendy accompanied them as they were concerned about her too. What had even happened? She was in shock too, and terrified.

The ambulance rushed to the hospital, as the paramedic questioned a sobbing and confused Wendy. She had no clue but remembered the lump of flesh in her fridge and the swim in the ocean. She related both events to the paramedic, hoping it would shed some light on what had happened.

Arriving at the hospital, Gabe, having come to but delirious with pain and shock, was rushed to an operating room while Wendy was escorted to a private room on the ER ward.

A nurse came to see her and had her change into a gown. She didn't need painkillers herself, but she was sick with worry, and the nurse assured her that everything was being done to assist Gabe. She left, assuring Wendy that a doctor would be in to see her as soon as they could.

She didn't have to wait long before a doctor popped into the room, sitting on a chair that he rolled over to her, a chart in his hands. He asked how she was before telling her he had bad news.

Gabe was about to be operated on, but he was missing part of his penis. They were afraid it was still inside her. She gasped in shock, and the doctor calmed her while stating they would have to retrieve the severed part if they could in order to try and reattach it if possible.

A nurse entered the room with a speculum, lube, and all the medical instruments needed to retrieve anything they found.

Wendy was guided to lie on the table, feet in stirrups, as the doctor positioned the light so he could see. Using the speculum, he spread open her vaginal canal and adjusted the light before his gloved hands gently touched her.

He gasped in shock and pulled back for a moment, before leaning forward, forceps ready.

"Dear God," he intoned, "What is that?" he said even as he remembered that it wasn't professional to say anything out loud, no matter how odd the situation was. But in his horror, the words had slipped past his nub lips.

"Doctor?" The nurse asked with concern as she let go of Wendy's hand that she had been holding and moved to assist him.

Wendy herself began to panic at the tone of his voice and what he had uttered. What had he seen inside her?

"What's wrong?" she gasped as fear took hold of her and made her heart pound, her chest constrict, and her mouth dry.

She started to shift, but the nurse steadied her with a hand on her abdomen as she leaned toward the doctor.

"Oh God, what..." the doctor began to say as he saw what was inside Wendy's vagina. Just as the words were uttered, he saw *it,* whatever in God's name it was, begin to move.

Without any warning, it detached itself and flew on its many legs straight at him, out of its former home as it sensed food and a better domicile for it.

It impacted the doctor's right eye and wasted no time burrowing into the socket, the eyeball bursting and optic fluid and blood spattering as the isopod buried itself deeper into his brain.

As the doctor fell screaming, his hand hitting the tray and scattering equipment in a clattering rain upon the floor, the creature found itself home.

Inside.

About The Author

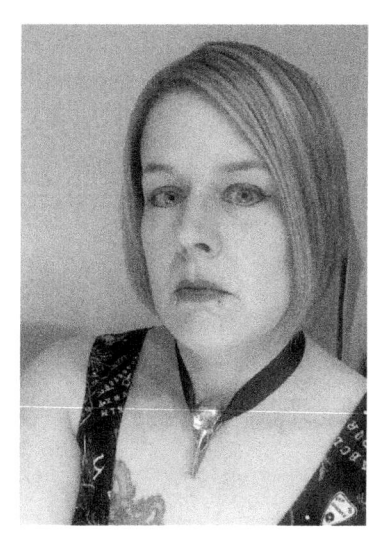

Ayralea Lander

Ayralea Lander, a visual artist for most of her life, recently started writing late in 2022 and found that she loved storytelling just as much as the ceramics and digital art she also creates.

Ayralea spent much of her childhood running naked and wild through the forests behind her house in northern British Columbia, Canada. Several moves and years later, she now resides in Central Alberta, Canada, where she is much more civilized and keeps her clothing on.

She resides in a small town with her husband, her dog, and a growing collection of tarantulas.

She consumes horror with ardor, especially indie horror novels that influence her own work as well. Adding to that is her favorite creature feature horror movies spanning the decades, but really, if it's creepy, she will be into it.

She is the author of the novella Cabal of Sinners.

Haunted

-E.B. Lunsford-

Haunted

It happened on a lonesome night in late October. The weather just turned, summer's heat disappearing to be replaced by the brisk winds and colorful foliage of fall. The smell of cinnamon and pumpkin spice hung in the air. My favorite time of year.

I was sitting outside, enjoying a few moments to myself at the end of a hard day. Seeing the decorations littering lawns up and down the block reminded me I still needed to buy candy for the upcoming holiday.

Luckily for me, my son wanted to wear the same costume as the year before. It would've been hard to find another one so late. I hadn't given much thought to Halloween, to be honest, though I loved spooky season as a child.

Back then, everyone dressed up. Even the adults. Now trunk-or-treating was replacing trick-or-treating much to my displeasure. It just wasn't the same. Maybe that's why the holiday didn't hold the same appeal as it used to.

It was nice out, not too cold yet. Relaxing even. The sound of the wind blowing almost putting me to sleep.

If only I could shake the gloomy feeling lingering in the back of my mind. Ever since my shift ended. The events of that morning replayed over and over in my head, an endless loop of tragedy.

The stress I faced everyday as an emergency room nurse was intense and relentless. I was on call pretty much 24/7 and worked rotating shifts, making it impossible to ever get enough sleep. Or keep up with appointments and important dates.

There was never telling if or when I worked on any given day. But I loved my job, wouldn't trade it for any other. What could be better than the excitement awaiting me every time I walked in? Never knowing what to expect but preparing for the worst. Anything could come through those doors next.

It was like constantly teetering on the brink of chaos, but I thrived on pushing my own limits, never hesitating to do anything. Bragging to anyone who would listen I was born to be a nurse. Forever a caregiver at heart. Helping others gave me pleasure like nothing else.

The hardest part was dealing with the loss of patients. Not everyone could be saved. We'd lost a patient that morning, and I couldn't stop thinking about it. Wondering what I could have done different, if anything. I wanted to save her so damn bad.

    A car accident brought her in, only eighteen years old. Endless possibilities ahead of her. She'd been driving her mother to chemotherapy as she did every Thursday afternoon, but they were running late. The car was acting up, an old Honda Accord. It broke down while they were driving on the interstate. Construction was being done on the section they were traversing, and there wasn't an emergency lane.
    Her mother died instantly. She was lucky. The daughter fought for hours, enduring unknown pain and desperate to survive. I did all I could, but it was too little, too late. She passed away.
    A young life snuffed out before it really even began.
    Imagine what it must have been like, sitting there in the middle of rush hour traffic, trapped in a disabled vehicle. Speed limit 65. Cars whipping by on either side. Like being in the eye of a tornado. Not knowing how they'd get out alive.
    Maybe they saw the black F-150 speeding closer at an alarming rate, growing larger in the rearview mirrors by the second. Hearts thudding as death hurdled at them

on four wheels with a lift kit and steel balls hanging from the back hitch.

There was nowhere for them to go, not a damn thing they could do to stop it. According to witnesses at the scene, the driver of the truck never so much as tapped the brakes before slamming into the smaller vehicle.
—Wham!—
Two lives destroyed in an instant.
Three if you counted the driver, but what kind of asshole couldn't see a vehicle stopped in the middle of the fricking interstate? Screw him. Totalled his truck but managed to walk away with only minor injuries, unscathed by the tragedy that befell the passengers of the car he hit. He would have to live with the fact that he killed them, though.
I hoped they at least had time to say goodbye to each other in those last few seconds. Maybe held each other's hands. Said 'I love you' one last time.
Poor girl…
Guilt ate at me for not being able to save her. I'd failed her. She held on for so long just to die anyways. It was a cruel hand life dealt her. What a shame.
But I couldn't save them all. It wasn't possible. Not part of the job. I was there to save the ones I could.

A scream pierced my eardrums, making me flinch. Shattering the illusion of a peaceful night.

It repeated a few more times before I placed where it was coming from, a tree on the other side of the fence separating my yard from the next. Hanging from the branches were assorted plastic weapons drenched in blood. Halloween decorations. Next to them was an animated axe-wielding figure that moved when my eyes touched it.

I jumped as it lifted its head and howled at the moon, slashing with the axe as another scream rang out. From a hidden speaker, no doubt.

Wicked.

It was an awesome scene, reminding me again of Halloweens past.

The wind picked up, tossing my hair in every direction. I shielded my face with one arm, holding my hair down as best as I could. Picking up the blunt I rolled before coming out, I stuck it into my mouth and grabbed my lighter.

A minute or two passed before I got the blunt to light, even while shielding the flame with my hand. I inhaled deeply as it finally caught and tried to hold my hit in for as long as possible.

My exhale exploded out of me in rush, making me hack uncontrollably. It passed soon enough. A smile came to my face as I wiped my eyes.

That was better. I took another puff and zoned out for a while.

Darkness prevailed in the yard, shadows hiding things in plain sight. This moonless sky made it feel scarier. I became more aware of my surroundings, a silent observer of the night.

A man jogged past on the sidewalk, oblivious to his surroundings. Earbuds in both ears. Not even wearing reflective clothing though it was after ten pm.

Dumbass.

Dogs barked from neighboring yards, the nearest one yapping insistently. Demanding attention My next door neighbor's chihuahua.

Answering yowls came from further away then gradually stopped.

A cat shrieked and hissed as a shadow moved near the stop sign at the end of the road. It took off running, disappearing into nearby shrubs.

I could hear crickets, cicadas, even a frog croaking somewhere in the backyard.

Nature fascinated me. This was the best part of my day. Relaxing on my porch, escaping reality for a bit. It was my happy place. Nothing bad could touch me there.

The porch was where I went to cry when I wanted no one to see, where I screamed my frustrations, and where I voiced what I'd never otherwise say aloud. It was a place to vent, release steam, to ponder past regrets.

Sometimes I hated myself for not being a better mother. A better person. Just better.
I was too hard on my son at times. He was still just a kid. I'd sent Keith to bed early that night because he forgot to do his chores. It wasn't like he did it intentionally, I should have let it slide. We got to spend little enough time together as it was.
The look Keith gave me as I sent him to bed said everything. I could see the hurt in his eyes.
As a parent, I struggled like most to balance the fine line of being too hard on my son and too lenient.
Wasn't it my job to remind him of things like chores? Keith was only twelve years old after all.
The chair beneath me bounced up and down in time with the heel of my right foot. The more I worried about Keith, the faster I seemed to rock. Back and forth.
I wished I could spend more time with him. It felt like school, work, and other things beyond control kept us apart. He was growing up without me and before I knew it, he would be gone. Time was flying by, whether I wanted it to or not. Time I would never get back.

Maybe I could cut my hours, spend more time at home. That would be nice. I didn't even need to work, my husband was the breadwinner, but I wasn't the type to stay at home all the time. It wasn't me. I needed to be on the go, to stay busy. But putting my career first also made me feel I was abandoning Keith.

I loved him more than anything else. I told myself that was enough, but was it really? No one knew how much time they had. Life could end in an instant. A finger snap, and one of us could be gone forever.

Death didn't spare anyone. Not sons or mothers or families or children. No one.

It definitely hadn't spared the high school senior driving her mother to the doctor that day. I could still see her in my mind, the life draining from her eyes as I stood by, unable to do anything to help her. Only now instead of red hair matted with blood, I saw Keith's blonde head lying there.

No!

I shook the thought away, refusing to think it. My worst fear imagined.

Other images rose to my mind. The little boy they brought in last week. He'd fallen headfirst from a shopping cart onto concrete pavement, while his mother stood less than a foot away, texting on her phone. Poor thing snapped his neck. He was already dead when they wheeled him in, but I couldn't stop thinking about him. Picturing his tiny body, bones sticking out from his neck. The mothers shrieking as we sent the body to the morgue haunted me after.

Poor woman would always blame herself for her son's death, but in truth, it could happen to anyone. They could glance away for a moment, reaching for a product on the shelf, hear the dreaded thud behind them. Heart racing as they turned to look, knowing it was too late. The unthinkable happened.

Life was brutal. I wouldn't be able to survive anything as awful as burying my child. Saying goodbye to him forever. It had to be the worst pain of all. Unimaginable. Unbearable to even contemplate.

Fuck!

I was depressing the hell out of myself. What was wrong with me? I took a couple more drags from the blunt, needing a distraction from my morbid thoughts.

The weed worked its magic, instantly relaxing me.

I leaned back and closed my eyes, just listening to the night. It was quieter now than earlier. Less people out and about as everyone retired to their homes and waiting beds. Even the critters were silent, hardly a sound to be heard.

I really loved being able to sit outside, get high, and enjoy my own company. There was nothing I'd rather be doing, not even making love to my husband. Not that the sex wasn't amazing, but out on the porch I didn't have to worry about satisfying anyone or meeting expectations.

    Another toke, and I was floating into oblivion. All my troubles, doubts, and fears melted away. I was weightless, feeling like I could drift right up into the sky and touch the stars above me. They shimmered like tiny mirages; there one minute and gone the next. Like my marriage.

    I kept forgetting Ronald was filing for divorce. I recently discovered him having an affair. It was like a plane crash, no one ever thought it could happen to them. I never even suspected.

    He told me only the day before the girl was pregnant with his child. She was twenty years younger than he. I couldn't even picture Ron chasing a toddler around at his age, especially with the back pain he'd been having recently. The thought of it was almost funny. Almost.

    If it didn't hurt so bad.

    I was devastated. Never saw it coming.

    Fresh tears sprang to my eyes.

    Damn him. Damn her. Damn them both to hell.

    Couldn't damn the baby, though. I wasn't that evil.

    I angrily wiped the tears away and took another drag.

No use crying over spilt milk. It's over and done with.

Wasn't worth another second thinking about. There would be plenty of time for that later.

My next hit had me coughing up a lung, or at least it felt that way. My throat burned in protest, and more tears leaked from my eyes.

That was okay. The desired effect was accomplished. I was stoned off my ass, my brain reaching the level of bliss it craved.

I took a final drag, then tossed the end of the joint into the ashtray next to me. I grabbed my cigarette pack and tapped one out. Put it in my mouth. Lit up.

Thoughts of Ron and his bimbo girlfriend drifted away like leaves in the wind.

The cigarette tasted great. I only ever allowed myself to smoke one a day. Only the one, and only when Keith was already in bed. He didn't know I still smoked, and I wasn't gonna tell him. One cigarette wouldn't hurt.

The combination of nicotine and marijuana left all my senses buzzing. I took my time, savoring each drag from the cancer stick. Smoking was the one addiction I just couldn't make myself give up. A bad habit I'd probably never entirely kick.

An inherited trait I came by naturally. Everyone had smoked in my family when I was growing up. I hoped Keith never started. At least I didn't smoke in front of him or in the house. Only outside.

Family was pretty much non-existent in my life now, aside from Ron and Keith. My mother died the year before, and most of the rest, I'd cut from my life long before. Lost souls every one, trapped inside their addictions. Even Mom before she died, but I learned I didn't need any of them years ago. I practically raised myself from the age of six, when I realized no one else was going to.

I loved my mother, despite her faults. She'd been the only one I kept in contact with. When she passed, I didn't have the heart to go to the funeral, not wanting to see any of the others. Not wanting to remember the abuse they dealt me all those years ago. But I did send flowers.

My past was dark and full of pain. Maybe that's why I loved working in the ER. Helping others deal with their trauma helped me forget my own. The blood and death that surrounded me in the hospital made everything I went through seem peaceful in comparison.

The cigarette was halfway gone. It was almost time to go back inside. Maybe I would finally bust open the bottle of wine my co-worker Cindy had given me the Christmas before. It was unopened, dusty and forgotten somewhere on the top of the fridge.

A glass of wine would be perfect right about then. I could even draw a bath, light some candles, pamper myself a little. It had been a long time since I'd been able to relax in the tub.

Why not?

Just the thought of it made me smile as I took another hit.

Leaves crunched nearby, just out of sight. Coming from near the fence.

My eyes probed the shadows, searching for the source of the sound. There was a dark shape, low to the ground, darker than everything else. It was big, whatever it was. And moving.

My heart leapt into my throat as it grew even larger the closer it moved in my direction, coming right at me before disappearing behind the shed.

What the hell was that?

"Whose there?" My voice boomed through the air like a megaphone, much louder than intended.

It was unnaturally quiet now, even the neighbor's yapping dog suspiciously silent. The only sound I could discern was my own breathing, heavy and uneven.

My mind went into overdrive, racing with possibilities. Could have been a possum or maybe a raccoon, but I doubted it. Looked much bigger than that.

Does Texas have bears?

I couldn't remember for the life of me. It had only been a couple years since we'd moved to the Lonestar state. I grew up in Tennessee and had no clue about Texan wildlife. I hadn't heard of any bear attacks, but that didn't mean they didn't happen.

Then again, why would a bear be in the back yard? And how would it have gotten there? It could have climbed the fence, of course, but wouldn't I have heard?

Besides, there weren't any woods nearby. Where would it have come from?

No, it had to be something else. But what?

Maybe someone casing the place, planning to break in as soon as I went to bed. Or I could have a stalker wanting to abduct me, and I'd never be seen again. It could have been anything really. Anything at all.

Even aliens. They could be real. They could beam me up into their spaceship and take me far away from here…

I giggled, laughing at the thought. What would aliens want with me? Or even with Earth for that matter? If they were the smarter species as many scientists predicted they were, they'd stay as far away from our planet as possible. Humans would be roaches to them. Pests. The scum of the universe. No, they'd wait for us to wipe ourselves out before claiming Earth for themselves.

A branch snapped. The sound came from the tree next to the shed. Leaves crunched. Another snap. Something was definitely moving over there. It was even closer than before, whatever it was.

Another shadow appeared, roughly the same size as before. From the other side of the shed. It was running right at me. Any second now, it would reach the porch steps.
I jumped to my feet, not sure whether to run or scream.
Keith's cat, Shadow, stepped into view. It slowed as it neared the porch and paused every few seconds to glance behind itself. Every hair on its back stood on end.
Shadow stopped right at the bottom of the stairs and turned to look again. He hissed once, then hightailed it

across the yard, disappearing through a hole in the fence.

Stupid cat.

I'd forgotten he'd escaped out the front door earlier when I got home. Another reason Keith was mad at me. Hopefully, Shadow would come back again. Last time he escaped, it took three weeks for me to find him. And then when I did, the damn thing clawed and scratched the hell out of me, like he didn't know who I was. Like I wasn't the only person who'd fed him for the past three and a half years.

Oh, well.

I'd worry about the cat later. The bathtub was calling my name.

All was silent in the house as I walked across the living room. Everything was clean and tidy. Just how I liked it. It was dark, but not so much I couldn't see as I made my way to the front hallway. I paused outside Keith's bedroom, listening for sounds of movement.

His soft snores greeted me. I eased open the door and glanced inside. Keith was fast asleep, his comforter on the floor at his feet. Must have kicked it off.

I tiptoed inside and picked it up, then carefully laid the blanket over him. He didn't stir at all.

As I made my way back to the door, I noticed a layer of dust covering everything. Like his room hadn't been cleaned in months.

I made a mental note to remind him to take care of it the next day as I left the room, easing the door closed behind me.

The kitchen wasn't as dark as the rest of the house. I usually left a small light over the sink on overnight, in case Keith wanted a drink or something after going to bed. It lit my way to the fridge. I rummaged around the top of it, standing on my toes, until my fingers touched the cool glass. Wrapping my hand around the bottle of wine, I pulled it toward me.

It didn't take but a second to grab a glass and fill it up. I put the bottle back and took the glass with me to the master bedroom. As I crossed the room, headed for the bathroom, I took a sip and swirled it around inside my mouth.

It was delicious. I enjoyed the sweet yet bitter taste on my tongue and savored it as long as I could before swallowing.

The tile was cold under my feet when I stepped into the bathroom. I crossed to the tub, grateful for the fuzzy bathmat in front of it. As I reached out to turn the taps, I heard a noise out in the kitchen.

Shit!

All at once, I realized I'd forgotten to lock the door on my way back in. And now someone was in the house. I could hear loud footsteps on the linoleum. Sounded like whoever it was wore boots.

I panicked. Fear washed over me like tidal wave, freezing the blood in my veins and making my heart race. I didn't want to die. How could I be so stupid?

I ran from the bathroom, wine splashing out of the wineglass, which flew from my hand and onto the carpet. Staining instantly. At least it didn't make any noise.

I darted to the closet and pulled the door to but didn't close it, not wanting to make a sound.

In my fear, my only thought was survival. I couldn't let them find me. I wouldn't.

There was a built-in caddy in the closet, meant to hold shoes. Climbing it like a ladder, I pulled myself onto the shelf above the hanging clothes. The whole time thinking the door would open behind me, and someone would grab me from behind.

The closet was dark, the air stuffy. I couldn't hear anything now. My heart was still going a mile a minute, my breath coming out in jagged puffs.

I wondered if they heard me. Imagined the door being yanked open, and light flooding the closet as the switch was flicked. I could almost see the pistol, hear the sound of the trigger being pulled.

But no one came.

I didn't hear anything for a while. And then I did.

A loud slam, like a door being thrown open.

Oh, no. Keith!

I felt like I'd been kicked in the stomach. In my panic, I'd forgotten all about him.

What kind of mother was I?

I was so stupid. How could I forget my own flesh and blood? My son. The one I spent sixteen hours bringing into this world.

Dread coursed through me. I didn't care about making noise now. I climbed halfway down the shoe caddy and jumped to the floor, almost breaking my ankle in the process. I limped to the door and threw it open, then ran across the bedroom fast as I could.

My injured ankle screamed in protest, but I didn't care. I was only worried about Keith.

He had to be okay. He just had to.

I was feeling sick and lower than low.

What had I done? Was I too late?

Please, God. No. Let Keith be alright.

The hall light was on, and Keith's bedroom door was wide open when I rounded the corner, dashing down the hall like something was chasing me.

As I ran, picturing a masked figure leaning over the bed with a knife in his hand, about to plunge the blade into my son's chest.

Don't let me be too late. Oh, God.

I knew it was going to be bad. I slowed as I neared the door and stepped into the room, then stopped in my tracks.

The bed was empty. It looked like it hadn't even been slept in. Neatly made, one corner tucked down.

What the fuck?

"Keith!" I yelled out.

There was no answer.

I called out his name again but knew it was useless. He was gone. Someone had taken him.

I ran back to my bedroom as quick as I could and grabbed my phone, which I'd left on the bathroom counter on my way to the bathtub earlier. I started to dial 911, then changed my mind. I called Ron.

This was a trick. He was punishing me. Teaching me a lesson. How many times had Ron warned me to lock the door before going to bed at night?

I just knew Ron was behind it. Everything bad that ever happened to me was always his fault.

The phone rang in my ear, once, twice, three times. It was answered before the fourth ring.

"Damn it, Jenny! Do you know what time it is? Why the fuck are you calling at this hour? Better be important."

He sounded different. Harsh. Like he wasn't even the same man that walked me down the aisle all those years ago. What happened to the love we once shared?

"Where's Keith? Where's my son? I know you took him!"

I was screaming, but I didn't care. I just wanted him back.

"Not this again. You know where he is. Do we have to do this now? Why can't you just accept it already? It's two o'clock in the morning. I have to be at work in three hours."

I could hear another voice in the background. Softer. A woman's voice. His twat girlfriend, no doubt. A baby squalled from further away.

"Great now you've woken the baby, too."

What baby? Did the girlfriend have another child? I felt confused and betrayed.

"What are you talking about? Not this again? Not what? What can't I accept?" I demanded.

Ron groaned before answering. "Keith's dead, you know that."

What?!

His words made me cold all over, like someone had thrown a bucket over ice water over my head. I shivered and shook my head.

"What? What are you talking about? Keith isn't dead. You took him, you bastard. Now tell me where he is!" My voice was so shrill, it hurt my own ears.

"He died eight months ago, remember? We buried him in the cemetery across from town hall." Ron's words were softer, but it didn't lessen the pain I felt at the words.

"That's impossible. I checked on him less than an hour ago… He was fast asleep in his bed."

Why was Ron doing this? Was he playing a sick joke? Getting back at me for something?

"I can't do this right now, Jenny. Our son is dead. He's been dead a long time now. Just let him go already. It's time. You have to move on."

"I'm telling you. He was in his bed. I put his blanket over him. He kicked it off in his sleep."

"No, he wasn't. He's buried, six feet under," Ron yelled into the phone. He took a breath, and then his voice was softer again. "Listen, I have to go. I'll talk to you later."

"Don't you dare hang up on me! Where the fuck is Keith! Give me back my son, you monster!"

I was done playing this game. It wasn't funny.

"Goodbye, Jenny. Don't bother calling back. I won't answer." With that Ron hung up.

I immediately called back, but it went to voicemail.

Fucking asshole, pick up!

He didn't, though. I called maybe thirty more times before giving up.

I sank to the floor and started bawling like a baby. Why was Ron doing this to me?

It didn't make sense. Nothing did.

Looking around, it didn't look like anything was out of place. The room was cleaner than I'd ever seen it, but everything was covered in dust. Same as before.

I stood up and flipped on the bedroom light. In the harsh florescent glare, the dust was even thicker. Making me even more confused. And the room was a little too clean. No dirty clothes or overstuffed backpack on the floor.

I climbed into the bed and hugged the pillow to my chest. It didn't smell like Keith at all. Smelled like it hadn't been used in a very long time.

I didn't understand. Keith was right here earlier. I raised the phone, about to try Ron again, but something tugged at mind. A forgotten memory begging for attention. It all came back to me in a rush. Everything. All of it.

I remembered the sleepover. The boys were so excited. Keith wanted a sleepover for his birthday. He wanted to camp in the backyard and sleep outdoors. I didn't like the idea at first, but then he asked could they sleep on the old couch in the shed. I agreed so long as he cleaned it up first. The shed was nasty, mostly used for storage.

That night was a blast. He spent a whole day cleaning the shed and preparing. By the time the three other boys arrived, everything was perfect. We even set up a small fire in the old pit, and they roasted hotdogs and made s'mores. It was the best birthday ever, Keith told me before I went inside for the night.

I checked on them a couple times, and once even had to ask them to quiet down. People were trying to sleep. It was too late for them to be so loud.

A little while later, I played a prank and beat on the door before rounding the corner and stepping into the shed with a flashlight under my chin.

—Booooo!—

The boys loved it. They begged me for a scary story, saying mine were the best. None of the other parents told stories like I did.

It was late, though. I had to work the next morning. I suggested they tell each other stories instead, just keep it down. Then, I went back inside.

It was supposed to be fun. I'm not really sure what happened. How everything went bad, why it ended in such tragedy. But it did.

The boys apparently wanted to make rocket fuel. They built a rocket together for the science fair a few weeks before. They wanted to make it fly. And made themselves fly instead. Up to heaven.

I don't know where they got the idea they could make rocket fuel by mixing household chemicals together. When I found them the next morning, the toxic fumes had killed them all. They'd closed the door, locking themselves inside with it. Probably trying to hide what they were doing from me.

Keith.

My baby.

My only child.

I remembered now. I could see the blue skin and fixed gaze all over again. He really was dead.

The memory of that horrible sleepover left me dead inside. It was all my fault.

I let it happen. Should have checked on them more times before going to bed.

No wonder I blocked it out. It was just too horrible. Their small bodies slumped over and dead. Four families that would never be the same again.

The truth I'd tried hiding from myself was finally out. Blocking it was my mind's way of protecting itself. A self-preservation tactic, locking the pain away deep inside where it could no longer hurt me.

I couldn't face it now, either. My biggest fear given life. Guilt tore at me, eating me alive.

I remembered his birth. His first birthday. Memories flew through my mind in a flash.

It was my fault. Keith was gone because of me. Dead. Taken away too soon. I'd never see him again. Never kiss him or read him a story before bed. Never hug him or smell that little boy scent.

I knew the hole he left inside my heart could never be filled. I'd never be the same again.

The knowledge of his death was suffocating. It was just too much. I was cursed to spend the rest of my life without the one I loved most. The only person who ever mattered. The owner of my heart and soul. Gone. Dead and buried.

I'd always be haunted by the loss of my child, forever screaming inside. Screaming for peace. The peace of death. And finally being reunited with Keith.

About The Author

E.B. Lunsford

E.B. Lunsford believes no horror is greater than reality. Reading was once her only means of escaping the hell she called life.
Nothing scared her more than not knowing what terrors she'd face next. Many people doubted she would ever succeed as an author, but E.B. was determined to prove them wrong. All she ever wanted was to share the dark and twisted stories her mind created. E.B. dreamed of doing for her fans what so many other authors did for her, give them a way of escaping the horrors of real life.

E.B. released her debut novel, No Escape, in 2020. She continues to make her impossible dream into reality with each new book she writes. E.B. resides deep in the heart of Texas with her family and an assortment of fur babies. Find out more by visiting her website, www.eblunsford.com. You can also follow her on Facebook, Instagram, and Goodreads.

Ukrainian Chimes

-Ronald McGillvray-

Ukrainian Chimes

The sound of rapid footsteps and heavy breathing mixed with the not-too-distant shouts of their pursuers. The pair crashed through the dark forest, aware of what awaited them if they were caught.

Branches whipped against their faces as they forced their way through the underbrush. Gnarled roots seemed to grab at them, as if to bring them to ground. Both men sweated profusely under the weight of their packs, gear and weaponry. Just hours ago, they'd been laughing with their comrades, but no more.

The darkness seemed to swallow them up and the forest was almost suffocating. Their surroundings were eerily quiet except for the excited voices off in the distance. How far off their pursuers were, the pair were unsure, but the fate that awaited them if they were caught was a certainty.

Dmitriy made a hand signal and Luka followed his gaze. Off in the distance were lights. Luka wondered if they should bypass the area or approach it in hopes of finding some kind of sanctuary. His decision was made for him as Dmitriy changed direction and moved towards the lights.

Dmitriy had always been the stronger one and Luka almost always deferred to his instructions.

The pair picked up the pace and crashed headlong through the forest, ignoring the cuts and stings of branches that slapped against their exposed skin.

Added to the sound of their pursuers, came the frightening sound of barking dogs.

How had things gone so terribly wrong?

The duo burst from the forest and were surprised to find themselves on the edge of a small community.

They stopped dead in their tracks.

Both men panted from exhaustion.

"I don't remember seeing this community on any of our maps," Luka said.

"Yet, here it is," Dmitriy said, still bent over, with his hands on his hips and taking in great gulps of air.

"I don't like it," Luka said, in between gasps of air. "We should bypass it and move on."

"And go where?"

"Anywhere," Luka said. "There may be militia here."

Dmitriy scanned the area and then looked back at Luka. "There aren't even any sentries watching the perimeter."

"That doesn't mean there might not be some waiting inside."

The sound of angry barking was getting closer.

"Do you want to wait for that?" Dmitriy asked.

Luka didn't answer.

"We'll keep to the shadows," Dmitriy said. "Now come on."

With that, Dmitriy left the shadows of the forest's edge and sprinted out into the open, towards a row of two-story cottages.

Luka followed close behind.

They pressed themselves against the wall of one of the cottages. Dmitriy made a hand gesture and the two inched their way along the wall until they came to a window. Dmitriy peered through it but could see no movement inside.

"I think it's empty," he said.

"Are you sure?"

"Of course, I'm not sure, but I'm sure enough."

Luka simply nodded.

They made their way around the cottage looking into the different windows they passed.

There was no sign of life in any of them.

They checked the back door, but it was locked.

"Should we kick it in?" Luka asked.

Dmitriy shook his head. "It would make too much noise."

"Should we make for the next one?"

"No, we'll go around to the front."

As they approached the front of the house, Luka stopped dead in his tracks.

Dmitriy noticed and turned to him. "Come on," he said. "What's the matter with you?"

Luka pointed at the doorway.

Dmitriy looked around confused and quickly crouched down. "What do you see?" he whispered.

Luka looked like he'd seen a ghost and simply pointed again at the doorway.

The wind had picked up and seemed to be carrying the sound of their pursuers ever closer. Luka shivered.

"Get it together and let's get inside," Dmitriy said, looking nervously in the direction of their pursuers.

Luka started to back away.

"What is wrong with you?" Dmitriy said. "Get back over here."

Luka just shook his head as he continued to back away.

Dmitriy gave up and followed Luka toward the next cottage but once again Luka stopped dead in his tracks. "What is going on with you?" Dmitriy asked.

Once again Luka pointed at the doorway.

Dmitriy stared at the doorway intently, in an attempt to make out what Luka was seeing that he was apparently missing. "What is it?" he asked finally.

Luka turned to him and it was clear from the look on his face, he was terrified of something.

"Spit it out," Dmitriy said. "I don't read minds."

"Ukrainian chimes," Luka said.

Dmitriy stared at him for a moment. "What?"

Luka pointed at the chimes dancing in the wind just by the front door.

Dmitriy stared at them for a moment and then turned and noticed the chimes hanging by the doorway at the cottage they'd just left. He turned back to Luka with a quizzical look on his face. "I don't understand what you're going on about."

Luka backed away from the front door toward Dmitriy. He scanned the area to make sure they were still alone and then looked directly at Dmitriy. "Those are Ukrainian chimes," he said.

"So what?"

"Look at them dancing in the wind."

Dmitriy smirked. "Yes, very pretty."

Luka frowned. "Don't you notice anything strange about them?"

"They just look like chimes to me," he answered. "My grandparents had some at their place."

"Not like these."

Dmitriy took another look at the dancing chimes. "Well, you've got me," he said. "Why don't you tell me what's so different about these ones."

"They're not making any sounds."

"Are you out of your mind?" Dmitriy said. "Let's get inside before we're seen."

Luka studied Dmitriy before he spoke next. "You don't find it strange that the wind is blowing, and the chimes are dancing around, but there's no sound coming from them?"

Dmitriy laughed. "Like you said, they're Ukrainian chimes."

"So?"

"So, what can you expect from something made in the Ukraine? It's obviously defective, like everything else in this god forsaken country."

"Why do you hate it here so much?"

"Because, I'd rather be home in Mother Russia. That's why."

Luka shook his head. "They didn't ask us to be here."

"Yet, here we are."

"Well, I'm not going into anywhere that has those chimes."

Dmitriy scowled at Luka. "What is it with you and those damn chimes?"

Luka stomped in place and hugged himself in an attempt to warm up. "Ukrainian chimes are placed to ward off evil."

"Are they now?"

Luka studied Dmitriy for a moment before going on. "It's said that the chimes remain silent, no matter how much they dance in the wind, until an evil presence passes under them."

Dmitriy laughed. "Good thing we're here to liberate our Ukrainian brothers and sisters then, so we should be safe since we're good and not evil."

"We're part of a Russian death squad," Luka said. "We've killed innocent civilians. I would suggest we're far from good."

"They were all resistance fighters," Dmitriy said. "I've killed no one that was innocent."

"What about the children we killed in the last town? Were they resistance fighters?"

Dmitriy's face grew angry. "I had nothing to do with that."

"We were complicit."

"We were following orders."

"And that makes it right?"

Dmitriy's face softened and he approached Luka and put his hands on his shoulders. "What's done is done and we're all that's left of our squad. So, unless you want to find yourself in an unmarked grave like our comrades, I suggest we get inside."

Luka shrugged himself free from Dmitriy's grasp. "I will not enter a cottage that has those chimes attached to it."

Beams of light broke through the forest tree line. The vicious barking of the dogs and the excited voices of their pursuers caught the pair's attention.

"Suit yourself but I'm getting inside before they find us," Dmitriy said, as he pointed his thumb over his shoulder towards the group now appearing out of the forest.

Luka turned and began to run across the lawn.

"What are you doing?" Dmitriy asked, following after him.

"There has to be a place without chimes somewhere down this row of cottages."

They searched the cottages, desperately looking for a place without chimes but there were none.

"What now, Mr. Chimes Expert?" Just as the words came out of Dmitriy's mouth another group of armed men appeared ahead of them. "Enough of this foolishness. We're going to get caught out here." Dmitriy turned away from Luka and took in the closest cottage. "I'm going in there. Are you coming?"

Grudgingly, Luka followed Dmitriy toward the cottage he'd pointed at. Sure enough, chimes danced maniacally in its doorway.

"The Ukrainian soldiers are everywhere," Dmitriy said. "We have to get inside." Without waiting for an answer, he walked under the chimes and tried the door. It was unlocked. He opened the door, stepped inside, and turned around. "Well?"

Luka glanced back at the approaching soldiers. He looked unsure but finally, making up is mind, he approached the threshold and glanced up at the chimes.

"See, they're still not making any sounds, so we must be welcome," Dmitriy said.

Luka was uncertain and nervous about passing under them, but his urge to survive won over and he followed Dmitriy into the cottage.

The cottage was deathly quiet as they searched downstairs and upstairs for any sleeping residents, but there was no one home.

"Where are they?" Luka asked, as he scanned one of the upstairs bedrooms.

"Who cares."

Luka seemed nervous. "You don't find it strange that there's no one home in the middle of the night?"

Dmitriy studied Luka for a moment. "I never realized what a nervous man you are. First with the chimes and now with empty houses. What's got into you?"

"Nothing's got into me," Luka replied, indignantly.

"Then pull yourself together. They probably evacuated this little town when they heard our squad was working nearby. I bet…

The sound of Ukrainian voices and barking nearby interrupted Dmitriy. The two of them quietly eased over to a window and looked out. Ukrainian soldiers, many of them, marched down the street, their search lights scanning every possible hiding place.

"Why are they not searching any of the cottages?" Dmitriy asked.

Luka didn't answer but instead watched uneasily as the soldiers and their tracking dogs passed by and continued down the road.

What seemed even stranger was that the dogs were now suddenly quiet. Luka and Dmitriy watched as the soldiers continued to move away.

Dmitriy turned away from the window. "And that's why they're losing the war," he said. "How can they expect to beat the greatest army on earth with that kind of undisciplined behaviour and laziness?"

"It's probably a trap," Luka said.

Dmitriy scoffed at the idea. "It would take better men than that to trap us."

"You forget, it was those same men that were able to ambush our squad and kill everyone but the two of us."

Dmitriy frowned and broke eye contact with Luka to take another look out the window. "I think they're gone," he said. "Let's go downstairs." Without another word he left the bedroom.

Luka stood alone in the bedroom for a moment, gathering his thoughts, when the sound of chimes drifted into the room.

His heart began to beat faster.

He had an urge to look out the window but decided he didn't want to know what might be out there waiting for him in the night. Instead, he hustled out of the room in search of Dmitriy.

Downstairs, he found Dmitriy struggling with the back door. "What are you doing?"

Dmitriy gave another tug at the door. "The door won't open."

"Did you try the front door?" Luka asked.

Dmitriy didn't answer but instead marched right by him.

Luka followed.

Dmitriy stopped to look out a window facing the front of the cottage. After he apparently felt the coast was clear he walked over to the front door. He tried opening it but he didn't have any success with that one either.

"What's going on?" Luka asked.

"I think they sealed the doors somehow."

"They didn't seal the doors," Luka said. "We watched as they walked right by."

The sound of the chimes suddenly caught both of their attention.

Luka opened his mouth to speak when Dmitriy suddenly spoke.

"Keep your mouth shut," Dmitriy said. "I don't want to hear any more of your chime nonsense."

Luka didn't answer, but instead brushed by Dmitriy and entered the small living room where he simply took a seat and sat there in deep thought.

Dmitry ignored him and walked back to the front window. He scanned the darkness looking for any kind of threat that might be out there waiting for them.

There was nothing.

Nothing but darkness.

And those incessant chimes.

Luka sat quietly listening to the chimes, the fear building inside of him with each passing moment. His grandmother had been Ukrainian, something he purposely neglected to inform his superiors about. She had been the one to tell him stories of the Ukrainian chimes and he had no reason to doubt her.

Dmitriy's voice broke him from his thoughts. "Get over here."

Luka reluctantly got up from where he was seated and approached Dmitriy. "What is it?" he asked, as he squatted beside him.

"Do you see anything?"

"You've been looking out there long enough," Luka said. "You tell me."

"Stop pouting and just look out and tell me what you see."

Luka looked at him quizzically but finally turned his gaze out the front window. He saw darkness.

Only darkness.

It didn't take more than a few more seconds for Luka to realize that he couldn't make out the lawn or even the street beyond.

How had it become so dark outside?

The sound of the chimes once again caught his attention. He turned his gaze away from the lawn and toward the sound of the chimes.

There they were in clear sight.

Just hanging there.

Motionless.

Yet the chiming continued.

"So, what do you see?"

Luka jumped, startled by Dmitriy's voice.

"Nothing," he finally said. His throat felt dry, and his answer came out more as a croak.

"Nothing at all?" Dmitriy asked.

"The chimes."

"Ah yes. The mysterious Ukrainian chimes," he said. "They no longer move an inch, yet they chime away as if in a gale force wind."

Luka met Dmitriy's gaze. "I told you."

"Yes, yes you did," he said. "Stranger yet is the fact that everything, but those damn chimes seem to have disappeared into utter darkness."

Luka got up from his squatting position.

"Get down," Dmitriy ordered. "Someone might see your silhouette."

"There's nothing out there," Luka answered indignantly as he walked toward the front door. He tried opening it himself, but it wouldn't budge. His mind raced. His grandmother had never mentioned anything about the outside world disappearing or being trapped inside. Was this something different?

There was a sudden knocking on the back door.

Dmitriy appeared out of the gloom. "What was that?"

Luka lifted his weapon. "Someone's out back."

Dmitriy readied his weapon and the two of them crouched down and quietly made their way toward the back of the cottage.

There was another knock.

"Maybe it's just a neighbour?" Dmitriy said.

Hope washed over Luka. Could they be so lucky, he wondered.

As they eased toward a back window, being careful to keep as low as possible, the knocking stopped.

"Maybe they went away?" Dmitriy said.

"Go check the door."

"You go check the door."

Luka grinned. "What are you afraid of?" he asked. "You're not afraid of the Ukrainian chimes, are you?"

"Don't be absurd."

"Would you like me to hold your hand when we go check?"

"You're getting on my nerves, Luka." Dmitriy eased away from the wall and slowly made his way toward the back door.

There was another knock at the door. This one much louder and much harder. So hard, Dmitriy could feel the vibrations from where he crouched. He turned and noticed Luka had come up behind him. It made him feel a bit better but not by much.

"Can you see anything?" Luka asked.

Dmitriy shook his head.

The two waited for another knock but there was nothing but silence.

"Should we go check or retreat back into the living room?" Luka asked.

Dmitriy couldn't seem to make up his mind. Finally, he said, "Let's go look."

Quietly they moved toward the window beside the door.

"Can you see anything?" Luka asked.

"Nothing."

"What do you want to do?"

Dmitriy hesitated for a moment as if deep in thought. Then he said, "If there's someone there, we'll blast them straight to hell."

Luka simply nodded.

"Ready?" Dmitriy asked.

"Ready." Luka gripped his weapon tightly.

The two sprang up and searched for any type of movement outside. But, just like at the front of the house, they could make out nothing but darkness. The two of them laughed nervously and relaxed their grips on their weapons.

"They must have left," Dmitriy said.

"Let's hope," Luka said. "Give the door another try."

Dmitriy shrugged. "I guess it couldn't hurt."

"If it opens, we should get the hell out of here."

Dmitriy smiled. "Agreed."

Dmitriy's hand rose toward the door but hesitated at the last moment.

"What do you think is out there?" Luka asked.

"Nothing that a few rounds from this can't handle." Dmitriy patted his weapon.

Luka's face turned serious. "No, I meant, out there, out there."

"I don't get your meaning."

Luka felt stupid about what he was about to suggest but it had to be said. "I'm wondering if there's anything actually out there," he said. "You saw it. The utter darkness, as if there was nothing out there anymore."

"Well, something must still be out there because someone was just knocking."

"I just have a bad feeling," Luka said.

"Just keep your weapon ready," Dmitriy said. "I'm going to try the door."

Just as Dmitriy reached for the doorknob, a shadow moved across the window. Dmitriy jumped back almost tumbling to the floor. "What the fuck was that?" He looked over at Luka.

Luka seemed shaken. He'd obviously seen it as well.

There was a sudden knocking.

This time at the front door.

"We're surrounded," Dmitriy exclaimed.

"I don't think it's the Ukrainians."

"Neighbours?"

"I don't think I want to know," Luka said.

Dmitriy's eyes darted from the back of the cottage to the front of it. "It has to be that Ukrainian squad."

"We watched them leave," Luka said.

"Well, they're back."

There's another knock at the front door.

"This is madness," Dmitriy said.

"No, it's the presence."

"The what?"

Luka looked defiantly at Dmitriy. "I told you. The chimes protect this place."

"By knocking at the doors incessantly?"

"The story goes that when the chimes play their song, it conjures up a presence who will appear, to defend the place."

Dmitriy looked incredulously at Luka. "And what does this presence look like?"

"No one knows because all who've come across it perish and can't tell the tale."

"That's idiotic," Dmitriy said.

Another knock, much louder this time, interrupted their conversation.

It stopped as suddenly as it began.

Yet, the Ukrainian chimes continued their haunting lament.

Luka and Dmitriy sat on the floor as they ate some of their leftover rations. Neither one spoke. They'd picked a spot in the middle of the cottage, as far away from the doors and windows as they could manage. There hadn't been a knock at the door for over an hour but both of them were still tense and exhausted. The chimes, however, had continued their eerie knell.

	Dmitriy swallowed the last of his ration. He stood up and stretched. Weariness was etched on his face. "Should we try the doors again?"

	Luka crumpled up the wrapper and casually tossed it across the floor. "Suit yourself."

	"Pull yourself together."

	"I'm fine," Luka replied.

	Dmitriy simply shook his head. "Those chimes are driving me crazy." He looked around their surroundings, but nothing had changed. He snatched up his weapon and without another word, slowly made his way towards one of the windows facing the front of the house. He hesitated at first but finally drew back the curtain to look out.

	He could see nothing in the complete darkness but the motionless chimes. This is madness, he thought to himself. A sense of frustration built up within him until he could take it no more.

He marched to the front door and tried to yank it open with all his might, but it wouldn't budge. He quickly turned around and went to the back door and did the same. Only to get the same result. He heard a noise behind him and spun around.

Luka stood perfectly still with Dmitriy's weapon pointed at his midsection. "No luck?" he said, seemingly unperturbed by the weapon pointed directly at him.

Dmitriy lowered his weapon. "No."

A sudden knock, as if on cue, startled the two of them.

"They're back," Luka said.

"I'm growing tired of this game," Dmitriy said.

There was another knock at the back door. Dmitriy rushed to the door, but the knocking stopped. He stared through the door's window and there was nothing but darkness. He inched closer and cupped his hands around his eyes and pressed them against the window. "I can't see anything. There's nothing but complete darkness out there."

There was a sudden knock at the door. Dmitriy, with his face still pressed against the door's window, felt the knock like a punch to the face. He jumped back in fright and fired some rounds into the door.

Luka rushed up behind him. His weapon raised and ready. "Did you get him?"

"I don't know."

They both stared at the door, now riddled with bullets, and then looked at each other. They moved toward the door and listened but there wasn't a sound.

There was a knock at the front door.

"Will this madness never end?" Dmitriy said, as he turned to go to the front door.

"Wait," Luka said. "Screw the front door. We've already made enough noise with the gunfire to attract anyone who might be within earshot. Let's just blast our way out of here and go out through the back."

Dmitriy grinned.

The two of them opened fire and shredded the door to pieces.

But still it stood.

"Try the door now," Luka said.

Dmitriy grabbed the knob, which was barely hanging from the door, and tried to open it.

The door didn't move.

"That's impossible," Luka said.

"I've had enough," Dmitriy said, as he brushed by Luka and into the next room. He stood in front of the picture window and opened fire. The window shattered into millions of pieces. "Let's get out of here."

The two of them approached the window and peered out into the darkness. It was unsettling. There wasn't a sound, except for the chimes, coming from out of the void.

"You first," Luka said.

Dmitriy nodded and wearily approached the new opening. The glass beneath his boots crunched under his weight. The complete darkness seemed to give him pause. "It doesn't seem right."

"Just poke your head out and have a look around," Luka said.

Dmitriy inched forward and leaned his head out the window. He stopped dead in his tracks and staggered back a few steps.

"What is it?" Luka asked.

"There's a barrier."

"What?" Luka rushed over and attempted to push his hand through the seemingly open space. His hand was met by a solid barrier.

"You see," Dmitriy said.

"How is it possible?"

Before Dmitriy could answer, a shadow passed by the open window and then another, and another.

The two slowly backed away, keeping their eyes on the opening, prepared for something to jump through, when there was a knock at the front door.

The two of them turned and opened fire, shattering the front picture window and shredding the front door.

They paused their firing and waited nervously to see what would happen next.

A shadow passed by the front window.

Dmitriy let out another short burst from his weapon.

Everything became quiet.

"Do you think there's a barrier at the front as well?" Luka asked.

"There's only one way to find out." Dmitriy, with his weapon ready, walked toward the shattered front window. Instead of using his hands this time, he poked the opening with the muzzle of his weapon.

Two grotesque hands sprang from the darkness and latched onto Dmitriy's weapon. Dmitriy was pulled forward but opened fire to no effect. Panicking, as he was pulled toward the darkness, he relinquished his weapon and watched it disappear into the darkness of the void.

Luka stepped forward. "Get behind me. We're getting the hell out of here." Luka slowly approached the open window with Dmitriy trailing along behind him. He let off a few bursts of gunfire and attempted to step outside.

His leg bumped against the barrier. He staggered in place for a moment before catching his balance.

Dmitriy stepped forward in a rage and began pounding with his fists against the barrier.

Luka dropped to the floor. "How can this be?" He held his lowered head in his hands.

Dmitriy didn't respond but instead, bent over at the waist, panted for breath.

There was a knock at the front door.

"Stop it," Dmitriy yelled out, covering his ears.

Luka wearily stood up and dragged Dmitriy away from the window. "Keep it together," he said, before collapsing onto the floor beside his comrade.

The knocking had stopped, and the cottage was silent, until the creaking of a door from somewhere upstairs broke the silence.

"They're inside," Dmitriy said.

The two of them listened as the door continued creaking.

Then it stopped.

Luka and Dmitriy both looked toward the ceiling and waited.

They didn't have to wait long before the sound of footsteps from upstairs caught their attention. They listened as the floorboards above them creaked with each footstep.

The footsteps stopped and then the creaking of a door was heard again.

They both jumped when the creaking stopped, and the door slammed shut.

The cottage once again became silent, except for the chimes.

Luka and Dmitriy looked at each other and then toward the stairs leading up. An unspoken agreement passed between them, and they stood up and quietly made their way to the bottom of the stairs. They stood there and listened.

There was nothing but the sound of the chimes.

Dmitriy made a hand gesture and Luka nodded. Slowly, they inched up the first few steps. They paused and listened for any movement. Just as they were about to continue, the sound of footsteps coming up from the basement caught their attention. Once again, the two of them looked at each other. After a moment, Dmitriy made another hand gesture and the two of them quietly stepped back down the stairs and toward the basement door.

They listened as the footsteps drew closer to the top. Luka's heart pounded in his chest as he lifted his weapon and pointed it at the basement door. Each step seemed to take an eternity, as if time was slowing down. Luka pulled his eyes from the door and looked at Dmitriy. Dmitriy's face was pale, and his thin lips seemed to tremble ever so slightly.

The footsteps drew closer still.

Luka felt perspiration forming along his hairline and dripping down his back. His hands were damp and shaking slightly so he tightened his grip on his weapon. What was coming up those stairs? He thought back on those strange arms that had shot out from the darkness and a shiver ran down his spine.

The footsteps continued coming closer.

Dmitriy gestured at the doorknob suggesting he might want to open it. Luka shook his head. He was in no hurry to see what was behind the door.

Finally, the footsteps stopped at the top of the stairs.

Luka and Dmitriy waited.

Both were startled by knocking at the back door but kept their eyes on the basement door.

Then there was knocking at the front door.

Followed by the sudden knocking at the basement door.

Luka and Dmitriy listened in horror as the knocking on all three doors continued. Each knock louder than the previous one. Luka felt like he was going insane. A switch went off in his head and without warning, he pressed the trigger of his weapon and unleashed a barrage of bullets into the basement door.

Everything suddenly went silent.

Luka watched as Dmitriy stepped forward and put his hand on the basement's doorknob. This time Luka didn't reject the idea. He watched as Dmitriy slowly turned the doorknob. Luka steadied his weapon and kept it pointed at the door.

There was a click as Dmitriy finished turning the doorknob. He looked at Luka and Luka nodded.

Dmitriy swung the door wide but there was nothing but utter darkness. They looked at each other quizzically.

Silence hung over them like a heavy weight.

Without warning, Dmitriy took a few tentative steps down into the basement.

"Wait." Luka's voice startled even himself.

"He has to be dead," Dmitriy said.

Luka shook his head. "I don't think it's a good idea."

"Do you have a better one?"

Luka stood there, unable to get a word out.

"That's what I thought."

Luka watched as Dmitriy disappeared into the darkness and down the stairs. Luka strained to see his comrade, but he couldn't make out a thing. "Dmitriy," he called out.

He waited for a reply, but none came.

"Dmitriy," he called out again.

And he waited.

"What?" finally came Dmitriy's reply.

Luka felt a sudden wave of relief wash over him. "What do you see?"

"Nothing," came Dmitriy's reply.

Luka inched closer to the doorway. "Have you reached the bottom yet?"

Luka waited for a reply.

"Dmitriy?"

There was no answer to his call.

"Dmitriy?" he called out again.

Still no reply.

Luka backed away from the door, making sure to keep his weapon pointed at its entrance. His mind raced with thoughts of what he should do next. He listened to the sound of chimes echoing in the night.

And then it began.

First there was knocking at the back door. Followed by knocking at the front door. The sound of a creaking door opening upstairs added to the terrors that were happening all around him. He backed away from the basement entrance and slowly turned in a circle, keeping his weapon pointed straight ahead of him.

He saw a shadow pass across the smashed front window. Then another one at the front door. The sound of crunching glass made him spin around and he saw a shadow pulling itself through the broken back window.

The sound of footsteps above him creaked on the floorboards.

Luka had had enough and ran for the basement. He wanted to fire off a few rounds before hitting the staircase, but he didn't know where Dmitriy might be.

He hesitantly entered the dark staircase. Slowly, he made his way down but couldn't make out a thing. It was as if he had been swallowed up by the darkness. "Dmitriy?" he called out. There was no reply.

Luka finally reached the basement floor. He fumbled around in the complete darkness until he stopped to listen to his surroundings. He could hear movement above him, but he seemed alone in the basement. He screwed up his courage and called out for his comrade. "Dmitriy?"

Still came no reply.

He moved slowly, inch by inch, across the basement floor until he bumped into something. It gave a bit but then bounced gently back into him. He instinctively stepped back. The sound of clanking chains echoed in the basement. The clanking gradually quieted until it finally grew silent.

Luka stepped tentatively ahead with an arm outstretched until he felt the object he'd just bumped into. The sounds of chains clanked again. Luka screwed up his nerve and felt around at the object. It wasn't long until he realized it was a body and it wasn't much longer after that, he realized it was most likely, Dmitriy.

"Dmitriy?" he said, almost in a whisper.

There was no reply.

Luka could feel the military issued fatigues that his squad wore and his heart sank. Amidst his inner turmoil, he remembered the lighter that Dmitriy carried. He felt around until he found the lighter in Dmitriy's pants pocket. It sank home then that his friend was right in front of him. He was unsure if he was dead or just unconscious but one thing he was now sure of, he obviously wasn't alone down here.

He pocketed the lighter and lifted his weapon. The roar of gunfire erupted in the darkness as he spun around spraying every last inch of the basement. He was panting and crying as he released his finger from the trigger. He waited for a minute, listening, but there wasn't a sound. Slowly, he reached into his pocket and took out the lighter. He felt the coolness of the metal against the palm of his hand. He played with it in his hand, hesitant to ignite it. He finally screwed up his courage and rolled his thumb over the flint wheel.

A flame burst from the lighter.

Luka gasped.

Dmitriy hung from the rafters, secured by heavy, rusted chains and splayed spreadeagle. Dmitriy's body began to spasm and thrash around as if in a vain attempt at escape. Lukas' mind went numb. Not because of the situation but because Dmitriy's body was missing its head.

There was a soft whisper from somewhere in the darkness and the lighter blew out.

Luka closed his eyes and screamed. He slowly dropped to his knees and felt tears begin to drip down his cheeks. He wiped at the tears as a sense of panic set in. He frantically felt around for the lighter before he realized he still held it in his grasp. He was about to try igniting it again when he heard footsteps coming down the basement stairs in the darkness.

Luka desperately attempted to ignite the lighter. He rolled his thumb over and over again against the flint wheel. Finally, the lighter sparked to life.

Dmitriy's body hung motionless before him. Luka looked down to avert his eyes from the gruesome site.

Staring up at him, inches from his knees was Dmitriy's smiling head. It slowly opened its mouth and the sound of chimes spewed out of it.

Luka began to scream.

As his screams echoed in the basement, from the darkest recesses of the basement came the sound of more chimes, slowly moving closer.

Out of the gloom of darkness, figures began to emerge. Nothing more than shadows, but each holding a set of chimes.

The chimes became louder and louder until they almost felt like they were emanating from inside his head. He slowly placed the still lit lighter onto the cold basement floor and lifted his weapon.

As he stared in horror at the emerging figures, he could see them now more clearly and they were no more than shadows. Dark, menacing shadows.

And the chimes grew louder.

Luka shouted obscenities and pressed the trigger of his weapon, but the chamber was empty.

Over the deafening sounds of the chimes came the haunting whispers from the shadowy forms.

Suddenly the lighter blew out and Luka screamed and screamed and screamed…

Until the Ukrainian chimes became silent once more.

About The Author

Ronald McGillvray

Ronald McGillvray is a writer from Ottawa, Canada. He writes short stories, scripts, novellas and novels. His latest horror novel, Cutter's Deep is available as a print or eBook on Amazon. His horror short story collection, Tales From The Parkland is also available as a print or eBook. His writing credits include the short story, The Garbage Collectors, which was published in Horror Library Volume 2 as well as in their best of anthology. An audio version of his story, Big Boy, was produced by Pseudopod and his story, A Night Out, was published by Dark Fire Fiction.

His children's fantasy novella, James' Journey To Dreamland is also available as a print or eBook.

Two of his film scripts, The Storm and The Goodbye, were produced by Cellardweller Projects. The Storm was chosen as one of the films to be screened at the World Horror Convention. It also screened at the Shocklines Film Festival in New York City.

His story, Head Case, was made into a film produced by Columbia College in Chicago. His film script, Magic Man, was optioned by Hyde Park Media.

His stage play, The Line, was chosen as part of the reading series by the Saint John Theatre Company.

Find out more about Ronald McGillvray at:
www.ronaldmcgillvray.com

Sweet Tea

-Leigh Pettit-

Sweet Tea

There are times when the comfort and safety of home are just that, comfortable, safe. Now that's all well and good, but there lies complacency and monotony. What stories could we pass to younger generations had we not lived an exuberant life full of adventure and danger? For some, the thrill of the unknown, no matter how perilous, outweighs the safety blanket of our familiar surroundings. The anticipation, the not knowing, keeps our souls alive. But, then, in hindsight, there are the moments you wish you had just stayed home.

    Leaving Cali felt good. It was just before six in the morning, and already the blacktop smouldered. The sunrise touched the sky with its peachy haze, and the palms drifted in the wind. Salt stung the air as it came in from the ocean. The Californian climate was enviable in comparison to the more northern states in early June.

    The Groms had already begun to flood the board shop, a revolving door of new blood. For Renn Garcia

Oceanside, California, had always been home. She had never really felt the urge to leave, but now it was time.

Cancer does not care if you have yet to achieve all you set out to do. It is merciless, it will hunt you, and for many, there is no escape, and Renn, being relatively young, felt the sands of time slipping through her fingers.

As vast as the ocean was, she had spent so much time on the waves that it had, in essence, become her prison, the infinite waters, her cage.

It is not until you harbour a ticking time bomb that your world suddenly appears so small, and it was now that Renn realised she had overlooked so much. The mountains, the prairies, pine-scented forests and roads that stretch so far you can fathom no end to them. Renn wanted to taste that. She needed it.

Leaving town just as the world series surf tour began was a double-edged sword. Renn couldn't bear to sit on the sidelines, knowing she no longer had the strength nor passion for something she had centred her whole life around. But, equally, catching one last wave seemed so final.

Her plan was to take her last breath there on the edge of the ocean with the waves lapping at her feet to be met by a giant swell which would swallow her whole, but not yet. She still had eight months.

The gentle morning breeze stroked her cheeks. The waves crashed against the rocky outpost as the gulls circled and soared above. Her chestnut brown shoulders held a scattering of freckles, Sol's kisses. Her blue-green eyes shone synonymous with the ocean she now gazed upon; this was farewell, not goodbye.

Bry's fingers tangled with hers, warm and homely, his tousled brown locks ruffled in the wind. Behind the tangled tresses, his amber eyes fell upon Renn's luminous skin. She had a light; it was always there, and it was that light that first drew Bry to the girl that rode the waves as though she were a part of them.

"Ready to hit the road, sunshine?" She was. Feeling the swell in her belly, the ocean's pull, the sparkling turquoise waters that cried, "don't go." Waters that loomed so high they would create a wall of water full of deep shadows. But it was too late. As the stormy petrels scratched at washed-up urchins, the sand melted beneath her feet, and without so much as looking back, she picked up her knapsack and vacated the beach and the only place she had ever known.

But now all was dark.

She couldn't remember how she got to this point, just the crash, the way they left the road before she could really fathom what was happening or why. The deafening sound as the roof of the car smashed against the ground, as her mouth filled with dirt.

For what felt like an age, Renn had sat in the dark. Even as time went on, her eyes barely adjusted to the opaqueness of the thick, inky air surrounding her, no light source offered to relieve her of this.

Her head swam as tinnitus rattled in her ears. Renn contemplated that she may, in fact, be dead. What a way to go, after everything, and if she were, it wasn't at all what she had expected. No pearly gates swung open for her here.

She had gone from a world of the west coast sun to the dark realm of cancer to this, an even darker place.

"Hello?" Hello, hello, hello… Her voice echoed back. It was cold, so, so cold. Her breath froze as it left her lips. She hugged her knees, pulling them under her chin to stop her teeth from chattering.

"Bry?!" There came no reply. Still, in her crouching position, she felt around a little. The rough, icy surface of the floor sent a chill through her fingers into the pit of her soul.

The warmth of the sun on their road trip had warranted only denim cut-offs and a light tee. Now a pang of regret over her choice of outfit writhed in her belly.

"Argh, where am I? Fuck!" This is just a bad dream, the little voice of reason whispered. You're going to wake up soon, Any. Minute. Now.

Then she heard something. A long raspy breath… "That you, Bry?" A trickle of cold sweat ran down her spine. She knew it wasn't him.

Bryan L Deichman, although sounding like a serial killer with a name like that, possessed the most gentle, fun-loving soul. Renn's lover and, above all, best friend. He had appeared on the beach, washed up with all the other Grom's. Travelling around in his late father's 1962 Oldsmobile Starfire, surfing the break, and waking up on a different beach every other week, hair full of sand. A simple life suited him. Then he met Renn, and Bry had found somewhere to call home.

Warmth filled her heart momentarily, and she almost forgot where she was.

Again, another long slow breath; Renn could feel it now inches from her face. Every hair on her body stood up as waves of fear ran over her flesh. The stench of its breath was putrid, reminiscent of raw meat way past its best.

"Who's there? Get away. Stay the hell away from me" Renn curled into a ball, covering her face and ears. Whoever or whatever was there was startled by the sudden outburst from its captive. Renn, who, although still unable to see clearly, could now distinguish even subtle movements in the vacuous silence of this makeshift prison.

Listening, waiting, unable to move and locked to the ground with terror, Renn stayed. Then a blinding light cut through the thick black as the phantom captor cracked open the door from the inside, perchance to slip away. It took a moment for Renn's eyes to adjust.

There its silhouette was, illuminated by the harsh light. A tall, long, ungainly figure stood in shadow before the exit. Renn rubbed at her eyes as pareidolia corrupted her vision. She was still cold, but the sight that greeted her inspired perspiration to form upon her top lip. Her hands became clammy and heavy as she sat rooted to the spot. The creature lunged at her without warning. Its long arms grappled out of the shadows, grabbing hold of the sleeve of her tee and pulling at her clothes. Renn lashed out in defence, scratching at her assailant's flesh. Letting out a gut-churning shriek, the thing retreated away from Renn. Then it growled a deep, irritable growl. The sound of which made Renn's heart sink.

The lump in Renn's throat became impossible to swallow. Again, the creature appeared from the shadows, moving closer this time, dragging its feet with an awkward gait. Seeing her nemesis more clearly now, Renn shuddered as her eyes followed its ghastly form. Its skin was a milky white, wet like a scaleless fish.

Shinbones protruded from its slender legs. Further up, the smooth tibia narrowed into what appeared to be notch upon notch of spinal segments forming the femur. Its flesh clung barely to its rib cage, only three rungs deep, distorted but much wider than a human's. The black stain of its heart pounded below the paper-thin flesh. Then Renn's eyes fixed upon its face, except this thing had no recognisable features. Just gash upon gash of open wounds. Like axe wounds on a fallen tree. Melting flesh slipped from its horrifying visage.

The smell of decay tore into Renn's nostrils, filling her lungs like roadkill left in the blistering heat. It reminded her of the hospital, and although the pungent aroma of disinfectant overpowered the smell of death, it was always there; the scent of defeat. The same sallow faces would show up week after week to be pumped full of viscous black goo with their plastered-on smiles and false cheer. They were drenched in toxic positivity until slowly, one by one; they stopped coming. Departed, snuffed out. The memory filled her with dread, and soon it would be her riding the long river with Charon as her guide. Had she done enough? At twenty-four, she knew she hadn't.

Before she knew it, the creature was upon her. Blood dripped from every orifice. Red spots of sanguine fluid appeared on her white tee, the only thing between her and the biting cold. The only thing between her and

IT. With her back against the wall, she scanned the room. Aside from the one escape route which the vile menace was blocking, her eyes fixed upon a broken slab of concrete just a few feet away. The creature cocked its head sideways as though it knew her mind. Taking another step toward her, its disfigured club feet scraped across the silver-grey concrete floor, leaving a trail of blood as it went. Renn saw an opportunity, and she lowered herself onto her belly, the creature's bony shins now just inches from her face. She could taste it; a bitter bile nipped at her tongue. The creature stood above, its head cocked this way and that, its long-pointed nail less digits reached out to no avail.

"It can't see me!" This, indeed, was a revelation.

The monstrous being's raspy, shallow breath cut through the silence. Renn used her elbows to push herself across the ground on her belly through the towering legs of the nightmarish beast until she reached the slab. It lay in two jagged parts, either piece large enough and heavy enough to cause damage. The harsh light from the door was now so close it burned into her eyes after so long in the dark, much like the fluorescent lighting of the hospital rooms. Oh, how she wanted to forget them.

Renn stretched out her arm, and as her forefinger brushed the edge of the concrete slab, her grotesque assailant grabbed hold of her leg and yanked, dragging her back from where she had come. The rough flooring tore into her tee, ripping her navel bar clean through her flesh. The pain was over quickly, but it was agonising, to say the least. Letting out a cry, Renn kicked hard, and the beast lost its grip. She took her chance and scrabbled back towards the slab. She pulled herself to her feet with the only weapon at her disposal firmly in her grasp. "Hey, ugly! I have something for you!" The gore-faced menace swung around, howling like a rabid coyote, raised its sinewy arm and backhanded Renn across the cheek, knocking her back on her heels and causing her to lose her footing. Her back slammed into the ground, and she narrowly escaped smashing her skull. The pain shot through her spine like a bolt of lightning.

    Standing above her, a gooey glob of bloodied spit fell from the creature and splashed upon Renn's cheek. Then the girl, the gentle Renn, found her fire. She rose to her feet, her eyes black as night, as a tempest slid across her irises, and before it could re-attack, she planted the jagged slab hard into its jaw, knocking it to the ground. For once, it lay assailed and confused. She leapt upon the beast, raining blow after blow upon the harbinger of hell's cranium. An ear-splitting thud rang in her ears like the sound of a hammer on an anvil until she heard a sickening squelch. She had reached the brain.

Using both hands, Renn slammed the slab upon the miscreation's shattered skull, again and again, until she felt she had annihilated it enough that there was no chance of the menace becoming reanimated. The blood-riddled corpse writhed, twitched, shuddered, and then fell still.

Blood slid from the mulched brain matter and began to creep across the floor, silently reaching out for something to touch. And there in the mirrored crimson pool, Renn caught sight of her reflection, familiar yet unrecognisable all at once. Looking back were wild eyes full of flame, a round face drained of colour except for the spatter of claret from the dead beast, and a smooth head bereft of hair. Before the cancer took hold, Renn had a head of golden blonde hair that always tousled and undone from the salty waves of her Pacific sanctuary. She looked deep into the bloody puddle; the sanguine pool swirled till her features became a distorted blur. The skin on her face started peeling away, melting. Red liquid oozed and dripped from her face. Her pretty eyes fell from their sockets. As she reached to touch her face, her fingers disappeared into the soft, sticky mess.

And she screamed a silent scream.

"Wake up, Renn, wake up!"

She opened her eyes; Perspiration soaked her skin, and her stomach bore the knots of a fated voyager.

"Hot damn girl, you nearly sent us off this wild road." Bry had become used to Renn's nightmares, and usually, a little dry humour quelled the aftermath. Renn gave Bry a sideways glance. They both looked ahead. Beyond the dust-scattered windscreen, the road before them stretched infinitely, straight as an arrow. The hazy midday sun sent ripples of heat off the surface. Vast prairies hugged the highway on either side as tumbleweeds rode the wind.

"Wild road, eh?" Renn retorted. They locked eyes and laughed. But Renn's face soon drained. Her smile dissipated a deep crevice formed upon her furrowed brow.

"That was the worst one yet. It felt so real." The sour, metallic taste of fresh blood still tainted her tongue, resting her forefinger upon her lips, she realised she had bitten a meaty chunk from her lower lip. The blood was her own.

Bry stroked her cheek. His warm amber eyes melted into her like hot butter. He had this way about him. Without uttering a word, he took her in his arms, holding Renn with such tenderness that he felt the sobs release from her body. He soaked it all up and took the burden as he always did. He would make her strong again.

The open road stretched out ahead. Homesteads were few and far between now, and Renn couldn't imagine living in such isolation. They had stopped at one town that consisted of a diner, a general store and a gas station that appeared to employ the same person running back and forth between the three. Or perhaps a doppelgänger. They had refuelled both themselves and their vehicle.

The small diner had rows of red leather seats, all well-worn, white-tiled walls, a checkerboard-tiled floor and numerous black and white photographs of 50s crooners that decorated the booths. A hearty brunch of cheese grits, warm biscuits, eggs sunny side up and maple-cured bacon, washed down with cool, long vanilla milkshakes, had most definitely filled a hole. The pair had freshened up in the adjoining washroom and got back on their way.

But now Bry stared at the dash. The thermostat gauge was a lot higher than he was comfortable with.

"Damn, I knew I should have grabbed some coolant at that last rest stop." The car was all he had in material terms, but it wasn't just that. It held sentimental value, too. As an only child raised by his father, Bry had spent his most formative years riding shotgun in the baby blue v8 hardtop coupe, travelling the Midwest, his musician father at the wheel, with few belongings but a 1959 Les Paul of the finest ebony with mother-of-pearl inlay.

Black Beauty was her name, and someday she would make them both famous. But it wasn't to be. Bryan L Deichman Sr had found solace at the bottom of a bottle of bourbon one too many times. Then, on a balmy Sunday morning in a motel in Medora, North Dakota, he was discovered in a pool of his own vomit, eyes white and glassy. All hell broke loose, and as the motel owner comforted the distraught maid, the chaos that ensued once word had gotten around, was nothing short of hysteria at such a gruesome discovery. But it had allowed teenage Bry to slip away unnoticed. He rode into the unknown, just him and the Starfire, forever one step ahead of child protective services.

Bry rested his head in his hands before Renn's soft touch took hold of his arm.

"Let's just let it cool down some, huh? While away the time in the backseat, then we can hit the road again and find another town. My crystal ball says it's gonna be A-OK." Renn's oceanic eyes sparkled. She scrunched up her pretty nose, peppered with golden sunshine. The sweet, sexy pout on her lips seduced Bry all too easily.

The back seat was roomy, with deep burgundy leather seats finely stitched into scalloped cushions. The warmth of Renn's wet lips merged with his as her soft breasts brushed her lover's chest. Grasping her peachy cheeks in his hands, the pair found their groove. Little beads of perspiration ran down Renn's spine into the small of her back, settling in the little dimples on either side. Renn moved so fluidly, grinding into Bry's lap. The warm mahogany tones of their sun-drenched skin merged. His lips and tongue traced the line of her throat, and as the sun disappeared behind the endless horizon, the lovers became one.

Renn rested her head against Bry's warm chest, feeling the gentle, rhythmic pulse of his beautiful heart. They slept in a knot of legs and arms until sunup.

The white picket fence stood out against the sun-scorched backdrop. Hues of ochre and pale yellow corn sat beside the deep black of the highway, and soft white clouds sailed through the ever-changing blue of the sky.

"Stop here!" Renn hung her head out of the window, soaking up the warm breeze. At the end of a long shingle path beyond the white picket fence was the prettiest little white house, double fronted with a wooden boarded porch that ran all the way around, a sunny yellow door, and mouldings along the roofline.

"I don't know, Renn. Something doesn't feel right. We should keep going."

Renn pouted a little and pulled the puppy dog eyes move, which always seemed to work. Bry, who was a real sucker in that respect, pulled over beside the parched lawn, and against his better judgement, they began the quarter-mile walk along the path leading to the house.

The breeze was light and refreshing, especially after being on the road for pretty much two days straight. Stretching their legs was a welcome relief.

Reaching the little white cottage, there on the porch sat a petite and elderly lady. She stood abruptly as the pair approached. The rocking chair in which she had been sitting continued to rock behind her with a creak, creak, creak, until, eventually, it stopped. The old lady squinted at the unexpected visitors, removed her glasses, and rubbed the foggy lenses on her apron before sliding them back on her nose. She peered through the glass at Renn and Bry and smiled.

"Well, what do we have here? I don't get much in the way of visitors." The old lady shuffled closer to the top step of the deck. "What can I be doing for you folks now? I keep nothing valuable if that's why you're here." She must have stood no more than five-foot-two, with sun-weathered skin and white hair swept off her face in a bun. Her white cotton gown fell just below the knees draped loosely over her frail form. An over apron scattered with little blue flowers tied neatly at her waist completed her outfit. She was suspicious, and rightly so. They took a step back from the bottom step. Neither wanted to seem intimidating.

"Oh no, we just saw your house. We've been on the road for two days, and we were hoping perhaps you could point us in the direction of a gas station or somewhere we can rest and eat?" Renn put out her hand. "I'm Renn, ma'am, and this is Bry."

The old lady softened immediately at the sight of the handsome young gentleman before her, and the warmest smile danced on her lips. Her little grey eyes shone behind the round silver-rimmed glasses that clutched the end of her nose. She took hold of Renn's hand. "I'm Mary, Mary Snedeker. Won't you come in? Rest your weary bones a while?"

The porch deck was a light timber. On either side of the yellow door, along the front wall, were dozens of well-tended plants, all potted in fine earthenware and terracotta planters, with muted, purple-tinged bell-shaped flowers and luscious blackberries amidst the green fan-shaped foliage. They were quite unusual. Secateurs, trowels, and little mounds of freshly dug earth littered the deck.

"It's potting season. These babies are getting too big for their boots, so they are." Mary chuckled as she shuffled through the door. Renn and Bry had warmed to her already.

Inside, the house was quite dim; the shutters were kept closed to keep the place cool, which was especially necessary during the dry season. A layer of dust covered the furniture, floral paper lined the walls. Upon the aged decor were a scattering of many portraits of what looked to be a young Mary with her beau. A timeline of their life together in various decades until finally a picture sat alone at the foot of the staircase of a solitary Mary as she looked now. The same white cotton dress ruffled at the neck and little round glasses perched upon her nose. It seemed such a sad portrait and without Renn needing to ask, Mary spoke.

"That's my late husband, Earl. Such a well-formed chap. All the girls would flutter their lashes and blush when he walked by, but he only had eyes for me."

They followed their host into the parlour room where, rather unexpectedly, there stood a dozen cages housing many pairs of yellow canaries, sitting upon their perches. The light Twitter of the birds filled the room.

"Now sit yourselves down. I'll go fix you up some sweet tea. Don't be minding that they're pooping. Those birds have no manners." She chuckled again as she shuffled out of the room.

Bry brushed off most of the bird droppings that scattered the snug beige two-seater couch in the corner. Renn reluctantly and tentatively sat down next to Bry.

"Poop," she whispered as she stifled a laugh and gestured silently at the room laden with avian faeces.

Mary returned a few moments later with a tray filled with cups of hot tea, a little dish of white sugar lumps, a plate of warm Bundt cake, and apple butter.

"So, what brings you youngen's out here? You reek of sex!"

Renn wasn't quite sure she had heard that correctly over the increasing din of the canaries.

"I beg your pardon, Mrs Snedeker; I didn't quite catch the last bit?"

Bry, who was staring blankly towards the cabinet behind Mary's chair, seemed oblivious to the elderly host's faux pas. Raising her voice, the widow spoke again.

"I said, what are you youngen's doing out here? There ain't much to see!".

Of course, Renn explained her illness and her desire to experience more of nature's beauty before her time ran out. Mary nodded in all the right places yet seemed quite indifferent to the pain Renn wore on her sleeve. All the while, Bry stared at the cabinet.

"We shouldn't stay long, Mrs Snedeker. Did you say there was a gas station nearby? We have a lot of ground to cover in order to reach the mountains before nightfall."

The widow, who had noticed Renn's male counterparts' attention was elsewhere, snapped her fingers at Bry, then turned her gaze back to Renn.

"I suppose you don't frequent church much?" Her voice had a haughty tone as it trailed off until it was but a whisper. "Sinners of the flesh should be boiled alive in hot oil."

Renn glanced at Bry, again unsure of what she was hearing, and spoke gently in reply. "I'm sorry, Mrs Snedeker, did you just say....?"

Before she could finish, the old lady interrupted, "Call me Mary," she snapped. Her eyes had now turned into what looked like black beads pressed into a soft dough, no longer dove grey and welcoming. Resting back in her chair, she rocked back and forth. The chair creaked on the bare boards. She wrapped her slim, leathery fingers over the edge of the wooden arms. Her nails, long, thickly ridged and discoloured, scratched across the wood with the kind of jarring sound that put Renn's teeth on edge. Again, the widow cleared her throat to speak over the gentle twitter of the canaries.

"How's the tea, kids?"

Bry, who had been snapped out of his trance, had been struggling to swallow much of the bitter brew. It was now quite tepid, and despite filling the cup with copious sugar lumps, he found the "sweet tea" still unpalatable. So he tried to stall further.

"What kind of tea is it? If you don't mind me asking, ma'am?"

Bry's eyes wandered once more to the cabinet housing a good many portraits of the late Earl Snedeker. His eyes scratched out. Or so it appeared. But being quite dim in the parlour, Bry wasn't sure if the shadows and the excessive sugar consumption were playing tricks.

"I make my own blend, dear. You can't get that in any of those fancy stores you got over there in Californiyaa, no siree! I got my own plants right there on the porch. NOW DRINK UP!"

The widows' sudden change of tune frightened her young guests, and with a few final gulps, they finished their tea. Her knuckles whitened as she gripped the edge of the chair. Her former gentle persuasiveness had given way to something more unnerving. Leaning in closer, the widow whispered through her pale, thin lips.

"Atropa Belladonna." A maniacal grin crept across her face, a smile that betrayed all innocence. "That's the secret recipe I serve up when I get unwanted, um, I mean unexpected guests, like you two!"

Renn had felt a heaviness upon her brow as the afternoon had worn on, becoming quite drowsy, and on more than one occasion, had misheard Mary. Bry had just stared into space the entire time. Renn became aware that her mouth was dry, filled with grit. A throbbing pain slowly slid across her forehead, and a veil of black crept over her eyes. Renn could feel herself slipping away; she could do nothing to stop it.

    A piercing light hit Renn's irises as she forced open her lids. Her eyes ached, and her head pounded.

    Still, on the poop-covered couch, she was lying on her side now, not sitting upright beside Bry as she remembered. She pulled herself up, perhaps too quickly, as her head swam violently, washing over her eyes in a multidimensional haze of colour. The taste of the insipid tea still filled her mouth. She wiped her lips, discovering that seemingly she drools in her sleep, although there had been no mention of such a thing from Bry. She realised she was alone. The standard lamp that stood tall in the corner with its dim, dusty bulb offered little light, leaving the rest of the room in shadow.

    The canaries were silent now. Dark cotton sheets had been draped over their cages, mimicking nightfall. The clock on the mantlepiece read a quarter to 4 in the afternoon. Three hours had passed.

    Renn stood up, walking on air yet feeling as though her legs were full of lead. She slowly made her way out of the room in which she had slumbered for so long. The door frame was a worthy anchor as her head swam, she steadied herself upon the aged hessian-coloured woodwork.

    "Hey! Where are you guys?"

A faint metallic grating sound came from above. Renn followed the sound, flicking light switches as she went, but only one of the bulbs illuminated. The silhouette of a dozen dead moths and bluebottles lay in the base of the glass shade. The scraping sound continued.

"Bry, are you up there??"

She ascended the dim staircase. The wooden bannisters wobbled and creaked, and as she followed the sound, she reached a door. The low amber light of the late afternoon sun streamed in and peeked under the cracks. Renn pushed on it, and it creaked open.

"You joined us just in time, dear. Rigor Mortis has set in, nice and hard."

Without turning her head, Mary ground back and forth, groaning gleefully.

"Ugh uhhh uh, ugh…"

The bed creaked as the old lady writhed upon the cadaverous Bry.

"Uhh, uh uhmmm hmmm."

The birds in the aviaries screamed as only birds could. Shrill, frantic, beating their wings against the bars in a deafening ruckus. Mary continued with her necrophiliac act, groaning orgasmically yet still managing to address Renn, who stood in the doorway, stunned at the horrifying sight.

"Deadly nightshade doesn't kill 'em all. Sometimes it just makes you sleep for a good while."

As the springs pinged and twanged their metallic melody, the filthy mattress bounced off the floorboards, and the birds screamed a deafening crescendo.

"Get off him, you vile old witch!"

The widow paid no mind to Renn and continued to writhe and slide up and down Bry's solid member.

"I said get off him before I cave your fucking head in!"

Renn took hold of the solid wooden chair leg beside the three-legged nursing chair and held it aloft, Renn's stomach still churning from the deadly nightcap. The cacophony of noises that pounded in her ears, the continuous shrieking of the canaries, the grating of metal upon metal of the bedsprings, and the moans from her host's lips all disappeared except the dull thud of her own heart. Fire surged through Renn's veins as she stepped toward the grotesque love-making scene before her.

"Come on, dear, hop on. He's stiff as a board, hard as a rock. Earl could never satisfy me the way these boys do. Seedless he was, left me childless." The old lady was practically foaming at the mouth. She spat as she spoke.

The room around Renn began to spin. The canaries shrilled and shook their cages, and she could taste blood on her tongue where she had bitten into the previously wounded lip. The widow continued to moan and grind atop her new playmate.

'There had been others?' Renn had seen and heard enough. Moving closer still until she could feel the cold of the cast iron bed against her shin, she tightened her grip on the makeshift club. The geriatric necrophile, midst the throes of climax, was oblivious to Renn, who was now directly behind her. As she continued to grind back and forth, her white cotton gown hitched up to reveal her thin, fleshy thighs. Varicose veins scattered the pale white flesh. Flashes of purple, a road map of all the other roads Bry and Renn should have taken, any road but the one that led them here.

As Mary threw back her head at the point of no return, her beady, black eyes met with Renn's. Letting out a cathartic roar, Renn smashed the heavy oak chair leg into the old lady's face and skull. The flesh and bone gave way like an overripe cantaloupe. The widow Snedekers' cavernous cranium exploded in a bloody shower, splattering the walls, floor and Renn with the metallic scarlet poison. Her teeth scattered the room like dice in a game of Yahtzee. Mary Slumped forward, still straddling Bry's molested cadaver. Then came a slow snigger. The old lady laughed a deep, throaty laugh.

"The look on your face. I gave him the best ride of his life." The beastly geriatric shrugged her shoulders before erupting into hysterics. Skin hung off the bone; blood dribbled from her eye sockets, and toothless mouth. Renn raised the plank, still fresh with flesh and bone meshed to the polished surface, and with every ounce of hatred, anger and despair, she slammed the leg onto Mary's head, delivering the final deadly blow. No movement nor sound came now from Mary. She was deceased, although Renn felt the widow had died long ago. And now Bry, too, was gone. A wave of nausea swam through her belly, up into her mouth, and exited swiftly onto the blood-soaked floor. Most likely the last of the tea. The guilt, however, would stay with her for eternity.

"Bry." Such sorrow fell from her lips as she spoke his name. The canaries had ceased their squawking, and silence descended in the still of the room. A black mist crept across the floor around her feet, sliding up her legs, around her ribs and into her mouth. She had allowed hate to consume her. The realisation of what she had just done hit her like a freight train, and she stumbled back against the wall. Her hands were now full of splinters, and her knuckles glowed white as she gripped the club tight in her fist. She couldn't let go. Tears stung as they left her eyes, blazing a trail across her blood-tainted face. Closing her eyes, she released her grip, and finally, the deadly weapon hit the floor.

She heard nothing except her own sobs as grief rocked her body.

And then…

A long, slow creak. A sound that Renn did not want to hear. She drew her attention to the source of the sound, revealing it to be coming from the large, built-in pine cabinet across the room, facing the bed, just as the door eased itself open slowly. There, amidst the rows of coats, stood Earl Snedeker.

"Is the seed planted, Mary?" He shuffled forward from the closet, his arms outstretched. His mouth hung open, aghast; his eyes scratched out just as they were in the photographs. "Mary, my love?" As he spoke, the canaries began again, furiously leaping about their gilded prisons, squawking and screaming. It was pure pandemonium.

Earl covered his ears, obviously distressed, then put his index fingers into each of his eyes.

"The birds!" He shrieked. "The birds, the birds, the birds!" Again and again, as he squealed, so too did the birds.

Renn could take no more. She had no strength left, and her arms and legs felt like jelly. She had already spotted the box of matches on the mantle, and without hesitation, she seized them, struck one against the side of the box, and held it to the worn chintz drapes. She watched the golden flames pull at the fabric, turning blue and yellow, warm and rich and powerfully destructive. She lit another and another. One for the bed where Mary and her beloved Bry lay, and the other she tossed at the widower, Earl Snedeker's feet.

    Renn sat upon the bonnet of the Starfire. The air was cooler now as dusk descended, and she watched the house burn. She felt empty, numb, cavernous, bleak, all the worst feelings one can feel. She didn't know how else to feel other than that. The flames reached out of the windows, wanting to draw her in where she too could blister and melt, charred and black. She looked on as the roof began to collapse in on itself and swore she could see Bry's face in the red and yellow inferno. Mary's, Earl's, the many canaries. She could hear the little yellow menace's screams amid the treacherous flames. They deserved it, too, stealing Earl's eyes and letting him continue on in darkness. Then, just the sound of crackling wood and the thunder in her heart as the fiery wrath burned on. Renn thought that if she were a smoker, now would be the time to have a cigarette. One of those old-fashioned woodbines, the ones that are all tobacco and not the other nasty stuff. But now she should leave. As desolate as this place may be, those flames would soon be seen far and wide. She reached into her shorts, only to discover there were no keys.

"Where are the keys?" She patted down her back pockets. "Fuck, fuck, fuck!!" She could see the keys right now in Bry's chinos. His flesh melted around them, with Mary still astride him. She slammed her fist down upon the roof of the only thing she had left of Bry.

"Arghh!" she screamed, beating her hands against the car over and over. Finally, she buried her face in her hands, defeated. She had nothing left in her.

Suddenly, she heard a familiar jangle through the window. The golden red flames illuminated the shiny silver fob.

"The keys! Damn it, Bry; you left the keys in the ignition, you clever son of a bitch!" Then a gut-wrenching feeling arose. Was it relief or dread? Perhaps both. "The police. Oh my god, but it was self-defence. They'll see that. I'll tell them everything." She tried to reason with herself. The conflict in her head twisted her insides. Then Renn realised nobody actually knew where they were. The widower had no other relatives and no close neighbours. She could drive, keep driving, and realise the dream she and Bry had concocted.

She watched the blaze in the rear-view mirror as she pushed her foot hard on the accelerator. This was goodbye, not farewell.

Twelve months passed, and Renn had surpassed her estimated expiration date. She stood upon the sand, her toes buried in the golden grains. As the clouds sailed above, the sky turned black. A velvet cape that turned the skies inside out as the sun disappeared behind it. Rolling thunder clashed, and flashes of blue tore through the tumultuous grey canopy. She breathed in, the air filling her lungs. It was electric. Eye to eye with the storm, Renn remained steadfast as the biggest maverick wave she had ever witnessed approached. She could taste the salty sting on her tongue as the wind whipped around her limbs. Her soft dress, the colour of summer corn, billowed against the grey, black, and blue of the ocean's wrath, and as the shadow of kahuna reared, she waded out and whispered the words to her and Bry's song…

This is the end, beautiful friend.
This is the end, my only friend,
The end.
Of our elaborate plans, the end.
Of everything that stands…

The end.

About The Author

Leigh Pettit

Leigh is quite the enigma, legend has it her remains were discovered in one of Vlad Dracula's vaults, and was reanimated by a mad scientist. This undead queen of the macabre now resides in Britain's first city, creating dark, melancholic freeverse poetry, born from an age long past, but hauntingly relevant today.
When asked of her influences she spoke of Poe, Byron, Lovecraft and lastly the Count. It became very apparent the love she harboured for her creator was all encompassing.

"In life we meet many people. Some destroy us and then there are those who inspire us, I believe he was capable of both, and yet that little spark from which the wildfires of my heart raged, continued to burn on. It is true that my writing is largely born from my own pain. I took my sorrow and made art out of it, From that I present to you my poetry" . L.P

Plastic – A Love Story

-Lee Richmond-

Plastic - A Love Story

Saturday

Eddie Wilson massaged his throbbing temples, desperately trying to silence the beast of a headache that punished him mercilessly since he'd dragged his sorry carcass out of bed not two hours earlier. Polly had told him not to go out drinking the night before his daughter's birthday party, but he'd ignored her as he often did. He had grown sick of her constant, demanding demeanour, and his Friday nights spent drinking with the lads were too important to forgo. A man needed to have an avenue of pleasure, and it certainly wasn't to be garnered from his marriage.

There had been a time when he loved Polly more than he knew how to express. He remembered the day she stepped into his auto shop, looking for someone to repair her blown exhaust. She was a vision of beauty in her floral summer dress and sun hat, her golden-blonde hair cascaded down her back and over her shoulders and Eddie was smitten from the get-go.

    Their relationship developed fast. Within a few months, they were cohabiting and planning their wedding. Things remained good for the following five years, and then Alice was born, and that's when their relationship took a nosedive.

    For the first time since they'd met, Eddie wasn't the sole focus of Polly's affection. Alice took up much of her time, and Eddie didn't like it one bit. Bitter jealousy spread through him, corrupting him, and twisting itself around every fibre of his being. Suddenly, Polly didn't seem so appealing. His sour resentment of the woman he'd married caused him to see her differently. Gone was the stunning, blonde beauty he had fallen for all those years ago, and in her place stood a frumpy, tired woman, spiralling towards middle age and leaving her best years behind her. The summer dresses became replaced with jogging bottoms and loose-fitting t-shirts, usually sporting some baby-related stain down the front.

    He was wrong, of course. Any red-blooded man would have agreed that Polly was still an extremely attractive lady, but Eddie no longer saw it. He had become a profoundly selfish man.

    Eddie sneered as he watched Polly and the other mums, or the Witches of Eastwick, as he called them, chatting and laughing. *'I bet they're laughing at me,'* he thought. *'You'd all have been burnt at the stake a few hundred years ago.'*

A quintet of excitable children came running past, screaming and shouting, and shook him from his gleefully sinister imaginings.

"Hey, kids. Keep it down to a quiet riot, will you?" He yelled after them.

"Leave them alone, Ed," Polly snapped. "They're just being kids."

"Well, they should be kids more quietly," he replied.

"Don't be a sourpuss just because you have a hangover. Nobody forced you to get drunk as a skunk."

'You did,' he thought. *'You drive me to hit the bottle with your bullshit.'*

Screeching four-year-olds and the morning after the night before did not make good bedfellows, and every high-pitched noise that the little bastards made had much the same effect as fingernails down a chalkboard. Eddie stood and reached into his jacket pocket, searching for his cigarettes.

"Where are you going?" Polly asked.

Eddie didn't respond. He held his pack of smokes up for her to see.

"No, you're not. We are about to do presents."

"I'll only be a few minutes," Eddie replied. "I need some air."

"Cigarette smoke is not air,"

The Witches sniggered at Polly's condescending response. Eddie scowled at them in return but chose not to say anything, as they would only accuse him of trying to ruin his daughter's party. He wouldn't give them the satisfaction of painting him as the villain. He slumped back into his seat with a huff.

Polly got up and began herding the kids around the dining table. Once they were all rounded up, she dumped a pile of presents before Alice.

"Okay, honey, you can open them," she said, holding her phone to film her child gleefully tearing into the wrapping paper.

"Ooh, what have you got there?" Polly asked as Alice finished unwrapping the first gift.

Alice held the present up with a grin to show her mother.

"Lego. Well, aren't you lucky?"

Alice pushed aside the Lego and tore into the next gift on the pile. She sat, looking confused at what she uncovered, before looking at her mum, puzzled.

"What is it, darling?"

Alice handed her the box with a shrug.

"Oh, it's a board game. I will teach you how to play it later."

Alice's confused expression became a toothy smile.

Eddie sat, fingering a thread of cotton that had unravelled on his jacket. Every now and then, he would look up and feign interest in his daughter's excitement as she opened her presents, but truth be told, he really couldn't give a shit.

A squeal from the table penetrated Eddie's brain like a hot needle. Its offensive pitch made his soul throb.
"Jesus Christ," he muttered, louder than he intended. He looked up and noticed the glares from the Witches.
"Sorry," he said, looking down at his feet like a scolded child. "Just made me jump, is all."
Alice hopped down from the table and ran around like a decapitated chicken, holding a box above her head.
"Mummy, Mummy, Look." She thrust the box at Polly.
"Oh, wow. You're a lucky girl," Polly said. "What do you say to your aunty Susan for such a lovely gift?"
Alice ran over to her aunt and threw her tiny arms around her neck.
"Thank you," she said.
"You are very welcome, sweetheart," Susan replied.

"Look, Eddie," Polly said, showing the box. "Alice has the Spring Break Sophia doll she's been obsessed with for the last three months."

Eddie looked up from the cotton thread that had held his attention for the last five minutes and glanced at the box in his wife's hand, and what happened next hit him like a rampaging bull. His eyes locked on the plastic doll in the box, and his pulse quickened. Eddie was instantly breathless, as if all the air had been sucked out of the room. He hadn't experienced feelings as intense as this since that day when Polly had wandered in off the street looking for someone to repair her car.

"Daddy, Daddy, look," Alice cried, snatching the box from her mother's hand and running over to Eddie. She ripped open the box and dragged the doll free from its packaging. "Look, Daddy." She held the doll for her dad to see. It dangled below her outstretched hand, suspended by its hair.

"Whoa, gentle. You'll break her," Eddie snapped, taking the doll from his daughter.

Alice's bottom lip dropped, and tears welled in her eyes. She wasn't sure what she had done to anger her father.

Ignoring the upset he'd caused, Eddie held the doll carefully in his hands and stared, unblinking, into its lifeless eyes. His heart jackhammered in his chest as he visually soaked her in. Her flawless plastic skin reflected the light from the bulb above. Eddie stroked the doll's hair, worried that Alice's careless carrying of Sophia might have somehow damaged it. To Eddie, she was beautiful, and it pissed him off that Alice handled her so poorly.

Alice began sobbing, wanting her new doll back.

"What are you doing?" Polly barked, yanking the doll from her husband, and handing it back to her daughter.

"I was just looking," Eddie replied, sounding wounded and slightly pathetic.

"You've made Alice cry. What is wrong with you lately?"

The Witches of Eastwick looked on, failing to hide the smirks that adorned their faces.

Alice took the doll and stomped out of the room, clutching it to her chest.

"I don't get it," Eddie snapped, standing up so fast that he knocked his chair over. "You moan at me for not taking an interest, and then you moan at me when I do. I can't fucking win with you." He shoved a cigarette between his lips and stormed through the door, slamming it behind him.

Sunday

It had been a long time since Eddie last woke up with an erection. Come to think of it; it had been a while since he'd last awoken and remembered his dreams. This morning, however, Eddie boasted both a full recollection of his subconscious fantasies and a boner he could hang a towel on.

He'd dreamt that he was in a woodland clearing. There wasn't another living soul to be seen. Just the sound of the local birds as they chirped merrily, a bottle of champagne cooling in a chiller bucket, and Sophia basking in the midday sun, wearing a tiny bikini.
Eddie lay on his side, gently running his finger along the doll's arm. In his dream, the cold, hard plastic felt just like actual skin, soft and warm and responsive to his touch.
"I love you," Eddie whispered as he slowly lowered Sophia's miniature bikini strap over her shoulder. He

leaned in and kissed the doll as he uncovered its ridgid, nippleless breasts.

The doll's head turned to look at him. "Eddie, wake up," it said. Its lips were the only animated part of its stiff, synthetic face.

"Eddie, I said wake up; you're drooling."

"Shit," Eddie yelled, sitting bolt upright. Polly's voice pulled him back into reality with a jolt.

"Morning," she said, ignoring his outburst. "Sleep well?"

Eddie took a moment to orient himself. He'd almost forgotten that he'd been forced to sleep on the sofa last night. He and Polly had spent the best part of the night arguing after all the party guests had left, and after reaching no resolution, Polly had demanded that he sleep somewhere else.

Breakfast around the table was quiet that morning. Having said all they needed to say last night, Eddie and Polly had no desire to drag it up again. Usually, the silent treatment would have driven Eddie nuts, but on this occasion, he couldn't have cared less. Instead, his mind was occupied with other things, foremost, thoughts of Sophia.

Alice, who was usually a chatterbox during breakfast, sat silently eating her cereal. She might only be four, but she was a clever kid for her age, and she could sense the atmosphere between her parents and decided it was best to shut up and get through her meal.

That way, she could disappear upstairs to her room and play with her presents she'd received yesterday. She hated it when her parents fought, but it seemed to be becoming more regular, and she always retreated to her room when the bickering began. She shovelled the last spoonful of Coco Pops into her mouth and then jumped down from her seat.

"Erm, excuse me," Polly chirped, breaking the silence. "Where do you think you're going, young lady?"

"To my room," Alice replied, her expression a mix of guilt and irritation at being held back from escaping.

"No, you don't. You know we don't leave the table without asking to be excused."

"Oh, let the kid go," Eddie butted in.

"Really?" Polly glared at him. "You don't want to back me up on this?"

"She doesn't want to be sitting here any more than I do," he responded. "Let her go and play."

Polly rolled her eyes, pissed at being undermined. "Fine. Go play, but next time you ask."

"Thanks, Daddy." She skipped out of the room and up the stairs, happy to make her escape.

Polly's eyes burned into her husband. He could feel her stare but refused to look up and acknowledge her.

"That wasn't okay," she said.

"The kid was obviously uncomfortable. Frankly, I don't blame her for not wanting to stick around."

"Well, whose fault is that?" Polly snapped, no longer trying to keep a lid on her anger.

"I suppose it's mine. It's always fucking my fault, isn't it? Because when do you ever do anything wrong? Fucking Polly perfect."

"That's not fair," Polly replied, sounding hurt.

"You're damn right; it isn't fair. I have to sit there being judged and scrutinised by you and the rest of your coven. It wears fucking thin, fast."

"You have to what?" She asked, baffled by his words.

"Fuck this. I'm going upstairs to watch the football in peace. You can stay down here with your hatred for me to keep you company."

With that, Eddie stomped up the stairs like a moody teenager.

"Fucking child," Polly muttered as she cleared the table.

Eddie hit the top of the stairs and crossed the landing, his blood still boiling from the fight with Polly. He stopped in his tracks as he passed Alice's room. Her door was open ajar, and her voice drifted through the gap and into his ears as he picked out one word. 'Sophia.' She was playing with Sophia. He pressed his face to the gap between the door and the frame to get a peek at the tiny doll.

There she sat, just as beautiful as she had seemed yesterday.

Alice had placed her on the floor and was pouring her an imaginary cup of tea from her toy teapot. "Would you like one lump of sugar or two, Princess Sophia?" She asked.

Eddie couldn't take his eyes off the doll. His heartbeat reverberated in his ears, and his palms felt sweaty as he ogled the seven-inch moulded effigy. Alice had received some clothes and accessories for Sophia from her cousin and had dressed the doll in a cropped pink t-shirt and three-quarter-length jeans. The sight of the plaything's midriff had Eddie salivating.

Alice spotted her dad and beckoned him in with a wave.

"Hey, honey. What are you doing?" Eddie asked, pushing the door open.

"We are having tea, Daddy," she replied with a smile. "Would you like some?"

Eddie made his way to the little table and sat down on the floor, crossing his legs. "I would love some, thank you."

Alice poured him a pretend cup of tea and handed him the cup. "Here you go, Daddy."

"Thank you," Eddie said, taking the empty cup. "Is Sophia enjoying herself?" He nodded in the doll's direction.

"Yes, she likes tea parties."

Alice poured another cup of imaginary tea and clumsily lifted the cup to Sophia's mouth.

"Careful," her dad said, leaning forward. "You might scald her."

"Don't be silly," Alice replied with a giggle. "She isn't real." She tipped the cup to its lips.

"I said, be fucking careful," Eddie yelled, lurching at Alice, and smacking the cup from her hand. "Do as you're told!"

Alice sobbed as Eddie grabbed Sophia from her little chair and inspected her for signs of damage.

Polly appeared at the door, having rushed up the stairs to see what all the shouting had been about. She leaned in, shocked to find her daughter in tears and her husband ignoring her, more interested in Alice's doll than his upset child.

"What the hell is going on in here?" She wasn't so much asking for an answer as demanding one.

"It's nothing," Eddie replied.

Alice ran to her mother's side and threw her arms around her. "Daddy shouted at me," she said between sobs.

"What? Why?"

"He said I wasn't being careful. He said I was going to spill the tea on Princess Sophia."

"Is this true?"

"She's overreacting again," Eddie said, rolling his eyes. "She wasn't taking care of her new things."

Polly stormed over to Eddie and snatched the doll from his hand.

"Hey!" Eddie shouted in protest.

"Stop being an arse and let the girl play," Polly snapped, handing the doll back to her daughter.

"Why do you never back me up?" Eddie asked.

"Well, maybe it's because you're completely unreasonable. Why did you come in here in the first place? Just let the kid play and stop upsetting everyone, for once in your life."

Eddie stood up and made for the door. "Fuck this. I'm going to the pub."

"Good," Polly yelled after him. "Don't return until you can apologise for being a dick."

Monday

Two nights on the sofa had taken a toll on Eddie's delicate back. He'd wandered in from the pub around 9 pm, inebriated and clutching a kebab to his chest. Polly lost it, and the following hour had been spent with Polly chewing him out while Eddie sat on the sofa and tried to stop the world from spinning.

    Having said all she needed to say, Polly had marched off to bed, and Eddie passed out soon after. Around two in the morning, Eddie awoke with a thumping headache and a bladder that desperately needed draining. He'd carefully climbed off the sofa and steadied himself for fear of falling on his arse before making his way upstairs.

    On his way back from the bathroom, he'd stopped outside Alice's room when an idea struck him. Eddie had snuck into his daughter's bedroom quietly so as not to wake her and carefully taken the doll from the sleeping child's bed.

Once clear of Alice's room, he made his way downstairs and back under his blanket where he'd fallen asleep hugging the doll, but not before tenderly kissing it goodnight.

His intention had been to wake up before everyone else and return the doll unnoticed, but due to the amount he'd drunk the night before, Eddie forgot to set his alarm. If Eddie thought Polly was mad the night before, it was nothing compared to how angry she was when she came downstairs and saw her husband clutching their daughter's toy against his face.

Words like weirdo and pervert were thrown his way. Questions about his mental state and statements about needing help. A barrage of insults and insinuations. Eddie heard them all, and he'd never been happier about having to leave for work.

Dinner that evening was an awkward affair. The three of them sat around the table eating a lasagne that Polly had prepared. Nobody said a word, which only thickened an already uncomfortable atmosphere.

Eddie ate little, his appetite lacking somewhat. But it had nothing to do with being in the doghouse. He couldn't get Sophia out of his head. She occupied his every waking thought. He yearned to be with her, cuddled up on the sofa, holding her near, as he did the night before.

He didn't love Polly anymore. Her anger towards him made her once beautiful face ugly. Frown lines had set in, making her look old. It never once occurred to Eddie that he might be to blame for her constant irritation. He was the victim, as far as he saw it. She'd pushed him into the arms of another woman, even if that woman was a mere seven inches of moulded PVC resin.

'Fuck her,' Eddie thought. He planned on sneaking Sophia down again tonight once everyone was asleep. He didn't care what his wife thought of it, and he wasn't too bothered with whether it upset Alice either. *'Fuck her too.'*

Eddie's watch read eleven-thirty. He lay on the sofa, patiently waiting for an opportunity to creep upstairs and liberate Sophia from his daughter's room. Then, figuring they'd had ample time to nod off, he tiptoed up the stairs and into Alice's room.

Sophia wasn't on Alice's bed as she had been the night before. He quietly dropped to his knees to see if she had fallen off the bed, but there was nothing. Frustrated, Eddie slowly pulled back the duvet, uncovering his daughter, hoping to find the doll under her quilt, but it was nowhere to be seen.

"Where the fuck is it?" Eddie said, a little louder than he intended.

Alice stirred as Eddie hurried to cover her back up. He turned to leave but was too late. Alice's eyes shot open, and she sat bolt upright, terrified by the figure that loomed over her bed.

"Mummy!" she cried. "Someone is in my room."

"Shhh, Jesus Christ," Eddie said, clamping his hand over Alice's mouth to silence her. Unfortunately, this only served to scare the girl more, and she started clawing at his wrist to get him to let go.

"That hurt, you little bitch," Eddie snapped, raising his hand to strike his daughter.

The bedroom light came on, its sudden glare momentarily blinding Eddie, who pulled his hand free from Alice's mouth to shield his eyes. His other hand remained in the air, ready to strike.

"What the hell do you think you're doing?" Polly yelled. "Get away from her right now."

Eddie stood, frozen to the spot. He wasn't sure how he was going to talk himself out of this one. With no words or excuses coming to his aid, he simply turned and smiled.

"I said, get away from her, now," Polly repeated, coming across the bedroom and towards Eddie like a charging bull.

"What?" Eddie said with a shrug, feigning innocence and instinctively backing away from his approaching wife.

Polly took a swipe, smacking her husband's still-raised arm with such force that he felt something pull in his shoulder.

"Fucking ouch," Eddie cried.

"Think yourself lucky it wasn't my foot in your nuts. You were about to hit your daughter, weren't you?"

Eddie held his hands in the air, a look of faux innocence on his face which suggested her accusations hurt his feelings.

"Don't give me that look, you bastard," Polly snapped. "How could you?"

"I wasn't going to hit her. I would never dream of doing anything like that. How could you even think so little of me?"

Polly wasn't having any of it. She wasn't stupid, and she hated being treated as such.

"Polly, please.?" Eddie continued, knowing his pleas of innocence were falling on deaf ears.

"Get yourself downstairs and stay on that sofa," she snarled, her finger pointing in her husband's face. "I don't want you coming back up here tonight, and tomorrow morning we can discuss what we're going to do about this shit."

"What if I need to use the bathroom?" Eddie asked feebly.

"You can piss in the garden." She turned and made her way over to the door, holding it open for her shameful-looking husband. "Come on. Off you fuck."

Eddie stepped past her, head down and shoulders slumped. He didn't bother to look at his wife as he made his way across the landing and towards the stairs.

Tuesday

"You're kidding, right?"

Polly shook her head. She'd never been more serious.

"Where am I meant to go?" Eddie asked, still not believing what he was hearing. He'd expected to be chewed out, having a wealth of excuses prepared for his behaviour last night. He'd not expected to wake up and receive his marching orders.

"I just need a break," Polly said. "I'm not saying that this is a permanent thing. I need to get my head together."

Eddie could feel anger boiling inside him. He swallowed it, knowing it wouldn't help his situation to give in and blow his lid. "What about Alice?" He asked.

"She's terrified of you now," Polly replied. "You scared the life out of her last night. You almost hit her."

"I would never hit her," Eddie snapped, once again looking offended. "She startled me when she woke up shouting, that's all."

"Even if that's true, what were you doing in her room?"

"I was upstairs needing the toilet, and I heard a noise coming from her room," Eddie lied. "I went in to check on her because I thought she was having a bad dream or something."

"Bullshit," Polly scoffed.

"Why bullshit?"

"You were looking for that fucking doll. You've been acting weird ever since that thing came into our lives. It's creepy."

"You leave her out of this!" Eddie yelled, his temper getting the better of him.

"Her?" Polly asked, dumbfounded. "Her? It's a thing, not a fucking her. Are you mental?"

Eddie could control himself no longer, and he lunged at his wife, grabbing her by the shirt and pushing her hard against the wall.

"Don't you dare call her a thing! You're not half the woman she is!" Flecks of spit landed on Polly's face as he screamed at her.

As tears filled her eyes, Polly pushed at Eddie with every ounce of her strength, but she was no match for his size and weight. He had her pinned, and as she regarded his rage-twisted face, she no longer recognised her husband. He wasn't the person she had fallen in love with. He would never have raised a hand to her or their child.

"You're hurting me," she cried, struggling to breathe as Eddie pushed against her chest.

Eddie didn't reply. He was too swept up in his anger to consider his actions.

Fearing what might become of her if she didn't fight back, Polly drew her knee up as hard as she could manage, and it connected with Eddie's testicles. He instantly released Polly and dropped to his knees, clutching his groin.

"You fucking psycho!" Polly screamed, running to the coffee table to retrieve her phone.

Eddie buckled, still clutching his privates as he gasped and wheezed, desperately trying to breathe through the pain.

"You have exactly ten fucking seconds to get out of this house, or I'm calling the police," Polly said, rubbing her sore chest.

Eddie slowly pulled himself to his feet. Still hunched double and holding his swollen balls, he tenderly limped towards the front door. His anger gave way to the nauseating agony between his legs. Polly had successfully knocked the fight out of him.

"Polly, I'm sorry," he croaked.

"Get the fuck out. I mean it."

Eddie opened the door and shuffled gingerly outside. "You're not going to get away with this," he sneered menacingly. "You can't keep me away from her."

"Don't threaten me," she replied. "I'll do what I have to do to protect my daughter."

Eddie made his way to his car, giving Polly the finger as he did so. He wasn't talking about Alice. He didn't care about not seeing his little girl. Eddie would be back for Sophia.

Wednesday

Polly arrived home, having been out to buy groceries while Alice was at playgroup. At first, nothing struck her as unusual. She'd come in through the front door, dropped her keys in the little bowl on a table in the hall and then wandered into the living room to kick her shoes off.

It was only when she walked into the kitchen to put her shopping away that she realised, to her horror, that someone had broken in.

The back door to the house had been kicked repeatedly until the frame splintered, and it now hung weakly on its hinges. Polly's heart thumped in her chest, her first thought being that she had been burgled. She dropped the bags onto the kitchen counter, grabbed a knife from the block, and rushed back into the lounge.

Polly scoured the room, looking for signs of anything missing, but everything seemed to be where she'd left it. As she searched through the rest of the house, she found nothing out of the ordinary. Whoever had broken in had taken none of the many valuable items that filled the residence.

'Mum's jewellery,' she thought suddenly. Her heart ached at the idea of someone stealing the only things she had to remember her mother by. Polly raced up the stairs and into her bedroom, where she kept the jewellery in a box on her dressing table. She threw open the lid and rummaged through the contents.

"Oh, thank god," she said, relieved that everything appeared to be in its place.

Knowing she needed to call the police, Polly headed onto the landing towards the stairs. As she passed Alice's room, she noticed the door was ajar. That wouldn't have struck her as strange were it not for the fact that she distinctly remembered closing it before taking Alice to playgroup. Polly froze. Her knees felt suddenly weak as fear took hold.

'What if the intruder is still in there,' she thought. Then it was as if something else had taken control. Her hand reached out for Alice's door. It wasn't Polly consciously gravitating towards the door—at least not Polly's common sense or sense of preservation. Instead, Polly's curiosity was in the driver's seat. She was just along for the ride.

"What the fuck am I doing?" she whispered to herself.

The door creaked open slowly, and Polly peeked cautiously inside. The sight that greeted her caused her heart to sink. Alice's room had been ransacked. All the drawers in her furniture had been pulled out, the contents of which were tipped all over the floor. Alice's bed was flipped over and left in the centre of the room. The curtains had been yanked open so violently that they had pulled free from the rails.

Polly dropped to her knees as tears streamed down her face. Now she knew who the intruder was.

Needing somewhere to bed down in a hurry, Eddie had crawled to his best mate, Greg, with a sob story about how unreasonable and spiteful his wife was. Greg somewhat begrudgingly offered his sorrowful-looking pal the box room, much to his wife's displeasure.

Nicki, Greg's wife, never much cared for Eddie, or Edward as she insisted on calling him, simply because she knew it wound him up. He'd been a thorn in their relationship since she and Greg had met fifteen years before. Eddie was yet to have met Polly at that point and resented Nicki for stealing away his mate. When Eddie met and settled down with Polly, she hoped things would improve, but they never did. She did, however, get on like a house on fire with Polly, which only made Eddie's new tale of woe that bit harder to swallow.

Eddie lay upstairs in the tiny bedroom, listening to his friend bickering downstairs with his wife. Nicki made no effort to keep her voice down, and he knew she was doing it intentionally so that he would feel unwelcome, but he didn't care.

His clothes lay strewn across the bedroom floor with careless abandon. Next to his discarded attire lay a tiny floral dress and a pair of miniature plastic high-heeled shoes.

Smiling from ear to ear, Eddie sprawled naked on the bed, gently running his finger back and forth across the two solid, nippleless mounds that were Sophia's breasts. His other hand worked furiously on his limp cock as he struggled in vain to get a rise out of it. He lifted Sophia to his mouth and kissed his way along her rigid, artificial body. Still, his dick remained flaccid.

'This is all that bitch's fault,' he thought, meaning Polly. Defeated, Eddie stopped playing with himself and lifted the doll to his face. He kissed it tenderly and whispered an embarrassed apology.

"I'm sorry. I love you."

"You know what you have to do," the doll said, turning her head to address the red-faced man that held her.

"I would do anything for you," Eddie replied. A single tear ran down his cheek.

Sophia smiled. "I know you would."

"Tell me what needs to be done, my love."

"We need to tie up a few loose ends," the doll said. "If we are to be together truly, we must first do away with everyone who would come between us, and you know who that is."

Eddie nodded. He knew exactly who and what she meant.

"I'll be strong," he promised. "Whatever it takes until it's just you and I."

"When?" Sophia asked.

"I don't know," Eddie replied. "I need to think…"

"Tonight," the doll responded.

"But I…"

"Tonight," she repeated. "If you love and want to be with me, it must be tonight."

Again, Eddie nodded. "Okay, tonight. I love you."

The doll didn't respond.

Pain was all she knew as Polly Wilson regained consciousness. The source of her pain was the bump on her head and the harsh light that invaded her tear-filled eyes. Groggy, and disoriented, she tried to call out for help, but the only sound that escaped her lips was a muffled cry, obstructed by the tape that sealed her mouth shut. She tried to get up, but the same tape that silenced her held her fast to a chair. Panic-stricken, she began thrashing from side to side in an effort to break free of her bondage, but it was futile.

Polly's eyes drifted to her left, and to her absolute horror, there sat Alice bound to a chair, unconscious, her mouth also sealed shut with the tape.

As her eyes adjusted to the light, Polly became aware of someone else in the room with them. A blurred figure that stepped towards her, coming into focus the closer it got.

The figure leaned in, its face becoming recognisable once it was mere inches from Polly's. Her eyes widened in terror as the distorted mass morphed into the familiar shape of the man she had married years earlier.

"Hey honey," Eddie said with a sinister smile. "Miss me?"

Polly strained against her bindings, her fear giving in to rage. She fought with the tape but lacked the strength to free herself.

"I'm going to give you a minute to calm down, and then maybe we can have an adult conversation," Eddie said, dragging a chair over and sitting in front of his struggling wife. "Take your time."

Sensing it was in her best interest to get herself under control, Polly stopped struggling and allowed herself to relax. It was then that she realised just how much she was shaking.

"Are we calm?" Eddie asked.

Polly nodded. She wasn't remotely calm. But she didn't want her husband to know that.

"Okay," Eddie said, standing up and walking towards her. "I'm going to remove this tape. If you so much as try to scream, I will break your fucking nose. Blink twice if you understand."

Polly did as instructed, blinking her eyes twice.

"Good girl," Eddie said, meaning to sound patronising. He took a corner of the tape between his fingers and, in one swift tug, tore it away from Polly's mouth.

"That hurt, you prick," she said, wincing.

"You'll live," came Eddie's sharp, uncaring reply.

Polly looked over at her still-unconscious daughter. A small trickle of blood had dried on Alice's forehead, and Polly felt her temper flaring once again. Sensing his wife's thoughts, Eddie allowed a stifled chuckle to escape.

"You think that's funny?" She snapped. "That's your fucking daughter!"

"I'm very aware," Eddie replied nonchalantly.

"What did you do?" She demanded to know.

"I had to get you both downstairs and into those chairs. I couldn't have done that if you were both struggling, could I? Not after the kick to the giggle-berries you gave me earlier."

Polly hadn't spotted it at first, but as her husband rambled on, her eyes wandered to a chair in the room's corner. An icy shiver ran down her spine as she noticed the tiny doll, Alice's doll, sitting and staring in their direction with its cold, dead eyes.

"What the fuck is that?" She asked.

Eddie followed her glare over to where the doll sat.

"Well?" Polly pressed for an answer.

"That's Sophia," Eddie replied. "You remember Sophia, right?"

"I know what it is," Polly snapped. "I mean, what the fuck is it doing there?"

Something inside Eddie snapped. He charged his wife and grabbed her by the throat, squeezing it tight as he pressed his forehead against her nose. Polly's eyes bulged, and her face reddened as her husband's grip cut her airway off.

"She isn't an it," he snarled. "She has a name. It's Sophia, and you need to be more fucking respectful."

Polly tried to tell him she was sorry but couldn't get the words out.

"What's that?" Eddie asked. "I can't quite hear you."

"Please," she croaked.

Eddie relinquished his grip and returned to his chair, leaving his wife choking and spluttering.

"Why are you doing this?" Polly asked, her voice hoarse. Tears streamed down her face.

"Okay, well, first, I'm leaving you," he said. "And before you ask, it's not me; it's you."

"Okay, then go," Polly sobbed. "Just leave us alone and go. I'm not going to fight you."

"Don't you want to know why?" he asked.

"I don't care," she croaked.

"I've met someone," Eddie continued.

"Let me guess. It's the doll, right?" Polly asked, laughing, even though it hurt her throat to do so.

"I told you; her name is Sophia!" Eddie roared.

"Oh, my god. It is, isn't it? Are you fucking it? How would that even work?"

Eddie swiped at his wife. The back of his hand connected with her cheek. Polly recoiled with fright, almost tipping her chair over in the process. Her face stung where he'd hit her.

"You bastard," she spat through gritted teeth. "If you want to go, fucking go. Take Sophia with you and leave me and Alice alone."

Eddie shook his head, laughing maniacally. "Nope, sorry, love. That just won't do."

"You want my blessing? Fine, have my blessing. I hope you'll both be very happy together."

"No, no, no!" Eddie yelled. "Sorry, Polly, but that's not going to cut the mustard."

"Well, what the fuck do you want, then?" Polly asked, frustrated and confused.

A groan from the next chair interrupted the bickering couple as Alice stirred. She opened her eyes and looked at her parents, clearly frightened.

Polly looked at her husband, trying to find some semblance of empathy that she could appeal to, but there was nothing there.

Unable to move, Alice cried.

"Eddie, please? She's your daughter. Your little girl."

Eddie shot her a blank, emotionless look.

"She's just a kid," Polly continued. Let her go. I don't give a fuck what you do to me, but not her. I'm begging you."

"I'm sorry," Eddie replied. "For me and Sophia to be together, you both have to go. That's the way it is."

Ignoring Polly's continued pleading, Eddie reached into a duffel bag he had grabbed from the garage before accosting his wife and daughter. 'Perfect,' he thought, wrapping his fingers around the handle of his cordless drill. Eddie squeezed the trigger, and the drill bit spun with a mechanical whirring, confirming there was plenty of life in its battery. Polly's heartbroken sobbing ceased after spying the power tool in her husband's hand. Abject terror took over.

"Wait," she demanded, her lips trembling. "Please, put that away."

Eddie examined the drill and then his wife's frightened expression. "Relax," he said reassuringly. "This isn't for you."

"What's it for?" Polly asked.

Eddie, ignoring her question, walked over to his now very awake daughter and gently removed the tape from her mouth.

"Daddy, I'm stuck," the little girl said. Her tired, blinking eyes struggled against the glare of the light.

"It's okay, honey," Eddie said, stroking her tussled hair. "Daddy's here now."

"Leave her alone," Polly begged.

"Daddy, I'm frightened," Alice said, her voice breaking as she cried.

"It's okay, baby. Daddy is here." He brushed her hair back and kissed her on the forehead.

"Please, Eddie. I'm sorry," Polly continued. "Take Sophia and be happy together. I won't stop you. You can have whatever you want."

Still ignoring his wife's pleas, Eddie lifted the drill and pressed the tip against his daughter's head. As he pressed the trigger, Alice and Polly began to scream.

The drill chewed its way through Alice's flesh with ease before coming up against the hard bone of her skull. Holding his free hand on the hilt, Eddie pushed harder, forcing the rotating tip to bore into the girl's cranium. The room filled with the stench of burning corn and hair, which caught Eddie off guard and caused him to wretch. Somehow, he kept himself from vomiting and pushed on.

Polly wasn't so lucky; the sight before her caused her to evacuate her stomach. She howled with sorrow as strings of bile hung from her chin.

Giving the drill one last push, the spinning bit broke through the little girl's skull and slid effortlessly into the soft tissue of her brain, silencing Alice's screams forever.

Polly fell silent, too, her daughter's death proving too much for her to process. Her head hung uselessly, her mouth wide in a silent scream.

Eddie pulled the drill free from the hole in Alice's head and placed it on the floor, its tip dripping in blood and mangled brain matter. He approached his wife and lifted her head, forcing her to look at him.

"Just fucking kill me," she said weakly.

"Don't worry," Eddie replied. "You're going to die tonight, but not before you witness what it is to truly be in love." He dropped her head and disappeared from the room.

Polly began fumbling with the tape that bound her wrists but couldn't summon the strength to free herself. She had lost the one thing that meant the most to her and no longer had any fight left.

Eddie reappeared moments later. He entered the room carrying a red Jerry Can with him. He placed it on the empty seat and quickly unscrewed the cap. The scent of petrol filled his nostrils. A smell he had weirdly always liked. It reminded him of his days as a trainee mechanic.
"I want you to watch this," he said. "This is a gesture of love and commitment I would never have shown you."
"Fuck you," was all the beaten down Polly could muster as she begrudgingly lifted her head to look at the man she'd once loved dearly.
Ignoring her, Eddie proceeded to strip. He tossed his clothing aside until he stood before her, butt naked, except for a lighter that he had retrieved from his pocket.
For the first time since they'd met, Polly found the sight of Eddie's naked form repellent. At this moment, she hated him more than she knew she was capable. Just looking at him standing there, as nude as the day he was born, made her blood boil in her veins.

"You disgust me, you fucking sick freak," she spat at him.

"I don't care what you think of me," Eddie said, laughing at her cruel remarks. Then, he turned to face where he had placed Sophia.

"Are you ready to take the next step, honey?"

The doll turned her head and smiled at him. "Whatever it takes for us to be together," it replied.

Eddie's smile grew wider. "I hoped you'd say that."

"Who the fuck are you talking to?" Polly asked, baffled by what she was witnessing.

"I'm trying to have a conversation," Eddie snapped.

"You're talking to yourself, you fucking lunatic!"

"Ignore her," Sophia instructed him. "She will never understand."

"I know, baby," Eddie replied. "Okay, let's do this." He walked over and lifted the doll out of the seat. Then, carefully, he removed the tiny clothing he had dressed her in before leaving Greg's earlier that night. He clutched Sophia to his chest and walked over to where he had left the can.

"What are you doing?" Polly asked. She already had an idea but was too horrified to accept it as a reality.

Still clutching the doll, Eddie lifted the can and tipped it over his head, dousing himself in the liquid fuel. It poured over his entire body, splashing onto the carpet at his feet.

"You want to know what it is to love?" He asked. "What it is to be at one with someone else? Well, here's your answer."

Polly watched in horror as her husband clicked the lighter. In a flash, flames travelled up his arm, igniting the petrol that covered him from head to toe. Eddie was engulfed in an instant. His screams echoed around the house as the inferno took him.

The sensation of burning alive was more agonising than he'd imagined possible. The heat from the fire attacked and destroyed every nerve in his being. His pain receptors were now completely overloaded as his skin melted away. Finally, he dropped to his knees; the flames having taken his eyes, rendering him blind. The doll, Sophia, the love of his life, bubbled and liquified, her once rigid body melting onto Eddie's chest until she was nothing more than an unrecognisable puddle of molten goo. Eddie's wish had come true. She was indeed now a part of him. Quite literally fused to him.

Finally, Eddie succumbed to the blaze. He fell, face first, onto the floor, a dead, blackened, burnt husk.

The flames, having travelled across the floor, had reached the furniture in all four corners of the room. They ate everything in their path as if they had an agenda. The chair on which Polly sat ignited with ease, taking her with it. As she surrendered to the hellfire that ended her life, Polly's dying thoughts were of Alice.

Her love for her daughter was as pure and unconditional as love could be, and it was stolen away in a moment of sheer insanity. Only in her last moments did Polly understand how fragile and finite everything was; it hurt her more than the flames that consumed her ever could.

The End

About The Author

Lee Richmond

Lee Richmond was born in the swampy marshlands of East Anglia. Fed on a steady diet of fast, snotty punk rock and 80s slasher movies, it was only a matter of time before the sick, twisted imagery that festered in his head eventually found its way to the page.
Lee was influenced from a very early age by the films of John Carpenter, Dario Argento, Wes Craven and Tobe Hooper and the books of Clive Barker, Stephen King and James Herbert.

Music also plays its part in influencing Lee's writing. His love for bands like The Misfits, Ramones, Fugazi and Sisters of Mercy and the works of such movie composers as Hans Zimmer and Christopher Young.

Lee's other interests include playing bass guitar and drawing. He also owns and writes for horror movie website, reelhorrorshow.co.uk along with fellow writer, Mark Green.

Lee is the author of 232 Jericho Avenue, Beneath, Tits and Teeth, and PolterGary.

Open House

-Rebecca Rowland-

Open House

Bill tore six slices of the precooked bacon from its plastic package and slapped them onto a paper towel. He placed the towel on a plate, put the plate in the microwave, and set the timer for two minutes. He liked his bacon crispy. "I like my bacon the way I like my women," he often told people with a wink. "Lean and salty... and a little overdone, if you know what I mean."

No one knew what he meant. But, people nodded and smiled accordingly. That's what people did around Bill: he had that kind of charisma. He could look you in the eye while he reached into your abdomen and took out an organ or two, and more than likely, you'd simply thank him for leaving you a kidney. Melinda suspected that about her husband when she first met Bill, she knew it when they married in a city park three years ago (no family in attendance—it was better that way: more intimate), and she blindly trusted it every time they walked into a new school auditorium amid the stale percolator coffee, over-baked PTO cookies, and sad brochures pleading with parents of potential students to apply.

Melinda, or Linda, as Bill called her, sat in a chair at the wooden kitchen table, the skin on the back of her thighs catching on one of the rips in the plastic-upholstered seat cushion. If she kept shifting, her skin would look like a road map, crooked interstates crisscrossing with blue rivers from the back of her knee to the curved ridge of her ass, and Bill would not like that at all: no sir-ee. So, she kept the lower half of her body very still as she stirred her coffee over and over, breathing in the sugary scent of the hazelnut creamer she had drowned it in.

Bill brought the plate of towel-wrapped bacon to the table, his last few steps quicker than the first, as the plate had gotten hotter than he had anticipated and holding it began to singe his fingertips. He snapped his hand back toward his body and rubbed his fingers quickly back and forth across his chest like a mad third-base coach instructing his pitcher not to throw the curve.

"Are you okay, baby?" asked Linda. "Do you want me to get some ice?"

Bill stopped the maniacal rubbing. "Nah, it's fine." He flipped open the paper towel, shoved a slice in his mouth like a cigarette, and began to roll it about with his tongue. Bill did the oddest things with food, Linda noticed. She was always afraid people were staring at them in restaurants, so they rarely ate out. "Hey, see what else is on," he said, pointing to the TV with his first and middle fingers welded together into a gun barrel shape. "We've seen this Law & Order, like, fifteen times."

The couple had two television sets in the house. One was in the kitchen, kitty-cornering the countertop next to the coffeemaker. The other was in the bedroom. "The living room is for sitting and visiting," Bill had said when he moved in a few months before their trip to the park, and Linda, of course, agreed. It was nice spending evenings in the parlor with Bill. Some nights, they'd each read books and bask in the silent hum that blanketed the house, but most nights, they spent hours just talking. Linda could listen to Bill talk all night. She thought that was pretty impressive: three years married and not once tired of his company.

Linda held the remote even with the set and clicked the channel button a few times. "Wait—stop: hold up. What's that?" Bill said, holding his hand in the air, palm facing his wife like a traffic cop. Linda watched the screen. It was a commercial for an open house at one of the local Catholic elementary schools.

Give your child the best educational opportunities available!

Choose Saint Benedict Joseph Labre Elementary. Open House this Friday, October 30 at 6 pm.

See what the gift of a Catholic education can do for your child!

Bill pulled the rest of the bacon slice into his mouth and chewed. Linda could hear the crunching of the driest pieces echo in his mouth. "Shall we go? It might be a good opportunity for Baby Jessica." When he smiled after he said this, Linda could see a piece of dark red bacon stuck in one of his teeth.

Bill and Linda did not have any children. They hadn't even tried for them. Sure: there was that one time that Linda thought she might be pregnant. Her breasts ached and her period was a full week tardy, so she drove to Walgreens while Bill was at work, bought a test, and smuggled it home, being careful not to let the neighbors see the bright blue and pink box practically glowing through the thin plastic pharmacy bag. She unwrapped the collection stick, placed it gently on the bathroom sink, and prepared to collect a cup of her urine for screening, but when she pulled down her pants to go, she found her panties stained with deep red blood. Her period had come after all—it had been playing a game of chicken with Linda and finally gave in. Of course, she had seen women on a number of daytime talk shows who claimed to have never known they were pregnant for months and months—they had even gotten regular periods—so she tested her urine just in case. Negative, but a close call just the same. If they had children, they'd never be able to play Baby Jessica.

    Linda had dropped out of college in the beginning of her junior year, but as a sophomore, she had taken American Lit II in order to fulfill the Humanities requirement. It was in that class that she read Edward Albee's play, Who's Afraid of Virginia Woolf. Truth be told, she was supposed to have read it, but it had been just as easy to rent the movie featuring Elizabeth Taylor and her real-life on-again, off-again husband Richard Burton. The two main characters speak of their absent son throughout the play as they use him in frequent attempts to goad one another into anger. At the end—spoiler alert—the audience learns that there is no son: George and Martha made him up to disguise their own shared regret at not being able to have children.

    Bill and Linda didn't use an imaginary child as a weapon in their domestic spats. They didn't suffer from shared psychosis either; Linda had learned about that phenomenon in her Psych 101 class, and they weren't imagining a child who wasn't there. No, Baby Jessica wasn't a real person at all. She was their code word for the game. Bill had come up with the moniker after watching some Reagan-era nostalgic news program: in 1987, an 18-month-old child in Texas became stuck in a well, and the cable news channels went berserk covering the rescue attempts. Baby Jessica, as she was known, was finally rescued, suffering only injuries to her foot. "Those goddamn news people couldn't stop talking about the kid. I mean, I know there are slow news days, but damn: gimme something better than some recycled Lassie script," he pointed out. "But you know what I think? I think the news was trying to distract America from all the terrible crap going on in the world. Oil tankers blowing up, people getting cancer and AIDS, the economy nose-diving... give the people a kid in peril and a cherry reunion at the end, and poof! All their worries, gone."

That's what Baby Jessica was to Bill and Linda: a distraction from their boring lives. A purging of their anxieties and regrets. For the last three years, they had played Baby Jessica every Halloween, and every year, they had walked away scot-free. And Bill was always extra passionate with Linda afterward: making love to her for hours, then curling up next to her in their queen-sized bed, nuzzling his face in the crook of her neck. "I love you, pretty girl Linda," he whispered to her last Halloween. He rarely told her he loved her. It had been a special evening.

Bill and Linda shook their rain-soaked umbrellas in the entryway of the Catholic school's gymnasium. Linda didn't want to carry the umbrella all night, but she didn't want to risk it getting stolen at the makeshift coat check, either. Bill hated when her hair frizzed and her mascara ran. He said it made her look like a dead hooker. She pulled the umbrella strap tight around the base and latched it, then wiped her damp palms on the bottom of her cardigan sweater.

Like a typical salesclerk, a stout woman with short-cropped salt and pepper hair wearing a navy skirted suit approached Bill and Linda within a minute of their arrival. "Well, hello! Welcome to Saint Benedict's. I'm Sister Monica." She grasped Linda's still slightly wet hand in hers and shook it up and down. "I'm the headmaster. And who is your little angel?"

Linda pulled her hand away as if she'd been bitten, then instantly regretted it. She was always nervous in social situations, and given what she and Bill planned to do, it was likely their every move could be scrutinized and their plan foiled before it had even begun. She had to act normal. What would a normal mother inquiring about parochial school for her child do? "Her name is Jessica. She's at home with a sitter because we weren't sure how late we'd be here," Linda said quickly, making sure to smile with all of her teeth. She knew she looked more sincere that way. "Do you mind if we look around?"

For just a moment, Sister Monica glanced at the space just behind Linda and Bill, then her eyes searched Linda's face and she brandished a tight-lipped smile. "Oh my goodness: please do look around. We have a number of tables set up by the children to showcase all of the activities and opportunities available for little Jessica." The headmaster seemed to spot the person she had been looking for, because she placed a hand on Linda's upper arm to show that their conversation had come to an end; then she excused herself and moved on to another arriving couple.

"Well, that was a quick sales pitch," Bill said under his breath. He nodded at the display tables. "Let's take a look, shall we?"

The two wandered from stand to stand, eyeing the sports, clubs, and specialized classes the private school boasted. Three to five children positioned themselves behind each display, some sitting painfully in worn, orange plastic chairs; others shifting from one foot to another in a nervous dance recital. Many were talking animatedly with their classmates; most appeared sallow, almost sickly, under the harsh fluorescent lights. Linda perused each activity: soccer teams, baseball teams, basketball teams; choral groups, a hiking club, even a knitting and sewing club. *What eight-year-old knits?* thought Linda.

Toward the middle of the gym was a table staffed by three children, all of whom looked to be about nine or ten years old. Linda and Bill checked the sign propped at the front of their display: "Baking and Cooking Club." Two of the children stood erect at one corner, facing each other: a boy and a girl. The girl was short with round brown eyes and a mop of curly brown hair pinned back with a pink ribbon barrette. The boy was tan—strange for the middle of the autumn—with hazel eyes and a willowy build. He wore a tall baker's hat, obviously a wayward piece from a child's dress-up set, jauntily over his dirty blond locks. They were playing some sort of game where the boy held his palms upright in front of him and tried to pull them away before the girl could successfully slap them. The girl kept making contact with the boy's hands and laughing hysterically each time the sound of skin cracking echoed across the room.

   Next to those two, however, was another child. A boy. This boy was sitting in a rickety wooden chair, his shoulders slightly hunched, his eyes staring down at the table in front of him. He was a heavyset child with dark hair, ruddy skin, and eyes that were slightly rimmed with the redness of fatigue. A cowlick stuck out defiantly by the back of his crown. He looked like he was willing himself to disappear, silently begging the staunch white tablecloth displaying cookie cutters and awkwardly posed photographs to rise up like an apparition and swallow him whole. Bill looked at Linda. This was the one.

Linda walked nonchalantly to the edge of the table. She placed a finger on the edge of her mouth as if deep in thought. "Say, what have you baked this year in your club?" she asked the trio, letting her eyes dance on each one of their faces.

The young couple continued their game as if they did not hear her. The girl slapped the boy playfully on the hip, and the boy yanked off his hat and threw it at her, softball pitch-style. Tufts of sandy locks stood at strange angles on top of his head. The girl shrieked with pleasure, caught the hat in her hands, and said, "Now it's mine!" and ran off into the growing crowd of the gymnasium. The boy followed, laughing a nervous boy laugh.

The sitting boy did not move. He didn't even flinch.

Linda paused and looked at the boy sitting in front of her. She peered down at the spot of floor still visible under the edge of the tablecloth. Next to the boy's worn, grey sneakers were three crumpled wrappers: two from Little Debbie chocolate snack cakes and the last from an Almond Joy candy bar.

"Do you bake at home?" she asked the boy. His body and eyes did not move, but Linda saw him swallow and pinch his lips together.

"Sometimes." His voice was small, almost a whisper. If his classmates hadn't run off, the cacophony of their game and giggles might have drowned him out completely.

Bill fingered a star-shaped cookie cutter. "I love sugar cookies: I mean love them. Mrs. Brady just baked a whole bunch for the party tomorrow night, too." Linda flinched slightly at the name "Brady." They had forgotten to agree on a fake last name before arriving. It was always something ironic, some adaptation of a utopian television family. Last year they were the Bradfords; the year before that, the Waltons. Linda always suggested the Huxtables in honor of her favorite show as a kid, but with that whole Cosby mess in the news, Bill said they needed to be less conspicuous. Bill always made the big decisions.

Linda held out her hand as if introducing herself at a job interview. "I'm Mrs. Brady, and our daughter is about your age. Her name is Jessica. What's your name?"

The boy was silent for a beat, then he lifted his head to look at Linda. "Sam." His eyes were bright: blue, or maybe green. It was hard to tell. He ignored Linda's hand, so she pulled it back and put it in her pants pocket.

"Well, Sam, we could really use a dessert expert at our Halloween party tomorrow. Are you trick-or-treating this year?" Linda asked, keeping the cheer in her voice. "What are you dressing up as?"

Sam blushed at the word expert. "I am a dessert expert. I help my mom bake cookies and cakes and brownies all the time." He smiled slightly but shyly. "I'm going as Batman."

"Reeeaaaallllly?!" Bill said, dragging out the response into multiple syllables like a cartoon character. "That's so cool! Jessica's party is superhero-themed! She's going as Wonder Woman, of course. What other superheroes do you like, besides Batman, of course?"

Sam's posture relaxed, and his smile spread like warm peanut butter on toast. "Um, I like Superman, too. And The Flash. Spider-Man's alright, I guess. But I like Batman the best. I play the Lego Batman game on my Xbox all the time."

Linda smiled. Of course the kid had an Xbox. He probably spent all day Saturday and Sunday with his round butt glued to the couch, his eyes cemented to the TV screen, a game controller in one hand and a fistful of Oreos in the other. She turned her head slowly and scanned the room. Where were this kid's parents? Didn't they come to support their son's extra-curricular activity?

"You know, I just tried my hand at baking these chocolate-covered coconut macaroons, but not everyone likes coconut. I hope people will eat them at the party,"

Linda said. She painted a worried expression on her face for good measure. She could see Bill smiling his sideways grin out of the corner of her eye.

Sam practically sprang from his seat. "Oh, em, gee: I love coconut!"

"Well," Bill said, leaning forward conspiratorially, "I know Jessica doesn't have many friends coming to her party. Jess has been homeschooled for the past three years, and she doesn't know many kids. They are going to trick-or-treat together around our neighborhood later afterwards... lots of houses on our street give out the good stuff: you know, like the full-sized candy bars. 'You know what I mean?" He winked at Sam.

Sam nodded his head so fast, Linda thought it might come unhooked and roll onto the table.

Linda searched the gymnasium purposefully with her eyes. She held her hand up to her forehead as if she were blocking out the sun to focus her view. "Where are your mom and dad? I'll go introduce myself and ask their permission... if you'd like to come, that is."

Bill and Linda held their breath. This would be the make-or-break moment. If Sam declined, they'd have to start all over with another awkward kid. Plus, they ran the risk that the slapping game stablemates would return soon and want to attend as well. They had to close the deal and get outta Dodge.

Sam stood up. Linda could now see all of his pudgy frame. He balled his fists and held up his arms in a Strong Man pose and jumped up and down twice. The skin on the sides of his torso bounced visibly up and down inside of his t-shirt. "Yeah! I want to go!" He beamed at Linda. "My mom isn't here. She's gonna pick me up at eight o'clock."

Bill reached into Linda's jacket pocket and took out the small notepad and pen he had placed there for just this reason. "Okay, let me write Jessica's name and our address and phone number on this paper. You show it to your mom and tell her she can call us tonight or tomorrow if she wants. The party starts at four o'clock sharp, so don't be late!" He scribbled furiously and handed a small slip of paper to Sam.

"And make sure you wear your Batman costume: there are prizes for the coolest costumes," Linda added. She watched the boy carefully fold the paper once, then slip it in his pants pocket. Bill folded his arm around Linda's waist, and the two walked slowly and deliberately toward the door, trying their very best to muffle the smiles on their faces.

It was three in the afternoon on Saturday: Halloween, at last. Linda had been certain to decorate the living room for a kids' party in case Sam's mother wanted to come inside and look around. That had happened last year: young Bethany's father, his chest puffy and broad, accompanied his daughter to the door, and he must have suspected something because he asked to use their bathroom even though he didn't reek of booze, didn't appear sick, and seemed to be old enough to hold his bladder until he returned home. Linda had opened her door wide, spread her arm out like a professional greeter welcoming a member of royalty, and ushered the pair inside. Yes, of course you can use our bathroom: it's right there—first door on the right in the hallway leading to the kitchen. Why, no, my husband isn't home: you just missed him. He took Jess to the party store to pick up streamers. Would you like to sit down?

    Linda had even invited the man to stay for the party. She felt her heart race as she said it, knowing it was a bluff from which she would have no way of recovering if the father took her up on the offer. As she placed apple after apple into the water in the wide washing bucket, she rambled on about the weather and the upcoming town election and had focused on keeping her toothy smile wide and genuine. After an awkward moment or two, Bethany's dad stood up, tousled his daughter's strawberry blonde hair piled daintily within the constraints of a plastic princess crown, and walked toward the door. He even thanked Linda for inviting his child: their family had recently moved to town, and the poor, introverted girl hadn't made many friends.

"We're going to have a super time!" Linda had said enthusiastically, more to herself than to the child or her parent. Later, when she drove Bethany home, she was so sorry to report that the girl had fallen down the cellar stairs when the children were playing hide-and-seek. A few scrapes and minor bruises, nothing broken. A few days rest and she'd be good as new. Bethany was too sleepy to argue, and her pillowcase overflowing with candy must have served as adequate hush money, because Linda never heard from the father again.

Linda secured the last delicate orange streamer to the crown molding around the doorway that separated the living room from the dining room. She had hung furry plastic spiders from the ceiling, draped black cloth over the end tables, and put out bowls of candy corn. The cookies cut in the shapes of cats and topped with black-colored sugar were spread across the wide, silver serving tray, each overlapping the next like tiny Rockettes performing a final number. She had stuffed an old pillowcase with the contents of three full bags of fun-sized candy and poured a fourth bag containing Almond Joys and Mounds bars into a bowl by the front door, as she had run out of time to make the macaroons.

If Sam's mother questioned why Sam was the only child there, Linda was prepared to affix her best sympathetic countenance and deliver her prepared response. She practiced while she straightened the chairs and brushed imaginary lint off of the sofa. "Gee, you're the first one here: the party doesn't start until five," Linda announced to the empty parlor. "Jess and her dad made a quick trip to Shop & Save. We forgot the Fritos: can you believe that? ...What's that? I said it started at four? Oh, gosh, I don't think so, but that's okay: Sam, you can help me set up the drinks and test-drive the cookies: what do you think about that?"

    She nudged a sugar cookie that had shaken free of the chorus line and touched the edge of the tray lightly with her finger. Arranging party snacks reminded Linda of the open house-style housewarming she had held when she first moved in. She had invited all of her co-workers at the dental office, as well as her mother, aunts, uncles, and cousins. All day, she ran from room to room, offering trays of tapas and crudités, spinning her sweaty head from guest to guest until she was dizzy. Her mother had told her that an open-house style housewarming was the classiest and most welcoming type of new home party, and that Linda was too white trash to ever be able to pull off such a thing. She hadn't warned her that because guests could come and go as they pleased, she would have to have fresh food and drinks available all afternoon if she was going to be an appropriate hostess. Linda's feet ached for days following the party, and she never wanted to see a mini quiche again for as long as she lived. As she ran frantically over her newly refinished hardwood floors, she had spied her mother leaning against the walnut sideboard, balancing a wine glass stem between two delicate, meticulously manicured fingertips, shooting her glares of disappointment and disgust. Thank goodness at least Bill accepted her, white trash warts and all.

She and Bill hadn't had a reception after the wedding. They had simply retired to the cozy craftsman-style bungalow, drank champagne, and fed each other the cake Linda had procured from the bakery down the road earlier in the day. There was so much less stress that way, and Linda had Bill all to herself: no sharing him with family or friends. She got such a limited amount of Bill as it was—he held his feelings so close to the vest—that she cherished her time alone with him on holidays and at special events.

The doorbell rang. Linda glanced at her watch. Quarter to four. Was he early? She straightened her blouse, smoothed her hair with her hands, and practiced her expressions. Big, toothy grin of joy. Furrowed brow of motherly concern. Wide eyes of confusion and astonishment. Her face clicked through the emotional flip chart she knew people expected of upstanding mothers and wives. She stretched her jaw, cocking it to and fro, then wiped the slate clean and swung open the front door.

Sam stood, round and sweaty, on the top cement step, his hand still hovering over the doorbell. A brown, beaten-up Chevrolet of 1980s vintage idled in the street near the curb. Linda leaned down and tried to spy the driver, but all she could make out was an outline of fuzzy hair and a faux-fur trimmed jacket hood. She pantomimed saying hello, then shooed Sam into the house with her hand on his shoulder. The car sped off without so much as a honk or a shadowy wave. Sam did not look back.

"Well, hey! You're a little early, Sam, but come on in and make yourself at home," Linda sang. She pointed to the couch against the picture window. "Have a seat. Would you like something to drink?"

Sam pushed up the black mask that had been covering his face from his nose to his forehead with his wrist. "Um, do you have any root beer?"

Linda thought for a moment. "Let me take a look! I'll be right back." She spun on her heels and walked briskly to the kitchen. She would have to work fast: she hadn't anticipated the boy being this eager to arrive. Grabbing her rolling pin from the counter with one hand, she pulled open the cabinet above the sink with the other and grabbed the thin, caramel-colored pill bottle. She shook out one of the mint-green tablets and quickly crushed it into powder with the rolling pin: Sam was a hefty kid, Linda thought, but a single 7.5 mg pill should be enough. She peered into the refrigerator, spied one lonely can of Barq's in the back, and put in on the counter.

"Excuse me," said a tiny voice behind her as she poured the soda into a glass. She turned quickly, keeping her body pressed against the counter to hide the tiny pile of green powder. She was frozen, unsure of what to say next.

"Well, Sam: it's nice to see you again," said Bill, suddenly appearing in the doorway to the butler's pantry. He held his arm above his head and pressed his elbow against the door frame. "What say you and I hang out in the parlor until drinks are served, yeah?" He shuffled up next to Sam and shooed him back into the front room like a shepherd. Linda brushed the green powder to the edge of the countertop, held the lip of the glass of root beer below, and dumped the drug into the fizzy drink; the bubbles raced to the top to meet it. She ran a spoon through the liquid a handful of times. She didn't want to over-stir, or the drink would get flat and the boy wouldn't finish it.

Back in the living room, Sam was again sitting on the sofa, his mask still pushed astray. He had moved the bowl of candy corn from the end table to the cushion next to him. "Here you are!" Linda handed him the glass of brown liquid, and the boy took it from her excitedly and began to gulp. He had imbibed half of the drink before removing it from his mouth to take a breath. Sam held the glass in front of him, searching the spaces nearby for a flat surface to rest the glass. Seeing none, he looked at Linda.

As if reading his mind, she replied, "Drink up! There's plenty more where that came from!" and like a trained seal, Sam emptied the solution into his stomach, let out a satisfied Ahhhhh!, and wiped his mouth with the back of his free hand. He pulled his mask back down over his eyes and nose and held the glass up in Linda's direction.

Linda felt an instant wave of irritation. Did he expect her to be his maid? To wait on him hand and foot? She wondered if his mother did. He certainly lacked for exercise. Her own mother never would have brought her a soda, let alone stood by like a lady-in-waiting. She snatched the empty glass from his hand and placed it on the dining room table next to the cookie tray.

"So, Bruce Wayne, are you limber enough for the party games we are going to play?" Bill asked Sam, the question dripping with honeyed maleficence. Most children's radar would have alarmed immediately at his tone, and Linda put her hand on her forehead as if to push the concern out of her mind. "How 'bout we fix you another drink, and then we'll start to practice the candy corn toss," Bill continued. "By the time the other kids get here, you'll be a master!"

"Uh... we're out of root beer, though: would you like a Coke?" Linda asked. She knew this was Bill's signal to give the child another dose. At the dental practice, a full-grown adult was prescribed one tablet of Midazolam for anxiety before a complicated procedure, and even then, the patient had to be driven to and from the appointment because of the sedative properties. Sam was a child, but he was a hefty child. A full fifteen milligrams might knock him out completely. She glanced at her husband. He cocked his head to the side and raised an eyebrow at her. You're not wimping out on me, are you, pretty girl? She shook her head slightly to show him she was not.

Sam nodded his head furiously again. His face was slightly pink, like he'd been running. The costume was heavy and thick, and Linda had turned the heat up to 75 degrees, even though it was still the season for light jackets. She returned to the kitchen, crushed another pill, but swept only half of it into the soda. The rest she brushed into the sink and washed down the drain.

Back in the living room, Sam was tossing candy corn into the air and trying to catch the pieces in his mouth. His head was tipped perpetually backwards, his mouth agape like a big fish scooping minnows from the air. Linda stood and watched him for a moment, then looked at Bill. His eyes were wide as saucers and wet; it was the same look he often gave when she presented him one of her gourmet dinners, a dish she had taken hours to prepare just for his pleasure.

Two pieces sailed into the boy's mouth without his making much of an effort. Sam's head dropped and he looked at Linda. "Here you go," she offered, holding the glass of cola toward him. He walked the three steps to meet her and accepted the drink without a word. As she watched him guzzle, Linda's worry button began to buzz. Maybe we should have waited longer to see how he's reacting to the first pill. Maybe this is too much medication after all. As the last drop slid effortlessly from the glass into Sam's mouth, Linda grabbed the tray of cookies from the table and thrust it in front of him. "Cookie?"

Sam stuck his hand out to grab one when Bill leaped to his feet and pushed Linda and the tray back toward the dining room. "Cookies later. Let's practice for pin-the-tail," he said. He pulled an old black bandana from his back pocket and pulled it through a loose fist on his other hand, appearing to caress the cotton fabric with his fingertips. "C'mere, Sammy. Let's practice balancing and focus."

Before Sam could protest, Bill tied the kerchief over the boy's eyes, placed his hands on Sam's shoulders, and with some force, spun Sam's body clockwise once, twice, three times. He gave Sam's collarbone a final squeeze and pushed the boy backwards softly. Sam teetered for a moment, then straightened. He attempted to walk forward. His body, still trapped in the centrifugal force, leaned right, then left, then right again. Sam took a tentative step forward with one foot but seemed unable to follow with the other, his body frozen in a strange half-warrior yoga pose.

"Uh... I'm dizzy," Sam said in a tiny voice. He raised his hand to push the blindfold from his eyes, but Bill jumped forward and held his arm.

"Oh, no you don't!" he sang in an unnaturally chipper tone. "Not yet!" He clutched Sam's shoulders again, this time harder. He spun Sam counterclockwise, and the boy's torso twisted ahead of its appendages, causing Sam to hold his arms out like a bird to keep from falling. As he tilted forward, Bill pushed him hard, sending the boy backwards and almost falling again. Bill began to circle the boy, running faster and faster around the boy, pushing him this way and that, until Sam looked like an animatronic rag doll. After a minute or two of this, Bill exerted one final shove, and Sam fell down into a sitting position on the brown carpet.

"Oh my goodness! Are you alright, Sam?" Linda said, pulling the handkerchief from his head and holding out her hand to help him up.

Sam pushed himself into a squatting position, then lost his balance and tipped sideways. On the second try, he managed to push himself back up to standing. He pulled his Batman mask from his head and dropped it onto the floor. "Yeah... dizzy. I feel dizzy."

"Stand right there, buddy," said Bill. "Get your balance back. Hey, how about we catch candy corn again? You stand right there: I'll throw them into your mouth!"

Bill pitched his hand into the bowl and pulled out a handful of candies. He held one kernel between two fingers of his opposite hand even with his ear. "Okay, buddy. Open up!"

Sam stood staring at Linda for a moment. Then he opened his mouth an inch.

"Wider," said Bill.

Sam opened his mouth a tiny bit more.

"Wider!" roared Bill.

Sam opened his mouth like he was preparing for a tonsil exam. Bill gently tossed the candy corn into the boy's mouth. Sam chewed it and swallowed but did not open his mouth again.

"Again," Bill instructed.

Sam opened his mouth an inch, heard Bill suck in a forceful breath, and opened his mouth as wide as he could manage. Bill lobbed another candy into it, then backed up five paces. "How about from here? Hey: here's an idea. Let's play horse. Linda, why don't you see if YOU can make all of my trick shots, huh?" He spun his arm backwards like a big-league pitcher preparing for a fastball. "Open up, Sammy. Don't make me ask you again."

Sam closed his eyes so tight that his lids seem to sink and disappear into his face. He put his hands over his ears as if to shield them, and opened his mouth into an O-shape. This is what Munch's painting looks like blinking, Linda thought. Bill began to run around the room, first throwing, then pelting the boy with candy corn. The pieces popped and binged off of the boy's white, soft flesh like an orange and yellow hailstorm.

When Bill had run out of candy to throw, Sam tried to walk toward the couch during the reprieve. His pace was wobbly, drunk-like. "I don't feel so good," he said, slurring his words.

Linda placed an arm around him and helped him to the sofa. "Lie down, Sam: it's okay. Let me get you some ginger ale and crackers, okay? You probably just had too much sugar, sweetheart," she cooed. Bill backed up against the doorframe and clicked his teeth—a tiny pout as the pause button was hit on his fun.

Linda walked with purpose back to the kitchen and poured a small glass of ginger ale—sans powder—and looked quickly for some saltines. Finding none, she returned to the living room with only the soda. Sam was half-sitting, half-leaning on the sofa, his eyes heavy and half-closed. "Okay, sweetie," she pleaded in her kindest voice possible. "Drink this up now. Take some deep breaths." She placed the glass in Sam's sweaty hand.

Sam's eyes rolled a bit in his head like wet marbles. He clutched the glass weakly and brought it shakily to his lips. Just as the brim tickled his mouth, his body lurched forward in a spasm. Ochre vomit spewed onto his black shirt. His body convulsed twice more, sending two sprays of the putrid-smelling sick onto Linda, who had to close her eyes and inhale slowly through her mouth to not begin retching herself.

Bill patted Sam's back forcefully, like he was burping a plastic doll. "Well now, that's unfortunate. More room for cookies though, huh?" He shot a glance up at his wife. "Get the boy a wet towel, would you, Linda? For God's sake, the kid's covered in throw up."

Linda retrieved an old hand towel from the linen closet and dipped it in the tub filled with apples and cool water. She dabbed Sam's face carefully, watching his glassy eyes follow her facial expressions suspiciously. "I think I want to go home now," he mumbled drunkenly. "I don't want a cookie."

Linda peeled Sam's soiled top from his round, sweaty body, being careful not to shake any of the vomit onto the floor. Underneath, he wore a ribbed white tank top, the kind Marlon Brando wore in A Streetcar Named Desire. As if reading her mind, Bill burst out laughing. "Stella!!" he yelled. "Stellllll aaaah!" He guffawed and rubbed his stomach.

Linda took two steps backward. "I'm going to rinse off your shirt in the sink, Sam." She paused and looked at Sam straight in the eye. "You drink that ginger ale and Bill will drive you home, okay? Do what Bill says and everything will be okay."

She brought the shirt to the guest bathroom and ran it under warm water, watching the light brown chunky mess pause momentarily at the drain, then disappear. Never had a child gotten sick before. She wondered if this would affect the amnesic properties of the Midazolam. She and Bill had to be more careful. She was stupid to give him so much of the drug without food.

She squeezed the shirt, twisting it into a long, wet log and wringing it three times. Once it was no longer dripping, she returned to the parlor.

Bill was standing behind Sam, who was bent in a wobbly right angle, his head almost completely submerged in the tub of apples. Bill was holding his shoulders and Sam was flailing his arms about wildly.

Linda thought she could hear a muffled, underwater scream.

"Bill! What are you doing? Stop! Stop! You're going to kill him!" Linda shrieked, dropping the shirt in a wet plop on the carpet. She stood next to her husband, half covering her face with her hands. "Oh my god, Bill: please—please let him up!"

Bill grabbed the top of Sam's tank top by the straps and pulled. Sam sputtered and gasped for air, his mouth stretched wide and angled toward the ceiling. "We're just bobbing for apples, Linda! What's the problem? Sammy here almost got a good one, too: didn't ya, Sammy?" He pushed Sam's face back into the water and held his palm firm against the top of Sam's neck. Water splashed from the bucket and onto Bill's t-shirt, soaking it to near translucence.

Linda pushed her husband hard: pushed him with all the force she could muster. Bill was a big guy—much bigger than Linda, and almost always much stronger. This time, she was able to gain the upper hand. She pulled Sam backward and away from the tub. He coughed violently, spraying Linda's face with spit and drool. "Are you alright?" Linda said, smoothing Sam's wet hair against his forehead over and over. "You slipped and fell forward... Oh my goodness: you're soaked: Let me get you a towel: hold on, Sam... just hold tight." She ran to the linen closet again and sorted through the piles of towels like a madwoman. She wanted to give Sam the cleanest, softest towel. She spied a fluffy yellow one, pulled it from the pile, and ran back to the living room.

"Sam, here is—" She stopped short. Sam was not in the living room. "Sam?" she called, walking cautiously through the dining room and into the kitchen. No Sam. "Sam?" He was not in the house. She stupidly opened a cabinet. Did she expect to find him hiding inside? She closed the door and leaned her back against the counter, crossing her arms in front of her chest. She supposed it was time to clean up.

She dumped the tub of water into the kitchen sink and laid the wet apples on the counter to dry. She rinsed the empty glasses of root beer and coke and ginger ale and stacked them neatly in the dishwasher. She removed the tablecloths from the end tables, dumped the remaining bowls of candy corn into the trash, and picked Sam's folded, wet Batman costume from the floor. She was nibbling the tail of a sugar cookie when the doorbell rang.

Although Linda wasn't entirely surprised to see a police officer standing on her stoop, she pasted her best bewildered expression across her face and smiled prettily at him. Think: wide eyes of confusion and astonishment. She remembered to show all of her teeth. She glanced over at the squad car parked against the curb, the same place Sam's mother had peeled away from after leaving her sad, doughy son in Linda's care just a few hours earlier. Sam's pale face stared at her from the back seat.

"Ma'am, we picked up a boy walking through the neighborhood who told us some very disturbing things about a party you are having here," the officer said. His steely grey eyes met hers and did not move. "'Mind if I take a look around?"

Linda stepped backwards into her foyer. "Oh my goodness: no, of course not! Come right in," she said.

The policeman stepped cautiously into the house. He followed Linda into the living room, looking at everything from ceiling to floor, seeming to memorize it. "So, what can I answer for you?" Linda asked, sitting daintily on the edge of the sofa.

The officer did not make a move to join her. "The boy tells us that you fed him things to make him sick. He says you assaulted him and tried to drown him in a tub of apples."

Linda laughed nervously, but the cop was not smiling. "Well, that seems like an odd story. Are you sure it was this house he visited?" Smile. Teeth. She cleared her throat.

"The boy was wearing an undershirt when we saw him walking one block over," he continued. "'Says you took his clothes."

Linda laughed again. "Well, isn't that funny?"

The officer did not think it was funny. In fact, he was very stern as he walked toward the dining room table and picked up the wadded-up, wet shirt Linda had placed next to the cookie tray. "What is this, ma'am?"

Linda could no longer evoke a laugh. "My husband... my husband may know what is going on..." she began. She looked frantically about the room. Where was Bill when she needed him?

"Your husband?" repeated the officer. "Is his name Bill, by any chance?"

"Why, yes," Linda said. Her face felt hot. She wiped her palms on her still-soaked t-shirt in an attempt to cool herself. "How did you know that?"

The officer took two steps closer to Linda. "I need you to come with me, ma'am. We have some questions for you at the station."

As if in a dream, Linda rose to her feet and followed the policeman outside and to his squad car. Sam had exited the vehicle and was standing next to a blonde policewoman on her lawn. As she passed by Sam, she saw the cop place her hand on Sam's upper arm, as if ready to pull him back if Linda made any unsightly movements. "She... she kept talking to some guy who wasn't there," Linda heard Sam say. "But it was just her. No one else was there."

The gray-eyed policeman opened the back door of the squad car and motioned for Linda to climb inside. As she did, she heard Sam's tiny voice squeak, "Can I just go home now? I just want to go home."

The officer closed the car door, and Linda wiped the humid glass and peered out toward her tiny bungalow. Baby Jessica was ruined. Bill would be mad when she came home tonight. She was sure of it.

About The Author

Rebecca Rowland

Visit RowlandBooks.com for more information!

Rebecca Rowland grew up in Western Massachusetts but spent her early adult life in the Boston area, and most of her fiction is set in those locations. She is the author of The Horrors Hiding in Plain Sight, Pieces, Shagging the Boss, Optic Nerve, and White Trash & Recycled Nightmares and the curator of seven horror anthologies, including the bestseller Unburied: A Collection of Queer Dark Fiction. Her short fiction, guest essays, and book reviews regularly appear in a variety of publications and horror websites. She is an Active member of the Horror Writers Association and a reticent member of the Horror Authors Guild and Whip City Wordsmiths, and her writing genres of choice are psychological, transgressive, and satirical horror heavily influenced by Joyce Carol Oates, A.M. Homes, and Chuck Palahniuk. Find her on Instagram @Rebecca_Rowland_books.

Uncaged
-Jesse Thibodeau-

Uncaged

Simon was caring and helpful but almost always getting taken advantage of. Often picked on and mostly bullied, he would jump to do favors in hopes of making friends. If Simon didn't help out or do what others wanted, they would beat him up and call him names. Most people he hung out with only pretended to be his friends so they could have free favors without feeling guilty of using a person's trust.

 One day Simon was walking home from school, past a house where a dog was outside, locked in a cage with no water or food. Its loud barking filled the air. Feeling scared of the large black canine, he didn't want to approach, even though he was concerned for its well-being. The size of the animal and ferocity of its barking kept walking by. Arriving home and feeling hungry, Simon made himself a ham and cheese sandwich. While eating, he began feeling guilty for not helping the dog and decided to walk back after making another sandwich to share with the caged animal.

Arriving back at the house, he approached the dog with shaking hands and legs, trembling as the powerful creature barked and growled at him.

After a few minutes of staring down the boy, the dog approached with hungry eyes and drool hanging from its lips. Simon unwrapped the sandwich he had made and passed it through the cage, jumping in shock as the dog snatched it from his hand and devoured it in one massive bite. As the dog licked its lips, Simon spotted an outside tap and poured water into a nearby bowl for the dog to drink. As he watched it lapping greedily at the water, a green car pulled up in the driveway.

The dog's demeanour changed. It stopped drinking and, looking scared, backed into its cage.

A man and woman got out of the car, and the dog shook more as they approached. Glaring at the boy, the man kicked the cage and yelled at the dog.

He turned to face Simon. "What the fuck are you doing here, boy?"

"I. Um. I wanted to see the dog, sir."

He told the boy if he wanted to visit the dog, he should pay the man by cleaning his home, then laughed and spat on the ground before turning and following his partner into the building and closing the door behind them.

    After a few minutes outside, petting the massive dog through the cage, Simon decided to enter the couple's home and maybe start cleaning. He was disgusted with what he saw inside. Used needles were scattered over the kitchen counters, empty beer bottles and cans flooded the floors, and harsh smells of burnt plastic filled the entire place.

    Simon felt more than a bit out of place and far outside of his comfort zone. Scared to go any further, he could see the couple through an open door as they took a black kit from under the bed. Looking up, the man saw Simon standing there and started to yell as he approached him. "Hey! What the fuck are you doing in here? Don't you know how to fucking knock?" Simon shook with fear, frozen in place. "But, you said if I wanted to play with the dog, I could clean your house."

    The older man laughed and adjusted his stained and dirty grey sweatpants. "I wasn't being serious. Well. Since you're here, you might as well fucking do something. Start by cleaning the empty bottles and cans. Watch out for the needles. Don't want to catch something." Laughing, he opened up a beer bottle. A voice from the bedroom called out, "John, what's the fucking hold up? Are we shooting up or what?"

"Not right now, Sabrina. That fucking weirdo kid is going to clean the house. Come on out and say hi, will you?"

Sabrina stumbled out of the bedroom, wearing nothing but a filthy pair of panties. Simon couldn't help but stare at her breasts. "Hi, kid. I'm Sabrina." She held out her hand to greet him, but before going further, John struck her across the face with his beer bottle. The glass smashed against her, cutting her skin and spraying beer over her. John yelled at her to put on a bra and get dressed, and terrified at what he had seen, Simon quickly ran away from the situation, not caring to clean the house or see the dog ever again.

Arriving home, Simon cried himself to sleep.

When he woke the next morning, he didn't want to go to school, but his grades needed all the help they could get. Leaving his comfy bed, he got dressed, not eating much before walking to school.

His journey would take Simon in front of the same house. Not wanting to make eye contact with the locked-up dog in his cage, he kept his head down. The green car was still in the driveway, and not wanting to risk seeing John either, Simon continued staring at his feet as he walked, despite the familiar barking from the dog.

He didn't notice his bullies in the near distance sharing a joint before school.

"Hey, bitch!" Christian, the larger member of the trio, yelled, catching Simon's attention a little too late. The other two, Mike and Joel, ran up to him and grabbed him from behind. The pair tackled Simon to the muddy ground and began kicking him. Christian laughed as he got closer. "You better have got our homework done because this will keep happening over and over 'til you are no more." Christian spat in Simon's face and all three bullies walked away, laughing and passing their joint to one another.

Simon stayed on the ground waiting for them to be gone from sight. Once it was clear, he dusted himself off and looked back to see the green car was gone. Deciding to avoid school, he walked back towards the house to play with the caged dog.

For hours Simon sat and talked to the dog, who he named Tito. Simon wanted to set the animal free but was afraid to let the dog loose, not knowing the outcome. What if it ran into the road, and got hit by a car, or attacked someone? He had some lunch in his bag and shared it with the dog, who again ate it gratefully. He wondered if John or Sabrina, had even fed it since yesterday.

It was getting dark when he noticed the green car heading down the road back toward the house. Simon ran to hide behind the garbage can. John and his girlfriend got out of the car, she was walking too slow for John, and he pushed her to the ground shouting at her to walk faster. Sabrina got up and ran inside the house as John walked towards the dog, undid the cage, grabbed it roughly by the collar and dragged it inside. He slapped the large animal a few times because, like Sabrina, the dog didn't move fast enough for him.

Once inside, John locked up the dog, once more, in another cage he kept inside. He followed his bruised and beat-up-looking girlfriend into the bedroom, wanting to shoot up, get high and get his dick wet.

Simon watched through the window with frustration building as he saw his new friend Tito trapped in another cage. Not knowing what to do, Simon walked back home alone, and that night, he cried himself to sleep once more.

In their bedroom, John and Sabrina fought. Sabrina punched John, then curled her hands into talons and clawed at his face. "You fucking asshole, always bossing me around and hitting me! I am done with you. Fuck you. I am out of here." John pushed her against the kitchen table, knocking back bottles of beer that rattled together. He pressed his weight on top of her, pinning her arms and screaming in her face. "You ain't going anywhere, whore. You are coming to the bedroom to get high and fuck, whether you want to or not." Pulling her from the table and painfully twisting her arms, John forced Sabrina to the bedroom. He pushed her to the filthy mattress and began tying a belt tightly around her arm. He grabbed a syringe from the little black kit and injected her with enough junk for two people. Deciding he wanted to get a buzz going before he stuck his dick inside her, John walked to the fridge for a beer. He could hear the gargles of puke and choking coming from the bedroom, and beer in hand, he walked to the door to look at her. He laughed at Sabrina and laughed as she twitched on the bed, puke sputtering from between her lips as she choked to death on her vomit.

After six more beers, John passed out drunk beside her.

Friday morning arrives. Same old routine. Simon wakes up and gets dressed, and walks to school. Only this time, he decided he was going to save the dog from the ungrateful owners. Arriving at the house, he sneaks quietly to the window and peaks through the glass, seeing John and his girlfriend passed out on the bed. He spots the syringe still in her arm, and her skin turned a shade of blue and knows that something terrible has happened. He walked towards the door, expecting it to be locked, and to his surprise, it opens easily, and he is inside the same shit hole he was in before. Except the smell was worse. Simon walked towards Tito, who was still trapped in his cage. He began barking loudly when he saw the boy, and Simon whispered to him to be quiet. But Tito was far from quiet as he barked in joy at seeing his new friend. Simon tried to get the cage unlocked, and just as he was loosening the catch, John woke up. He staggered into the kitchen and seeing Simon playing with the cage door, began shouting as he picked up a discarded beer bottle and started approaching. Remembering seeing John hit Sabrina with a bottle, Simon ran away. Tears ran down his face as he dashed to school, knowing he would never be able to return and save his friend. His Tito.

    John kicked the cage and screamed at the dog to shut the fuck up. Picking up a glass of water from beside the cluttered sink, he threw the liquid on the dog's face. The over-a-hundred-pound canine head-butted the cage door so hard it broke the latch that Simon had already loosened, not knowing his actions had freed Tito. The dog plunged at John, using all his weight to push him down, not giving him a chance to rise or fight back. Tito started biting John's neck and face, devouring and ripping his skin off the bones. Shredding the meat from his face until nothing was left.

John's screams quickly stopped as the dog kept chewing and biting, chewing down John's lips and nose. Once the dog had his fill, he saw the front door was standing open.

Finally, the dog was uncaged and ready for more.

Simon ran till he couldn't breathe any longer, breathlessness and exhaustion kicked in, and he staggered to a halt. His heart pounded, and his breath wheezed painfully as he gasped from exertion. A familiar voice greeted him. "Hey, bitch. You got my homework?"

Looking up, Simon saw the familiar forms of Christian, Mike and Joel.

Simon gave them an explanation. "Look, guys, I've been having a rough week. Please let me go."

Christian laughed as Simon stood vulnerable and weak. With no warning, Joel and Mike rushed Simon, tackling him to the ground and throwing punches as he curled himself into a ball.

Simon cried as punches landed on his face and kicks landed on his chest. His face was bloodied, and tears soaked his cheeks. And then, he heard it, and a wicked bloody smile grew on Simon's face at the familiar bark. In the next few minutes, Tito was closer, knocking Christian back against a brick wall and biting at his face as he had done to John. Tito loved the taste of fresh blood. Joel and Mike were too scared to move and watched in horror as the massive dog bit into Christian, one of the fangs bursting an eye before he tore the boy's throat out. Quickly the dog turned to Joel, who raised his arms in defence. The dog started chewing and biting through his arms and hands, fingers being ripped and torn off his body as the dog chewed away like he was a little chew toy. Mike started running away, but Simon found a discarded beer bottle and threw it at him. It hit Mike right in the back of the head and knocked him down. The dog approached the last bully with a bloody coating on his fur. Simon walked beside Tito, speaking to the bully as the par reached him, "You shouldn't have fucked with me. This would have never happened. Now you will get turned into dog food." Tito started ripping the young boy to shreds.

    Simon was happy to have his new friend uncaged and safe against harm, knowing they would always watch each other's back.

    THE END.

About The Author

Jesse Thibodeau

A Canadian, born and raised. In his spare time, he loves to play the guitar, sit back and listen to music while playing video games and write the crazy stories that pop into his head. Jesse wants to share the artistic side of beauty and horror with the world. So, whether it's a slow song or a short story, a fast and heavy song that screams angrily in your face or an epic rollercoaster of a horror story, he's sure it will leave you with a satisfied smile plastered across your face.

I Hide In The Shadows

-Kristen Vincent-

I Hide In The Shadows

I hide in the shadows,
Wearing only what
I could escape in
From a life
That is now,
Out of my grasps.

Several months have passed,
Our worlds collide,
Explosions
Siren's
And screams
They are everywhere,
Leaving my ears
Ringing.

A war
That didn't have to be,
A war

That I wish would stop,
For it is out of greed.

I hide in the shadows,
Children and mother's
Hunched in the dark corners,
So lost and scared,
For you see the fear
That lingers in their pleading eyes,
Begging for help,
Begging for this war to stop.

I hide in the shadows,
I hear the tanks,
I hear their orders,
I hear their steps,
As they walk
Through our apocalyptic home.

About The Author

Kristen Vincent

I am an upcoming author who writes raw and dark poetry from what I have experienced and what life throws at me. I have been writing since I was roughly 12 years old to help cope and sort through my emotions; pen and paper were my therapy and continues to be so. Apart from my writing, I am also a student working on my teaching degree, an avid horror reader, watcher, and animal lover.

The Missing Return
-Adam Watts-

The Missing Return

I don't know why he insists on waving the paperwork in my face. It achieves nothing other than making me want to punch his nose through the back of his skull. It'd almost be worth getting fired for.

'This needs to be a priority,' he says, tossing the papers onto my keyboard.

This is because I swore at him in that e-mail yesterday. I might also have strongly implied my wish to physically harm him.

'I'm a case manager, Dean,' I tell him, pushing the papers to one side. 'Which means I'm too busy managing cases to play detective on another one of these missing return interviews. They always end up getting messy.'

'Look around, Pete. Half my staff are off sick, so my options are you or Lloyd.'

'Then give it to Lloyd.'

He won't, because he knows if he gives it to Lloyd, then Lloyd will cry foul and then Lloyd will make another complaint and then Lloyd will take another fortnight off because he's stressed. He hates Lloyd. I know this because Dean and I used to talk. He was alright back then, before he put ambition above friendship.

'It's literally over the road and round the corner. It'll take half an hour, that's all.'

'These things never take half an hour.' I glance at the front page of the report, scanning the particulars. 'He was missing for *three fucking days*. That's gonna take longer than half an hour to unpick.' I slump back in my chair, my temples already starting to throb.

'That's why it needs doing today. You know we've gotta make these things a priority after what's been happening. Everyone's in a blind panic.'

He's right. The absolute bastard. When kids go missing and turn up dead it does have a tendency to put a little fire under the issue of missing children, even the ones who eventually turn up safe and well.

Dean slumps with frustration. 'Look… just do the missing return interview and if there's any follow-up work I'll allocate it to a case manager. A *different* case manager.'

I stare at the paperwork, trying to imagine where I might accommodate it amongst all my other tasks. But there's *never* a gap. Time can only be stretched so far. A point almost entirely lost on our management team. Sometimes I feel like the pack-mule in that Buckeroo game, item after item loaded on; the pan, the boot, the banjo, the hat, the fucking missing return interview assessment… then BUCKEROO! What merriment. But nobody's laughing when it's some kid's welfare that's been kicked to the sky or when it's another good worker who's lost their mind and done something regretful. Still, despite the pressure, despite the ridiculous caseloads and the unnecessary paperwork, we always get the job done, because we're fundamentally helpful people.

'Three days missing,' I say, shaking my head. 'How old is he?'

'Twelve.'

'Where does a twelve-year-old go for three days?'

Dean seizes on this whiff of curiosity. 'Be interesting to find out, wouldn't it?'

The bastard has me hooked. *Curse my professional curiosity!* I look around the office. So many empty desks. So many blank spaces. Who knows when they'll be back. Days, weeks, months. Never?

'Just down the road, is it?' I say, the familiar feeling of defeat settling over me. A keen conscience is a curse in this job.

'I've already spoken to his dad, and apparently the kid's saying nothing, so the chances are it'll be a quick visit, just a tick in a box.'

'I'll go over this afternoon. Got boxes of my own to tick first.'

'Okay, but this missing return needs to be a priority, you understand?' he says. 'Oh, and that last assessment you sent me, I can't sign that off until you've seen all the kids.'

'But there's seven of them! I've contacted the schools, they've got no concerns, nor does Mum, nor does anyone else.'

'They still need including in the assessment.'

'Is that a priority too?'

'And the dads. Get contact details off mum. I'm not having another unsatisfactory audit,' he says, turning tail, back to the managerial pig-pen.

'You're welcome!' I call after him, waving the paperwork above my head.

Let the fucker fire me. I'd welcome it. Buckeroo!

It's June but you'd be forgiven for thinking it's January. The cold pissy drizzle makes the two-minute walk feel more like an hour. The rain dribbles down the back of my neck and my shoes are leaking. By the time I reach my destination my socks are sodden. Maybe I'll get trench-foot and score a few days off. A man can dream.

The house itself is no place of note. A modest detached home built of dark grubby brick, seemingly constructed with the sole purpose of sucking in the daylight and sending it someplace else. I'm guessing it looks dark and cold irrespective of rain or shine. The brick façade is broken up by three small windows which squint down at me. I knock hard on the door, which stands bare and flush with the line of the wall. There's no porch to keep the rain off my head.

'Either don't be in or hurry the fuck up,' I mutter to myself.

After a couple more knocks, I stand back from the house to check for movement at the windows, but those dark little squares give nothing away. They seem to watch me harder than I dare watch them.

I step back to the door and knock again.

'Waste of my time,' I murmur to myself, already settling for non-engagement. I tried and I got cold and wet in the process, what more does Dean want? Blood probably. These missing return interviews are always a bust. Especially since the pandemic. No fucker answers the door anymore.

'Yes?' comes a quiet voice from my right. A small doll of a man stands prim and expressionless, feet together, a pair of too-large spectacles perch upon his nose, the frames obscuring his eyes.

'Oh, hi,' I say, searching my pockets for my ID badge. 'I'm Pete. Here to have a chat about your lad going missing.'

'We don't use the front door,' he says, paying no consideration to the soggy badge I present to him. 'Please come around the back of the property.' He moves quickly, disappearing as I blink the rain from my eyes.

To the rear I find an open door, the man stands to one side but stays silent.

'Through here?' I ask, stepping into the house. An odd sensation comes across me now I'm inside. The house itself seems to be vibrating. Such an odd feeling… like it's vibrating *through* me, buzzing in and around every cell like a warm electrical current.

'It's the plumbing,' the little doll-man says, clearly noticing my bewilderment. His tone is peculiar; soft and ungraspable, as if spoken across a velvet cushion.

'That's not like any plumbing I've ever heard,' I tell him.

'It's an old house.'

I make a show of glancing around the room. 'Doesn't look very old,' I say. And it really doesn't. It's more of a utilitarian 1960s cuboid than a grand old townhouse.

He smiles, or seems to. 'The house is older than it seems.'

'I'll take your word for it. This shouldn't take long, by the way, I just need a few minutes with your son. It's standard procedure when a child goes missing.'

'A few minutes?' Again, with the peculiar smile. 'That's fine. Though it's important you take what he might say with a pinch of salt. He's rather prone to emotional flights of fancy.'

I notice he doesn't have a drop of rain on him. Guess that's what happens when you're so small; you can dodge the drops.

'Which way am I going?' I ask.

'Through the door behind you,' he says, stood upright and unyielding like a nail hammered into the floor. 'You'll find the boy in there. No rush. Please… take your time.'

Take my time? What time does he think I have?

I'd expected a living room, but it's more like a small library. There's no telly, no sofa, just bookshelves, fit to bursting, absorbing light and sound, coddling the room in an uncomfortable gloom. The air smells old and biscuity. A boy – *the* boy – sits in a chair in the corner reading. A book? Why's he not poking a phone screen or wielding a knife like any other kid his age?

'Are you George?'

He glances up for the briefest of moments, and then returns to his story.

'What are you reading?' I ask. I can already tell this is going to be like pulling teeth. My own teeth.

He glances up again. Holds the book towards me so I can see the cover.

'The Tempest?' I say, squinting. 'Bit of Shakespeare. Any good?'

'It's okay,' he says, his voice deeper than expected for a twelve-year-old, especially one so small and pale.

'I've never heard anyone describe Shakespeare as okay. People usually love it or hate it, don't they?'

George shrugs and turns his eyes back to his book. Stone-walled in favour of The Barde; a first for me. There's something unsettling about this kid. How he sits, stiff and contorted like an armature, like his joints have been prematurely set by rigor-mortis. He's baby-bird thin, his skins almost translucent and his eyes are red and puffy. I guess that's what happens when your house is all dark wood and dour paintings. It feels like a museum; nothing here is dusty, but all of it should be. The house seems to shush and tut behind my back. Maybe that's what that curious humming is.

'My name's Pete, by the way?' I say, sitting myself down on what I swear is the hardest chair in the universe.

'I'm George, but you know that already,' the boy says in return. He doesn't look up, he could be talking to anyone.

I shift myself in the chair. Damp clothes cling to me, make my skin itchy. One of the uprights digs into my spine. I can't imagine any consideration was given to comfort when this chair was made, but maybe I'm missing the point.

'You must be wondering why I'm here,' I say. I give George some time to reply but he doesn't. 'Well, I work for the local authority, but I'm not a social worker or a policeman or anything like that. My job is to help young people, and any time a young person –'

George looks at me sharply over the top of his book. 'It's because my Dad reported me missing.'

'Yeah, that's it. I wondered if we could talk about what happened.'

'I already told my dad what happened and I told the police, so why do I need to tell you?'

'That's a good question. I guess people are worried about you.'

'That's not what it is.' He hides his face behind The Tempest once more.

'I bet your parents were worried.'

He glances up at me with a pointed look in his eye. 'I doubt very much my mum is worried, given that she's dead.'

And with those words I am well and truly skewered. You see, this is what happens when you're not afforded the time to do the necessary prep work. A dead mum probably explains why this kid went missing. Grief can make you do crazy things.

'I'm really sorry to hear that,' I say. 'Was it recent?'

He seems to struggle with the question. 'I don't know anymore,' he says.

That was not really the answer I expected. He doesn't know *anymore?* So... when *did* he know? He notices the ill-concealed look of confusion.

'I don't really remember her.'

'That must be really tough,' I say. Stock response.

He shrugs. 'She wasn't well. My dad says it's for the best I don't remember.'

'And what do you think?'

He visibly composes himself, like he's reminding himself of his lines, pre-performance. 'What I think is, my dad wants to protect me and keep me safe.'

'Well, that's good to hear. But just out of interest... what's he trying to protect you from?'

George looks a little stricken now. I've thrown him.

'Everything he does is to protect me, to keep me safe and well.'

Those don't sound like his own words. More lines. More script. No wonder the poor kid ran away.

'I understand that, George. I suppose what I'm trying to get at is what you're being protected from.'

'Illness. Disease. Death. Failure. Sorrow. Violence.' His voice is slow and methodical, reading off his list. As he's talking the light in the room shifts. George doesn't seem to notice the shadows lengthening and then shrinking back, sliding across the spines of all those books. Light turns to darkness, then back to light, before fading into grey shadow. That curious humming sound intensifies just for a moment, reverberating through my bones. It's a sound I'd very much like to shake from my head.

'There's a lot of bad stuff in the world,' I say. 'But don't we need to learn how to deal with that stuff? Don't we need the opportunity to experience all of the good things life has to offer, so it balances out the bad?'

The boy tucks his legs under the chair and closes his book. He holds it tight to his chest. 'It's for my own good, my own safety. You never know what might happen... out *there*.'

Shadows sweep across the room again, followed by a dappled light, then the grey returns. Perhaps the weather is turning. Not that it matters to this kid. From what I can gather he's not allowed out, rain or shine.

'Humour me, then. What might happen out there? Specifically.'

'Just something bad,' he says. He examines his hands.

'To you?'

'Maybe. Or somebody else.'

'What might happen to somebody else if you went out to play?'

He doesn't answer that, but he looks worried. He pulls the sleeves of his jumper over his hands.

'George. Before I ask you this next question, I want you to know that I am here to listen to you and I am here to help, so whatever's happened, please know that you can be honest with me and that I'll do my best to support you. Do you understand what I'm saying?'

He nods but doesn't make eye contact. He looks tense, like he doesn't quite understand the words he wants to say but they're bursting to get out all the same.

'Did something bad happen when you were missing?'

The boy seems to turn in on himself, he shrinks, and though he speaks, he does so quietly. 'I wasn't missing.'

'You were gone for three days.'

'I wasn't.'

'The police report says you were.'

'I know, but I wasn't, that's what I keep saying. I wasn't missing. I stepped out the door for a minute, that's all. I don't care what you, or the police report or my dad says. It was a minute, not three days.' He stares at me wide-eyed, dares me to contradict him.

My head spins, something starts to unravel in my brain. This was supposed to be a quick visit.

'So, you stepped out of the house for a minute, and when you came back in it was three days later?'

His shoulders sink, he looks forlorn and confused. 'Nobody believes me.'

'It's a tough story to buy, George. But maybe we can figure it out.'

'You must think I'm crazy.'

'I don't. But I wonder if there's something you're forgetting, or maybe your brain just doesn't want to process the–'

'I'm not lying!' George snaps. 'And I didn't forget anything.'

'Okay, okay. I'm sorry, I'm definitely not accusing you of lying. What I've heard is that you've been under a lot of stress, that you're not allowed out, and that you've had to cope with the loss of your mum. I suppose I wondered whether you'd got to a point where you'd had enough, and you needed to get out and somehow your brain had blocked the memory of it. Our minds can do weird things when we're under pressure, when we're worried or stressed.'

He stares at me, like I've not heard a word he's said, like all he wants is for me to believe the unbelievable, that three whole days simply evaporated when he left the house. This isn't the first time I've had to believe the unbelievable in this job. Most of what people tell me is a front of one kind or another, and you can scream *bullshit* all you like, but butting heads achieves nothing. Sometimes you have to take the lie as truth and work with it.

'Tell you what, George,' I say, attempting a reset. 'Let's agree that time is a funny old beast.'

'What do you mean?' he says.

'I mean, hours can feel like seconds when you're asleep, but if somebody were watching you sleep, it'd still feel like hours to them. The same amount of time passes for both people, but they each experience it differently. Am I right?'

'I suppose.'

'So what if we just agree that your dad's perception of time during those three days away differed to your own? Nobody is lying, nobody is mistaken, it was just time being a funny old beast.'

'Okay,' he says, not looking entirely convinced. Perhaps he still feels fobbed off. Perhaps he knows how crazy he sounds.

'Can you tell me what happened before you left the house?' I ask.

He just stares into the bottom corner of the room, which suggests *something* happened. A trigger event.

'An argument… or a disagreement… a friend that got in touch.'

Still, he stares.

'Something to do with your dad?' I venture. An educated venture.

He wants to say something but holds it back. It's only a matter of time until he discloses something, though. I can feel it. I should probably back off because if he discloses it becomes *my* problem and that'll be at least a whole day wiped out. But for some reason I can't stop loading this little pack-mule with those miniature plastic items, heavier and heavier, knees giving way, pushing down until… BUCKEROO! There's something unusual at play here and my professional curiosity has got the better of me.

'Did you fall out with your dad?' I ask.

'I shouldn't have argued back,' he says, looking genuinely ashamed of himself. 'He was only doing what's best for me.'

'Keeping you inside is what's best?' I ask.

'He was right, though. He was right about what would happen if I…' I give him a moment, but the sentence hangs incomplete in the air. Tears spill, a bead of snot runs from his left nostril. He sniffs it back, but it soon dribbles out again.

'What did he say would happen?' I ask.

'Something bad. That somebody would have to –'

His eyes snap wide open, like somebody just flicked a switch in him.

'I'm not sure our friend needs to know the details,' comes the voice from behind me. I spin round to see his dad stood, back pressed against the door. How long had he been there watching and listening? How had he entered the room without us noticing?

It takes me a moment or two to find my voice amongst the confusion. 'The details are important,' I tell him. 'Especially when George tells a very different story to the paperwork. It's important that we finish this conversation and establish a clear timeline.'

He regards me for a moment, and when he eventually breaks his silence, the words are spoken softly but with considerable weight. 'And what would somebody like *you* know about timelines?'

'That's an odd question,' I say.

He smiles. 'Yes, I suppose it is. But your response barely masks your ignorance. An ignorant mind has no right to question matters of time. No right at all.' His tone remains cool and measured, but there is something in his eyes. A rising fire.

'The paperwork says George was missing for three days. He says he has no recollection of that time, so forgive me if my curiosity comes across as ignorance. But when nobody seems to know –'

'I know exactly what happened during those three days.'

'Then why did you report him missing?'

'The same reason you're here. Protocol. Some rules are made to broken, but some need to be followed, to pay the toll and restore balance.'

The light in the room shifts again. The thrumming vibration intensifies before dissipating into an idling murmur.

'For the purposes of your report you can simply state that the circumstances surrounding George's episode are *unknown*.'

'Or… we could let George finish what he was saying. Something about you warning him against leaving the house.'

'The boy's a fantasist, nothing more.'

'He's confused, and he deserves to know what's happened to him,' I say.

The boy's dad steels himself, fixes my eyes with a piercing stare. It strikes me that he's remarkably imposing for such a small man.

'You will state in your report that his whereabouts were unknown, that he was unable to remember, that he returned unharmed and is now safe in the care of his father. Do you understand that?' he says.

'I understand very clearly. And what I would like *you* to understand is that I will also be filing a report to Children's Social Care and the police.'

'On what grounds?'

'That depends entirely on whether you're willing to let George finish what he was telling me.'

'To your room, George,' he says, calm and matter of fact.

'I don't want to go to my room,' he replies.

'I said, to your room. Do not disobey me again.'

'Or what?' I ask. I'm aware I shouldn't be needling this guy, but fuck it… I've come this far.

His jaw twitches. Like he's having to stop the words wriggling out of his mouth like maggots from a wound.

'Or what?' I ask again. 'What happens when he disobeys you? Clearly something bad enough to make him disappear for three days.'

'I warned him about that,' he says. 'But he wouldn't listen.'

George mumbles something, and it's not just me who registers a particular word.

'Do not mention your mother to this stranger!' his dad yells. 'Don't you even dare insinuate that –' He catches himself before he hurtles over the cliff-edge. 'She wasn't well,' he says, softening his tone, probably for my benefit.

'That's what you tell me,' George says. 'But what's that got to do with keeping me locked up?'

'You are not locked up. I have a duty to protect you.'

'Is that what you used to tell Mum?'

His volume rises again, he seems to bulge at the seams, on the verge of erupting. 'She was unwell, and you know the lengths I went to save her. The lengths I continue to go to. Don't pretend to this man that you've been kept in the dark. I told you what would happen, I warned you and you didn't listen.'

'You don't tell me anything! Why were my hands covered in dirt? Why did you have to burn my clothes?'

From the look on his face, I'd say he hadn't expected this boy to say anything? Has this conversation really come as a surprise to him given the intense strain their relationship is clearly under.

'Go to your room,' he tells him.

'Why were my hands covered in dirt?' he repeats. 'I need to hear the answer. I need to hear it from you, because I don't remember… but I feel it… I feel cold and empty… I feel sick to my stomach, and you won't talk to me about it.'

'I said go to your room,' his dad repeats. He's working hard to measure his tone. I can only imagine how he responds to this boy when they're by themselves. 'And take your book.'

George hurls the book across the room, narrowly missing his dad's head before colliding with a picture on the wall, shattering the glass then landing with a thud amongst the shards.

'Why won't you tell me what happened?' he yells. 'Why won't you tell me where I went and why I can't remember?'

'Because you're a child!' comes the reply, screeching like a worn-out motor. 'You have no idea...'

'I may be a child, but I hear you whispering, I hear the things you say, and I know what you're working on. Your machine. Your experiment!'

The boy picks himself up and retreats. He is no longer in the room, but the last word he spoke remains. *Experiment.* The whirring vibrations start up once more, the lights shift in the room. Mr. Huxley stares at me, dares me to ask. To link the boy's final word to the sensation pulsing through the structure of the house and through our very selves.

'The pipes again?' I enquire.

'The boy's words should not be given undue validation. Especially by a manipulative do-gooder like you.'

'I've not manipulated anything, Mr. Huxley. I've been in your house less than twenty minutes and I'm hearing things which don't make a great deal of sense. I'd like you to explain exactly what's going on here.'

He regards me through his owlish spectacles, the lenses magnifying his wide pale eyes. 'You. You're a speck, that's what you are. A temporary, mindless speck. You were born, you live each day, working and feeding. Then… one day, you die. In that precise order.'

I have to laugh at that. Even if I don't mean to. 'So?' I say. 'That's an incredibly well-worn assessment of the basic human condition you've just made. Surely you can do better.'

'I don't owe you better. My son was missing. He has returned unharmed. You've seen him and you've confirmed he's well, but you're unable to elaborate on his three absent days.'

'But that's the issue, isn't it? He has no recollection, yet you insist you know exactly what happened. Why not put my mind at ease and tell me where he went.'

'How could your mind be eased by something it's fundamentally unable to comprehend? It would change nothing. The body of your report would still amount to circumstances unknown.'

Now it's my time to stare him down, but he remains resolute, nailed down, inscrutable. 'You drugged him, didn't you?'

His lip curls to a sneer. 'Drugged?' he inches towards me and pushes a chisel-sharp finger into my chest. The vibration through the house intensifies. 'This is how your mind works, isn't it? It's so simple to you. He must've been *drugged*. Pathetic.' He drives the finger deeper into my stomach yet somehow, I feel unable to stop him. It's like I'm a moth pinned to a cork board. 'Are you drugged, currently? Can you tell what is happening to you?'

I don't know how to answer that. The vibration intensifies, the room seems to turn now; or is it the light playing tricks as it skitters and twirls across the spines of the books?

'You… drugged him…' I manage to say, my voice pale and faded. 'Your experiments… your machine…' The boy says he can't remember. Maybe he just doesn't want to. *Why were his hands covered in dirt? Why did his dad burn his clothes? What happened?*

The room spins faster, the lights flicker and dim and now the only thing I can hear is the droning through the walls. *The pipes!*

Amidst the din I hear the man chanting. His words are unknowable. Louder and louder, his finger drives deeper into me. The room now whirling like a top, the lights strobing. Chanting… chanting… but what is he saying?

And then. It stops. No sound, no movement, no finger pushing through my guts. Just me and him stood a meter or so apart between the book-lined walls. It all stops in a finger-snap.

'What just happened?' I ask. My voice tattered and empty.

'I've answered your question,' he replies.

'You've answered nothing,' I tell him.

'I have answered your question, but you'll wish you never asked.'

'I'm not interested in your empty threats, Mr. Huxley,' I tell him as I back away towards the kitchen. He stays rooted to the spot, watching me like a small stone reptile. The light shifts across him again. His expression contorts to a ghoulish leer as the shadows pass across his over-sized spectacles.

'I am not a man to make empty threats,' he says. 'I warned the boy! I told him of the curse that would burden him. I wanted him to believe me, but he was always so wilful. Just like his Mum. But now he sees. He'll settle and he'll see this is all for him.'

'You're out of your mind,' I say. 'All this talk of experiments and curses and matters of time and death. It's madness! When I leave this house, I'll be contacting the authorities. I have significant concerns about –'

'Believe me when I say,' he bellows, 'when you leave this house nobody will believe a word you tell them. There is a cost to everything, a toll to pay. I found out the hard way, so too did my wife… and my son. But now, the curse, the terrible toll… it will belong to you.

And it will end with you. Blood for blood. That's the rule.'

'Fuck yourself,' I tell him. Not knowing where those words exploded from. 'I'm leaving this house.'

He smiles. 'Blood for blood,' he says again. 'I can't thank you enough.'

'You won't be thanking me in about an hour's time,' I say as I hurry through the kitchen and towards the door at the side of the house. The room starts to spin once more, the whirring and grinding in the walls fizz through my skin, my muscles, deep into the marrow of every bone in my body. I shove hard at the door, barely able to keep myself upright. My legs fail and I tumble backwards, cursing myself. I can't stand, I can't get up, the room is spinning at full clip. I do the only thing I'm able to do. I kick out at the door. The first blow does nothing, but the second lands more squarely. It's the third kick that dislodges it from its frame, and the forth that sends it clattering open. The outside world presents itself; stable and welcoming, not whirling and buzzing. I drag myself towards the opening, inch by inch, trying desperately to gain some traction as the floor beneath me spins like a top. I manage to curl my fingertips around the splintered door frame, and with fire burning through every sinew and muscle, I pull myself free of the house. The change is jarring. One second, I'm on a tilt-a-whirl, and the next, everything around me is still and steady. There's no residual dizziness like when you step off a round-about and need to take a minute to find your balance again. The shift is instant.

What the fuck just happened in there?

I look back to the house. It's the same house I stepped into not less than an hour ago. The same brown cube with its uncaring eyes staring down at me. Looking in through the broken door there is no suggestion of anything unusual. The house looks just as still on the inside as it does on the outside.

'How the hell am I gonna write this up?' I ask myself, backing away from the place lest it reach out with some invisible claw and pull me back in to the maelstrom. It's not until I'm round the corner that I realise it's stopped raining. Despite the welcome change to the weather, I still feel cold and damp, perhaps more so. I realise I don't have my bag with me. I could've sworn I grabbed it before retreating. Fuck knows. Best just keep moving.

The walk back to the office felt so much longer than it should've. Visits can do that to you. They drain you, wring you out, and even the most ordinary of encounters can distort your senses, so it's no surprise my mind is a bit out of sorts considering what I experienced. Inevitably, you bring a piece of those families out the door with you, you can almost hear their footsteps chasing you down the street, doubly so today. Did any of that really happen?

After what feels like an age I reach the office, and after the madness I've just experienced there's comfort in the sound of the murmuring chatter coming from behind the door; the chance to momentarily escape the administrative drudgery of the process. I have a story to tell them, and even though they may well scoff at the details, we will at least drink tea, have a biscuit, and agree how fucking mad it is out there. Then the work will start, there will be calls to make and reports to file, but for a few minutes at least I'll be grateful of the reprieve.

As I open the door there's a second or two where the muffled din of the office clamour becomes immediate and loud, and then it drops, and the room is silent. Everyone stares, mouths hang open, eyes are wide and it's like time has stopped. My eyes peck nervously around the room, and I try to smile like I'm in on the gag.

'Everything okay?' I ask, moving with small tense steps towards my desk.

The gaping heads gradually turn towards Dean, who stands and moves nervously towards me. I want to sit but somehow, I can't, not with everyone watching. Something else is expected of me.

'Pete?' Dean says, his brow furrowed. He places a hand on my shoulder.

'Dean?' I reply, mocking the measure of concern in his voice.

Dean quickly looks round to the rest of the team, then back to me. He talks slowly, like I might not understand his words. 'Where have you been?'

'Missing return. And thanks for that, by the way. Turned out to be a right shit-show.'

He turns to the rest of the team again, then back to me. He squeezes my shoulder this time. 'Pete. Do you wanna come sit with me for a moment?' He looks genuinely concerned, a look I've not seen in his eyes for a long time.

'Not really, no. I was hoping somebody might want to make me a cuppa. Never in all my years have I experienced anything like that, I thought I was losing my mind.'

'Pete? Look at me,' Dean says, his eyes staring hard into mine, scrutinising them, searching for answer I don't know how to give, because I don't really know what the question is.

'Are you gonna tell me what's up?' I say.

'That case...' he says. 'I sent you out three days ago.' He glances back at the team who all wear the same concerned expression he does. Dean forces a friendly smile, but he's nervous. Almost fearful. 'Where have you been?'

A dozen grim faces stare at me like I'm a pitiful curiosity exhibit.

'You all in on this?' I say to them.

Nobody replies.

'I think we need to have a sit down and a talk,' Dean says, gesturing towards the room in the far corner. He nods at Shelia. She nods back like they've just agreed something.

I shake my head. 'I'm up to my eyeballs with work, so I should probably just crack on.'

'Pete, it's Friday afternoon. You've been gone since Tuesday. Everyone's been out looking. People thought you were –'

'But I've only been up the road, Dean. I didn't want to go but you sent me!' I look around, panicked now. 'You sent me!' I dig my phone out of my pocket. And there it is, plain as day on the front screen. It's Friday afternoon. I let out a frantic burst of laughter, point a shaking finger at the faces in front of me. 'I was gone less than an hour. I just went to that house and then I came back.' My voice is loud now, I'm trying to smile through it. The faces soften, to concern, and then to pity. But there's something else there too; an almost fearful wariness.

'Pete, just come with me, will you?' Dean says, heading for the small meeting room towards the back of the office.

I plod after him, into the room, and place myself carefully down on a chair. My legs have gone weak, I can't keep them from shaking.

'I was gone an hour, that's all. You believe me, don't you?' I ask.

Dean sits himself opposite me, near the door. 'Of course I do, Pete,' he says, his voice quiet and careful. 'And I'm glad you're back. We've all been so worried. The police will want a –'

'The police? Why are we involving the police? I wasn't even missing, I was only gone an hour. Just tell them I'm back now. No harm, no foul.'

'It's procedure, that's all, but you'll need to tell them what you know.'

'And what exactly am I supposed to know?'

Dean glances over me, his eyes linger on my clothes.

Instinctively I glance down too. My clothes, which were clean on this morning (or what I thought was this morning) are filthy… they're covered in grime, dirt and mud. And something else… but how could that be? Is that… blood? Who's blood?

Dean sees it. He's made sure he's sat near the door. It's what we're told to do… never get yourself penned in by somebody who might pose a risk. 'We've all been worried,' he says. He certainly looks worried.

'I told you I didn't want to go on that visit.'

'I know, and I should've listened. I recognise you've been under a lot of pressure. It's understandable that you might've needed... some time.'

'Time?'

'Yeah... time away from all the... stress and –'

'This isn't about work stress, Dean. It's that house! The same thing happened to the kid I went to see. It's his dad, he has some weird experiment going on... a machine! Fuck knows what it does but he said I was a speck, and Jesus he kept talking about time and–'

'It's okay, Pete. It's okay.'

'Please don't talk to me like I'm some delusional junkie. I'm telling you, there was this weird sound through the walls and his dad was a freakshow. The kid told me... he lost three whole days, but to him it felt like minutes. And the dad... what was it he said just before I left? Just before the whole house felt like it was spinning.'

'I'm sorry, Dean, but none of this sounds real. You've been under a lot of pressure.'

'Fuck the pressure,' I spit. 'He kept saying something about a toll to pay, a curse, he said it's mine now, and that it ends with me. He said the same thing would happen to me that happened to the boy. *And the boy!* He said, his hands were covered in dirt, and the dad, he burned his clothes.' I'm rambling now, spitting out the details, it all sounds like nonsense. The man's words ring in my ears. *When you leave this house, nobody will believe a word you say.*

Dean's jaw tenses. He eyes my dirty blood-stained clothes again. 'I'm sorry.' he eventually says. 'I really am sorry.'

'I don't want your fucking apologies, Dean. What I want is for you to come with me. We'll go back to that house, and you'll see. Talk to the boy. And we'll take the police too.'

'We can't do that, Pete.'

'Yes! Yes, we can! We owe it to that kid if nobody else. I'm telling you now; that kid hates his dad, some bad shit's gone down, something about his mum dying, and I think it had to do with his dad's experiments. The kid will back me up, I know it.'

'We can't do that, Pete, and you know we can't,' he says. 'Are you understanding what I'm saying?'

'Of course we can. We can leave right now.'

'No,' he says. 'We can't.'

'Well, why?'

He stands, glances through the glass panel in the door. He looks pained, like he wants to say something but can't. He looks through the glass again.

'What is it, Dean?'

He shakes his head at me, I can see his eyes welling up. 'You're covered in blood, Pete. You've been gone for three days and you're talking like you've lost your mind.'

'Look, I can't explain it, but please, let's just go back to the house and –'

'They found the bodies, Pete.'

The room falls away. Or I fall away. Something is falling. I don't feel real. I want to scream; I want to ask what the hell is going on? But all I can do is look at the blood and the dirt and the look on Dean's face. Like all the blood has drained out of him, like he wants to be sick.

From a far distant place I hear Dean asking, 'Where have you been?'.

I wish I knew.

The police come. They handcuff me. I must look more capable of violence than I am.

'You need to go to the house,' I tell them. 'We're going to drive right past it.' But they're not willing to engage.

But sure enough, the route to the station takes us right past the house. 'That's the place I yell! We have to stop! Just two minutes and you'll see!'

I'm wasting my breath. I beg them, but they pretend not to hear.

The house glares from the road-side at me. That same cold hard square of brick and cement regarding the world with contempt. Only this time there is a difference. Stood in the upstairs window is the boy. And he's staring right at me, look he'd been expecting to see this very sight. But that's not the thing that makes the blood stop dead in my veins. Stood behind him is a woman. A woman I recognise from the picture that fell from the wall in the living room. The boy's Mum.

'Wait!' I yell. 'Didn't you see her? We have to go back! She's supposed to be dead, don't you see!'

'Pipe down back there,' one of the officers barks.

The final words the boys dad spoke to me echo in the far corners of my mind. *Blood for blood. I can't thank you enough.*

About The Author

Adam Watts

Adam Watts is the author of Like Rats, The Miracle, and Mr. Bloody Sunshine. He's had several short stories published by 88 Tales and has featured in a Halloween anthology. Adam is an avid horror fan, has a beard as dense as lead and lives near Nottingham in England with his partner and three children. Unlike most writers, he doesn't own a cat.

Elly Wilson

Elly Wilson provided the cover art for this book. She is an incredibly gifted artist from the UK. You can find her on Instagram @emerald_neon_suicida

<u>More From Elly Wilson</u>

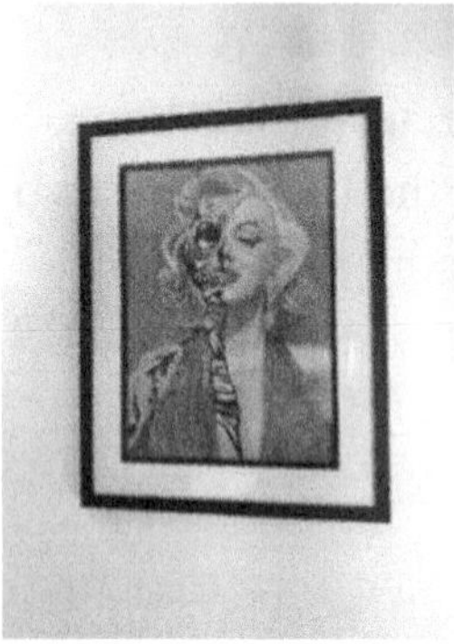
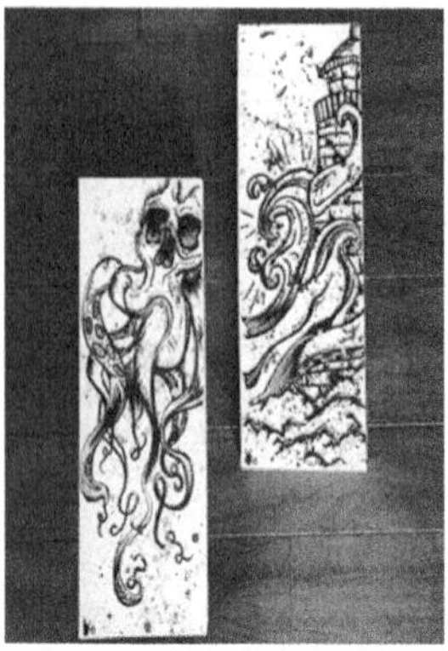
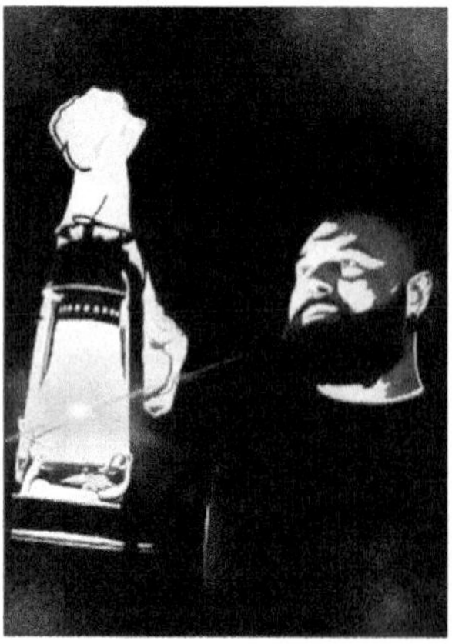
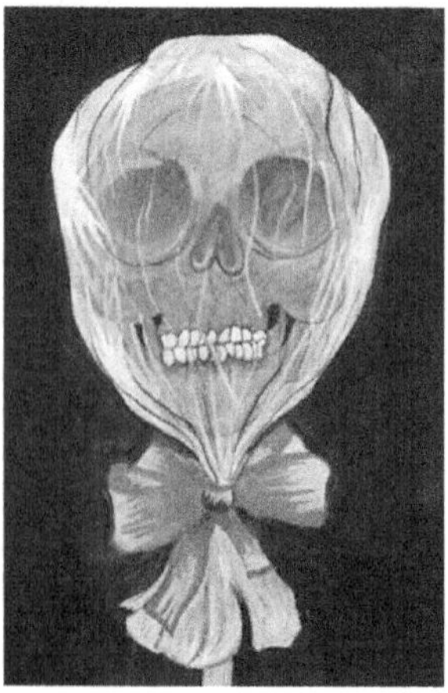